ALTHOUGH CO[...] INTELLIGENT, RUPER[...] TO THE DARK SIDE[...] NEW JERSEY FEAR[...] THE DRUG DEALER PARTNERS HE HAS BETRAYED. BUT GETTING TOO CLOSE TO RUPERT IS LIKE BEING SWALLOWED BY A POWERFUL VORTEX FROM WHICH NO ONE EVER EMERGES.

Early Praise

"Brilliant 'entertainment' in the Graham Greene sense. *The Broken Light of A Different Sun* gradually eases you to the edge of your chair, then keeps you there with a combination of terror and pleasure that only a superb thriller can achieve. Lawrence does a masterly job!"—***Ron Felber, bestselling author of Mojave Incident and Il Dottore, The Double Life of a Mafia Doctor.***

"Michael Lawrence has written a cautionary tale about the dark side of the American dream in the leafy, privileged suburbs of northern New Jersey. *The Broken Light of A Different Sun* has characters you won't soon forget and an ending you won't see coming."—***AJ Murphy, Former National Accounts Manager- Macmillan Publishers***

"Michael Lawrence's novel is not quite the usual crime thriller, it prefers to take a dead bead on the inner lives and the dark logic of the north Jersey narco underworld. Lawrence takes the reader on a roller coaster ride that ultimately reveals a worm's-eye view of an alternate reality–one inhabited by Rupert, the murderous impetus for this absorbing and dark tale. For a prosecutor like myself who's "seen it all," staring into the vacuum of Rupert's eyes reminded me how much I will never know."—***Georges de Pompignan, former Assistant Morris County, New Jersey Prosecutor***

"*The Broken Light of A Different Sun* explodes from a hidden source. The story launches from an appropriate setting; a region of subterranean worlds from which industrial America was birthed. A world hidden in plain sight, and whose history and presence are unknown to the tens of millions who live adjacent to it. Michael Lawrence has created a parallel world of characters who emerge from hidden places, revealing the unexpected."—*Steven Magasis, Aerospace Explosives and Environmental Engineer*

"Enthralling. The dark motivations of the characters drive this novel's compelling, nefarious plot. Combining suburbia's violent underworld with brilliant character psychology, this suspenseful thriller takes on a gritty realness that will leave readers astounded page after page."—*Dr. John Parras, Professor of English, William Paterson University, Graduate Coordinator of the MFA program in Creative and Professional Writing, Author of Fire on Mount Maggiore*

"*The Broken Light of A Different Sun*, Mike Lawrence's debut novel, starts with a big bang then dives deep into the spiritual darkness that the explosion has wrought with propulsive action, realistic dialogue and a story that never stops surprising. I can't wait for his next."—*Scott Krantz, author of the The Dogs Dance and The City and the Sky: a book of photography and poetry, Manager of Legendary NY Night Clubs: The LoneStar, The Blue Note, The Village Gate, Stand Up New York and Catch a Rising Star and 25 year member of The Friars Club and AA*

THE BROKEN LIGHT OF A DIFFERENT SUN

Michael J. Lawrence

Moonshine Cove Publishing, LLC

Abbeville, South Carolina U.S.A.

First Moonshine Cove Edition SEP 2022

ISBN: 9781952439414

Library of Congress LCCN: 2022915395

Copyright 2022 by Michael Lawrence

This book is a work of fiction. Names, characters, businesses, places, events, conversations, opinions, and incidents are either products of the author's imagination or are used fictitiously. Any resemblance to actual events, locales, conversations, opinions, business establishments, or persons, living or dead, is entirely coincidental and unintended.

All rights reserved. No part of this book may be reproduced in whole or in part without written permission from the publisher except by reviewers who may quote brief excerpts in connection with a review in a newspaper, magazine, or electronic publication; nor may any part of this book be reproduced, stored in a retrieval system or transmitted in any form or by any means electronic, mechanical, photocopying, recording or any other means, without written permission from the publisher.

Front cover image by Alan Dino Hebel, courtesy of the author; back cover and interior design by Moonshine Cove staff.

About the Author

Michael J Lawrence has a Masters in English with a Writing Specialization from William Paterson University and has published in literary journals such as *Mobius: The Journal of Social Change* and *The Paumanok Review.* Although his first love has always been literature, he has had an enjoyable alternate career in the fitness industry in management and as a trainer. Michael currently lives in Northwest New Jersey with his son Joshua, wife Kathleen and pupchik Pasha

THE BROKEN LIGHT OF A DIFFERENT SUN

Chapter One

One side of the oak, front double door blew off its hinges and smashed to the floor. Two figures preceded the others and stepped through the breached entrance way. They dropped the heavy, cylindrical battering ram they carried and it bounced off the splintered door and rolled back toward their feet. Men wearing black helmets and body armor held assault rifles in front of them and advanced, halted, and advanced again. They moved almost serpentine-like into the atrium. The entranceway opened into four separate rooms spread out in a semi circle with a huge stone stairway in the center that led to the second floor. Rupert heard the clatter of something small and metallic. It came skittering across the tile floor toward the sunken living room where he was sitting with Pam watching TV. The stun grenade blinded and deafened them, but he managed to roll off the sofa and sprint toward the French doors that led out to the pool and to the deep back woods.

"Pam," Rupert yelled with everything he had in him, but could not hear the sound of his own voice. He barreled through the doors crossing his arms in front of his face to deflect the splintering glass. He was fast and surprisingly agile for a big man.

As he ran down the hill behind the pool his vision refocused and then his hearing came back with a roaring from which emerged, the shouting DEA agents behind him. A bullet whizzed past him and he heard the shouted command.

"Stop or the next one is in your back!"

Another bullet whizzed over head and he knew then that they would not shoot him. There were bigger fish to fry and they needed him to betray everyone else involved in the mess E had created. It was a pile of shit and he should never have listened to the bastard.

He felt, after sprinting across the backyard, like he was surely going to die. He could not catch his breath and his heart was pounding so hard that he felt with any extra effort it would explode and he'd be heaving and gagging and drop dead right there in the grass. But when he heard the agents pounding behind him, grunting, swearing and snorting, his fear gave him new energy. He entered the woods on an angle running to the right in full view of the trio of agents just now approaching the gate to the back fence. Once he had entered the dense woods and was out of their line of sight he made a sharp left and began running toward the deepest part of the forest rather than through the strip of woods that bordered Rt. 23. There was a gulley full of brush and leaves and he dove in trying to pull as much forest detritus over him as possible. He lay there like a corpulent log trying to stay as still as possible, but was betrayed by a trembling left leg. When he heard the agents running past him, no doubt figuring he would head toward the highway and try to highjack a car or something, he got up and began the two-mile hike straight back into the woods and then up onto a ridge of ancient, layered rock where an old hunter's cabin stood. He had hidden some supplies and money under the floorboards for just such an event.

He had no idea what had happened to Pam. The last thing he saw was Pam rising to her feet as the front door hit the stone floor in the foyer with a crack that was as loud as the stun grenade.

Could they have shot her as she jumped up thinking she had a weapon? Poor, poor, girl. Dead? Lying on the floor of the living room drenched in her own blood? He clenched his teeth and squeezed his eyes shut hard. He couldn't believe this was happening to him.

When he pushed open the door to the cabin there wasn't a repeat of the fireworks like in his Green Pond McMansion. There was a man standing calmly in the center of the room with Rupert's go bag hanging from his shoulder. He was holding Rupert's Glock in his right hand and pushed a magazine into the receiver. He pulled back the slide, let it spring forward and pointed the Glock at Rupert's head.

"Oh God," Rupert wailed and dropped to one knee.

The agent frowned, walked behind him, pushed the Glock against the back of his head and kneed him between the shoulder blades. The pain pushed him up and off his back leg and forced him to stand.

"You're going to help us. You're going to help us put away all your buddies, and then you're gonna help us get the big boys. Put away the big boys and you can go live your entitled little life any way you want, or I can just shoot you in your fucking head right here."

Rupert looked at him and knew then that he was going to give the guy everything he wanted. He and Scheiner and E were in way over their heads and he should have known it would lead to this.

The drugs and the money were in the pool house. Having never dealt on this level before he really didn't know what to do with it all. He had built a false compartment in the rear side panel of his Escalade and was carrying a couple of kilos at a time down to a small but ambitious street gang in Paterson. They had a lab where they cut the product, chopped it up into ounces and converted much of it to rock. The street gang known as Los Fuerte had their associates sell rock on the street, and powder in Morristown and Parsippany.

The DEA agent walked him back to the main house in a relaxed almost amiable style. He acted as though they had been touring the grounds together rather than beginning a series of actions whose culmination would be Rupert ratting out everyone he had ever come in criminal contact with. And it would probably all wind up with Rupert dead, murdered by the hand of his associate's associates, or locked away in a maximum security prison for at least a decade living a life that really was as good as being dead.

They walked past the pool house door and he could see the packaged cocaine piled up with the boxes of money beside the floor tiles under which he had buried it all. He had dug through the concrete the pool house rested on and dug out a nice sized hole in the ground into which he hid money and drugs double bagged in heavy duty garbage bags. Every time he took out product and put in cash he fitted plywood into the subfloor over the hole, re-grouted the tiles meticulously and replaced the throw rug he had covered the tiles with. Perhaps it was all pretty obvious to the DEA who knew the psychology of assholes like him who were trying to fake it, but it was all he could think to do. The other agents had brought in a dog and were slicing open the sheetrock walls with a box knife.

"You got it all," he said to them with such resignation that the agent stopped momentarily to look him in the eyes. The agent stared at him with his own brand of world weary resignation, and then a tight smile suggested itself at the corners of his mouth. It said to Rupert, "there isn't anything here I haven't seen a million times before." Rupert knew at that moment with a kind of revelatory certainty, the sheer folly of what they had attempted.

The agents brought him to a holding cell in Morristown and then drove him into Newark in the middle of the night. Unlike the agent who had surprised him in the hunter's cabin, they were arrogant and very aggressive. They punched him between the shoulder blades to get him up and moving and then dragged him by the handcuffs from a windowless van in a dark parking garage into a dirty, creaking elevator. He was led down a long hallway and shoved along through some offices and into a windowless room, with a metal table and chair. The interviews were intensely, physically debilitating. There was a lot of shouting and ridicule. The verbal attacks harped incessantly on his, Scheiner and E's naïveté and arrogance.

"I told you before but I'm going to tell you again and keep telling you till you finally get it! You motherfuckers were in so far over your heads that your obliviousness was probably the only thing keeping you alive. Brashness doesn't make up for street smarts with these guys. It's quickly seen through. The worst thing that can happen to you in Paterson is when predators like Los Fuerte size you up and realize you got nothing. You, E and Werner Scheiner are just a bunch of spoiled, middle class kids from the suburbs trying to fake it. Now you're nothing but walking corpses in their estimation, and they'll get around to you in their own time. It won't take long."

The agent stood up and put his foot on the chair he had been sitting in. He put his elbow on his raised knee and leaned over the metal table, his shirt stained by coffee and perspiration. He smelled sharply of sweat, but also garlic, and in the small, hot interrogation room it was acrid and suffocating.

"E and Scheiner are on the run, but listen, and if you hear anything I've said today this is what you'll want to consider. The luckiest thing that could happen to those two assholes is if we find them first. You understand? You've actually got three different factions that want to kill you. There's Los Fuerte, your mobbed up supplier in Montclair who had the contacts with the Mexican Cartel and the Cartel itself. I'm sure the Cartel has at least a couple of Sicarios running around North Jersey anxious to be called into service and nail down any potential liabilities to the organization. Los Fuerte and the Mob guy know you'll rat them out. They saw through your shit pretty fast. They just strung you along, Los Fuerte to see how much dope you had and the Mob associate to see how much money you had. It was all about to fall apart and the luckiest thing that ever happened to you was the DEA coming in and busting you."

Rupert told him everything. After the second day, held in that brightly lit windowless room, without sleep, other than slumping and blacking out in the metal chair he was chained to while the Agent went out to get more coffee, he began to blubber like a kid who skinned his knee. He was a toddler who looks down to see torn skin and spouting blood drenching his leg and begins to wail like a fucking siren. Rupert's wailing rose up out of his pendulous belly, into his chest and then out of his throat. He couldn't do anything to stop it.

He was done, cooked, and he gave the Agents so much that they didn't even need E or Werner Scheiner who were caught and prosecuted fully for conspiracy when they might have been able to negotiate with the Feds. And the one thing he didn't know, but soon found out about his buddies from the North Jersey suburbs was that they could be as vindictive as any other sociopath in this world of murder and mayhem they had immersed themselves in. Their sense of vengeance didn't just die, it festered, and the poisons oozed and flowed and the infection grew.

He gave them the location of Los Fuerte's lab and headquarters which, when the DEA surrounded it and chucked in a few flash grenades, ignited and enveloped the entire Patterson block in fire. It was filled with highly combustible chemicals used in the manufacture of rock and meth. Three gang members came running out of the warehouse fully engulfed in sprouting flames that fanned out behind them like wings. They were shot before they hit the street. The DEA claimed they were shot because they pointed weapons at the agents. A dubious assertion Rupert thought, but shooting them was an act of mercy at that point.

Los Fuerte were decimated and a Bodega and Colombian restaurant were incinerated along with some staff and perhaps a customer or two. It was difficult to tell exactly how many had died due to the intensity of the conflagration and the difficulty in differentiating between the mostly featureless, charred lumps that were once people.

E's mob associate was spotted on Bloomfield Avenue in Montclair. After a car chase that lasted all the way into Newark and caused three collateral car crashes and killed a pedestrian trying to cross at a light, he was stopped in front of Rutgers Medical School. The agents rammed his car and pushed him into a parking lot. An agent hopped out and the mob guy fumbled on the seat beside him. He came up holding a Taurus 44 Magnum and the agent emptied a clip from his automatic rifle through the windshield directly into the perp's chest. His torso was literally blown apart and almost separated from his lower body.

After a week, Rupert was still being interrogated, now in Morristown at the Morris County Correctional Facility. He was held in solitary and not allowed to have any contact at all with the general prison population.

"For your own safety," the prosecutor said.

All of his assets had been seized and he was forced to have a public defender clown for a lawyer who spent more time joking with the agents than talking to him.

He was kept apprised, much to the enjoyment of the Morris County detectives, who had taken over the case from the Feds, with detailed and graphic descriptions of all the repercussions of his confession. But if they thought he was upset with what his criminality had caused other people to suffer, they were utterly mistaken. Even though ratting out practically everyone he had ever known or had any criminal contact with had won his own freedom, everything he built had turned to shit. It was all gone, swallowed whole by the justice system. The fruits of all that risk and effort had disappeared and was forever unretrievable. He felt like he was standing above a yawning abyss and the precariousness of his perch terrified and infuriated him. What he really cared about, the thing he obsessively went over and over in his mind, was whether he would also be swallowed up and what he would have to do to save himself.

The arrogance of his captors was intolerable. Anyone could plainly see that he had been victimized by E and Scheiner. Victimized by Los Fuerte and organized crime. Victimized by a legal system who used and abused him. He wasn't a fucking pinball bouncing off bumpers, ringing bells, getting clubbed and thrown back into play for the enjoyment of those who had, at least temporarily, some power over him. He was going to make his own fucking rules and woe to those who had taken advantage of him. There would be no more "weepy tragic parts" of the Rupert story. People sucked. The world sucked. You lie down on your back for a massage and perhaps a relaxing hand job and find yourself cut open from throat to scrotum while the masseuse steals your wallet. It was a wicked, wicked world.

No more. No way. Beat them to the punch. Pull the trigger first.

Push them into the conflagration before they know that you know. Let them all go to hell and burn to death in a world they set on fire.

Chapter Two

After it was all over, and Rupert had been freed from protective custody, or just plain custody, he wasn't really sure which it was, he felt alone and unable to muster the energy to do much about this new situation at all. Rupert needed a strategy to guide him through these unknown and dangerous waters. He went over and over what had happened to him and yet nothing materialized that was at all like the sudden inspiration which had guided his life in the past. This was new. He had always felt in control right up to the moment the flash/bang grenade had exploded in his atrium. Despite the therapist the court system reluctantly referred him to, he now felt out of control and could not bring coherence out of the jagged fragments his life had shattered into.

The Morris County Prosecutor who the DEA had turned the case over to after it had become apparent that Cartel members could not be implicated, had taken his confession and orchestrated the courtroom trial of E and Scheiner. Los Fuerte had been pretty much annihilated in the fire and it could not be determined whether there were any surviving members. When the trial ended and Rupert had been instrumental in sending E and Scheiner away for a good, long time, the Prosecutor suggested a move to someplace rural and hard to trace. He said Rupert should thank his lucky stars every night that there was insulation between himself and the Mexican Cartel. If he moved, and was discreet in keeping his name out of the news and his head low, it would be enough to protect him from E and Scheiner. The Cartel however, was a completely different matter. Once you came to their attention your fate was pretty much sealed and ultimately there was little law enforcement could do for you.

Despite the Prosecutor's suggestions, Rupert asked for witness protection and was told he should have thought about that a long time ago. He hadn't retained a proper lawyer and hadn't even sought any advice outside of his court appointed defense and the deal the Prosecutor had worked out for him by ratting out everybody in sight. He was on his own at this point.

"Look Rupert, you fucked over all your buddies and associates, I got you off the hook legally and everybody else is dead or in jail. Frankly, I don't really care what happens to you now."

What was he supposed to do? Park in the woods behind Indian Lakes and live in his fucking Escalade? He should have put the Green Pond McMansion in Pam's name and the state wouldn't have been able to take it away from him. He didn't because he always had to own everything. He liked having everything in his name because when it came down to it there wasn't anyone on the planet that he trusted, but he had to admit it wasn't always the right thing to do. When he left protective custody he had nothing and nowhere to go besides the Escalade which he stuffed with his clothing and some meager belongings they allowed him to take out of Green Pond. The Escalade's title and registration listed his dear, dead dad as owner. If he had assumed ownership the bastards probably would have taken that away from him too. There was also the cash from previous weed and ecstasy deals. They hadn't had the profit margin of what he attempted with E and Scheiner, but over the years had accumulated to a good bit of money. Rupert had secreted it all away in a safety deposit box in a Credit Union in Rockaway. He always had his stashes, never having full confidence in what the future would hold.

Rupert did not have anyone he could ask for shelter. He called an old client in Morristown whose heroin habit he had supplied discreetly for may years. His client was a physician who was well known in Morris County, but after the notoriety of the trial would not come within miles of Rupert.

When he checked in at the Sheraton in Parsippany he paid in cash. His credit card accounts had been frozen, investigated and then cancelled by the court and he had to hand over his driver's license for ID. The desk manager's name-tag said Isabel Vasquez. She grimaced very slightly when she looked over his documents, but he noticed. She looked up at him with a forced, scared looking smile. She took his license into a back room allegedly to make a copy of it although there seemed to be a copier right behind her.

"Broken," she claimed when he pointed this out. "It's broken, sir. I couldn't make a copy on the other machine either, but, you know, you paid cash, so, you're good to go."

No docs for him to sign? No ID or anything? Well, he supposed, the cash he paid with gave her the opportunity to pad her income a little. The lack of paperwork made her intentions pretty obvious. It wasn't anything he wouldn't have done himself.

Before checking in he had made a stop in Dover where one of the junkies at "The Wall" hooked him up with a few bags of dope and a small caliber Glock he had velcroed nice and high above the compartment in the back of his SUV. It was where he had hidden the coke when he transported it down to Paterson. When he got to Parsippany he put the Glock and 200 rounds of .22 LR hollow points in his attaché case wrapped in his socks and underwear, but available for fast retrieval. He had no idea what was coming next, but anyone with bad intentions was not going to find him an easy day's work.

He ordered a light dinner and planned to snort some dope afterward and lie around and watch movies. There was a knock at the door and figuring it was his dinner he opened it without the Glock and without taking any other precautions. No dinner. No hotel staff. Rupert scanned the hallway before something caught his eye hanging next to his door. Scrawled on a bag and fixed to the wall by a nasty looking blade was a note with his name misspelled prominently over the top.

"ROOBURT. Yeah motherfucker we find you. No big thing.

And we gonna kill you too. We kill you in our own time and where we fucking decide. You dead already. Just like in the movies motherfucker. Walking dead man."

At the bottom, written in larger letters than even the body of the message was the signature. "We The Strong."

He removed the knife, folded it and put it in his pocket. Once he had gotten the gist of the message and realized it was from his old employees, Los Fuerte, he stepped back into his room quickly and locked the door. He pulled the attaché case from under the bed and took out the Glock and filled a magazine with rounds. He pushed it up into the receiver and tucked the handgun into the back of his pants. He filled two more magazines with rounds and put them in his pocket. And then he waited.

His dinner arrived, but he was too nervous to eat much. What he did eat stuck in his throat and he gagged and choked and vomited into the toilet. He turned on CNN and tried to watch, but was so distracted he could not really follow any of the news stories or commentary. Scenes from the last few months of his life came back as a procession of images in his mind that he could not seem to stop. Rupert remembered how much the DEA Agents enjoyed telling him in grotesque detail about taking out his mobbed up contact with the Cartel and the horrendous fate of the members of Los Fuerte. He saw, with a scary feeling of actual presence, the faces of E and Scheiner as they were handcuffed and led out of the courtroom at the end of the trial, craning their heads and struggling to turn around against the guards pushing them forward, straining to get one more look at Rupert.

He waited until 3 a.m. and then carried his luggage over to the next wing and as quietly as was possible shuffled down the back stairway. He stepped outside and stashed his stuff behind a dumpster then took the most circuitous and darkest route to the Escalade. It was sandwiched in among a ton of other SUV's and did not stand out as much as he had feared. He had the Glock out and pulled back the slide and let it snap forward and chamber a round.

He was so scared he feared accidentally shooting himself almost as much as coming face to face with Los Fuerte.

He stopped and squatted beside the driver's door of a Ford Explorer. He put a hand over his forehead and took a moment to steady himself.

Fuck it, they weren't going to win. He wasn't going to go out like that. Bastards lived the life and took their chances just like him. They were going to pay if they fucked with him.

He moved his finger outside the trigger guard and folded his other hand over the fingers below his index finger. When he stood he held the weapon out in front of him and was ready to shoot anyone who challenged him.

He saw two figures walking slowly toward him. They wore hoodies and when they got closer he could hear them talking in Spanish and English. One was complaining to the other that he was hungry and tired and didn't like this 24-hour shit.

"Meu Amigo, this is for our dead. You remember that when you feel tired. This we do to honor Los Fuerte and our brothers. Someone has to pay."

They stopped at the back of the Explorer and Rupert dropped and rolled under the SUV whose high ground clearance he was thankful for. He rolled to the other side and came out behind the two gang members. He stood and crept to the back of the Explorer stepping away from the truck and holding the Glock out in front of him with two hands. Because he was a big man his movements were almost impossible to perform noiselessly. Los Fuerte spun around and then paused when they saw the handgun.

"Whatcha gonna do with that popgun," one of them said smiling. "Whatcha got there, a fucking .22? That maybe sting a little, but you know, I tense up hard and that shit just bounce right off."

He started to reach for his waistline where Rupert could see the outline of a handgun and Rupert popped off three rounds in a tight pattern in the center of his chest and then turned his gun toward his friend. The guy he shot dropped and was dead in seconds, a groaning exhalation while lying on the asphalt the last sounds he was to make in this world. The other guy looked at him aghast and began to turn to run. Rupert got off a shot that winged his shoulder and the guy ducked between the Explorer and the next car and scrambled up between the rows of cars and was gone.

Rupert saw a splotch of blood on the asphalt under the parking lot light post and thought perhaps he could follow the blood trail. He walked up a few rows of cars and abandoned this idea realizing the best thing he could do now was just get the hell out of there and disappear. He didn't know how many Los Fuerte had survived. He didn't even know how many had come to the Sheraton to kill him. The woman who checked him in must have been an associate. The gang probably had a network of informers all over Northern New Jersey. Best just to go at this point.

He found the Escalade and drove over and retrieved his stuff from behind the dumpster. He threw it in the back of the SUV and opened the driver's door with his foot up on the running board when he heard a revving engine. He turned and saw a Toyota Corolla come careening around the row of cars nearest to where he stood and accelerate toward him. He managed to jump in and throw it into reverse and slam down on the gas. The Escalade flew back, the tires spinning on the asphalt. The Toyota hit the dumpster dead on and the front end nosed down with the impact throwing the rear wheels up in the air. It was a horrendous crash. Rupert saw smoke from the engine compartment and then flames which licked the windshield of the Toyota from under the hood and then spread through the passenger compartment. He heard the screaming of the trapped driver. Rupert spun his truck around and in his rear-view mirror saw the car engulfed and burning furiously and then heard the whoomph of the igniting gas tank.

He smiled and paid homage to an ambitious Paterson street gang who with a bit more luck might have pretty much run Paterson and who knows what else.

"To Los Fuerte," he said aloud, "some tough motherfuckers,

who I fervently hope are now as extinct as the dinosaurs."

Chapter Three

He had no idea where he was going, but when he saw the entrance for Rt. 80 it was like a beacon and he turned onto the ramp and headed west. Once past Stanhope and then through the toll and into Pennsylvania he began to feel like yes, he had done the right thing. There wasn't any evidence he had ever been in Parsippany and he doubted rather strongly whether Isabel would give the police any information given her obvious complicity with Los Fuerte. Perhaps however, it would have been a good idea to pay her a visit before he retreated.

But still, no one knew where he was. He stopped at a rest area on the highway and hid the Glock in the hidden compartment in the back of the truck and threw away the drugs he had bought in Dover. He had in mind to start over clean. Or as seemingly clean as he could be and still pursue the life he wanted, exactly the way he wanted to live it.

In a little tourist town, Ridgeway, Pennsylvania, that seemed to him to be an attempt to create a New Hope/Woodstock atmosphere near Allegheny State Park in rural Northwest Pennsylvania, he stayed for a week in a bed and breakfast. He spent some time ingratiating himself with the townies and shared breakfast and dinner with them at the local eateries and it felt like an investment. It wasn't easy to turn on the Rupert charm after all that had happened to him, but it was still there when he needed it. His interaction with these people was an investment in a kind of tilling of the soil which might produce something useful at a later date.

The town reminded him of some very pleasant summer weekends he had spent with Pam in New Hope, wandering around the galleries during the day and eating at sensational restaurants gay communities always seem to have in abundance. He missed her. He wanted her back. In no time he was back to chipping some dope. He considered it medicinal to counteract the anxiety and depression over his awareness that he was in fact the rat motherfucker E had called him at the end of the trial.

He knew the look of the guys who could give him what he wanted. He was looking for just street level, a bag at a time heroin, and he knew the pieces of shit he'd be dealing with like the back of his hand. No illusions. An inquiry here and there with likely looking scum bags and he soon had a meeting to cop some dope.

He met the guy the scumbags set him up with at the trail head to the Little Troby-Clarion River Rail Trail. He figured he'd be meeting some jerk off with a couple of bags of mediocre heroin, but that was all he was up to at this point anyhow. Instead, a tough but professional Latino guy told him he had the good stuff and he could buy a quarter ounce or take his chances with the Ridgeway dopers who sold shit filled with fentanyl and God knows what else and he'd be taking his life in hands every time he scored.

"We see whatcha been drivin, man. You don look like just no tourist chipping motherfucker. I take good care of you. You see. But you got to put up some cash, man."

Rupert handed him five one-hundred-dollar bills and the guy beckoned with a right index finger for more. They settled for a price Rupert thought he would never pay for dope, but he figured he'd be set for quite a while as far as his own use and could sell off a little here and there for extra money and bring down the cost of his own usage.

"*Te agradezco mucho,*" Rupert said with a courtly wave of his arm.

"Yeah, yeah, man. Whatever."

He thought he'd be snorting once in a while and it was good dope, but it wasn't enough. His anxiety was removed temporarily but rebounded with a vengeance. The doctor from Morristown whose addiction Rupert had kept well supplied, phoned in a prescription for syringes and boxes of needles. Chemically he was all set, but he still missed Pam.

And then Messages on his iPhone went BING! When he saw it was Pam he began to think he was on his way to rebuilding a life, under new circumstances certainly, but a life in all its potential for fullness and even, who knows, happiness.

He texted and then she called and told him over the next couple of nights how the DEA had arrested her on a conspiracy charge after his bust, but they knew from the extensive surveillance they had done that she was uninvolved. They threatened Pam with decades in jail hoping to scare her enough to corroborate everything that Rupert had told them and perhaps add to what the Prosecutor had on him in order to insure his compliance. While in custody and unable to get any drugs, her heroin use that Rupert had told her was occasional enough to not cause addiction, resulted in first cold sweats at night that left her and her sheets drenched, and then full out convulsions on the floor of her holding cell.

They were done with her anyhow and allowed her parents to stick her in a posh rehab place in Massachusetts. It wasn't far from the campus of the Insight Meditation Society where she learned to meditate and was taught a new way of understanding how to deal with her addictive impulses. She described her practice in detail, but Rupert couldn't get a solid sense of what it was all about.

"An intellectual understanding of this stuff isn't any good, Rupert. I don't know if you are using or not, but your addiction is probably still there lying in wait for you. You might not be using but you're still a junkie and its just a matter of time really. I'll come out and we'll practice together. You have to experience these mind states. It's a realization that only comes through the practice. You must provide for your own salvation, sweetie. You are the only one who can save yourself."

When her Forester pulled up outside the apartment he had just leased he felt so many things that he kind of froze up, but then she was in his arms and he choked up and she noticed. She pushed him back to look him in the face. It was tear streaked and sincere. She was well acquainted with the bullshit Rupert, the one who could talk just about anyone into just about anything, and she could see that Rupert was at least temporarily emotionally overwhelmed. It was reassuring. It was his truth shining through all his accretions of bullshit and she was the catalyst. When they walked upstairs to his apartment, he announced that this was an event that demanded a special kind of celebration.

"What do you mean?" Pam asked suspiciously.

"Honey, we've been through so much and for so long. I was miserable and alone missing you everyday. Some days I couldn't function at all ... couldn't eat ... couldn't sleep. I felt like after all we had done and what it cost me, that everything had turned against me, you know, like my life was corrupted and now I was separated from it. I literally felt, you know, life out of balance and nothing I could do would bring me back to it."

He went into the bedroom and came back with a dark teak case whose lid was inlaid along the edge with a thin strip of lighter almost blonde wood. It contained his works and a vial of powder.

She was shaking her head from side to side and muttering "No, no, Rupert you can't be serious."

She tilted her head down and began to cry softly. When she looked up with wet eyes and her mouth contorted and ugly, his happiness that she was finally with him again seemed to diminish. What he felt instead was a kind of clinical interest in just how much he could get her to submit to him.

"C'mon," he said, "Just a little taste. We both know how much we love this shit. We shoot a little dope and lie around in bed and watch TV and later make love. We know its gonna be great. We deserve it. We do this once. We don't have to do it again. Honey, its special. After all we've endured ..."

She knew she was a junkie. She was a junkie who hadn't been using, but she was a junkie just like him and this was all too much for her. There was the bust, the separation with Rupert and there had often been times when she did not even know her lover's fate, or even if he were still alive. Now there was reunion. She did not want to lose him again. It was all so overwhelming and what she had learned at IMS now seemed somehow weaker. They went into the bedroom where he shot her up and she nodded, her chin on her chest and it was what he said, she loved it and she loved him.

He cleaned his works and then got high himself. They lay back on the bed and the TV was on that ridiculous channel with the Pawn Shop and the Pickers and it was a background drone that he alternately watched, intertwined with Pam and then would fall into the most delicious, golden reveries — sensual, with Pam's semi conscious, warm, body sliding across his deep, deep, deep in his plush, benevolent and infinitely safe bed.

But it wasn't going to be just once.

She could feel the power that drug had over people. She only got high once since the bust, but the next day she was edgy and all she could think about was that feeling of perfect well-being, like a stoned reverie inside a bubble of self sufficiency. It was a a state whose analogue in un-stoned reality she and Rupert had not experienced very often in their lives. They woke up the next morning and showered and ate breakfast at the local coffee shop. She was hungry and the strong coffee cleared her head and she could feel her energy coming back into the body.

"It was good wasn't it honey?" he asked pushing his eggs around his plate not yet fully back to the land of the living.

She looked at the floor and shook her head emphatically. "Rupert, let's never do that again." She looked into his eyes imploringly. She put her hand out and clasped his forearm. "It's important we make this decision now. That drug ... it's, ... you know, it's just too good."

"Yeah," he said giggling. "Exactly! That shit is just too fucking good!"

While walking back to the apartment after eating she convinced him to spend some time with her hiking and camping in the mountains.

"I'll teach you a simple practice and it's something that deepens as you become more skillful. Let's go someplace quiet, sweetie and we can meditate and hike and eat good food at some new places down in the valley. This is good, maybe we needed a last dance with the devil before going in a different direction, but lets get healthy. Body, mind, and spirit. This is where we need to be right now."

They bought some gear and looked on the web for information about hiking trails and places to camp. They paid for a week at the State Park and it had clean showers and toilets just a short walk from their camp site.

It was early evening when they found their campsite. Rupert set up their equipment and built a fire in an open pit around which he put their foldable camp chairs and a canvas backed quilt they could lie on. Pam threw a couple of meditation cushions on the quilt and carried over the big Styrofoam cooler they had bought and showed Rupert the beer and marinated chicken they could grill.

She sat on one of the meditation cushions and folded her legs.

"C'mon, honey. I've been looking forward to showing the practice to you. Let's give it a try."

Reluctantly he sat next to her and when he folded his legs his knees were sticking up at alarming angles and he could not sit upright.

"Oof, you're so stiff," she said. "We're going to need a little yoga too."

Rupert frowned. She got her sleeping bag and folded it up into a one-foot-high square. She perched the cushion on top and Rupert sat and his legs were down and he was stable. She gave him instructions and Rupert closed his eyes and folded his hands in his lap.

But he couldn't do it. Not even close. The harder he tried, the more frantic and energized his thoughts and fantasies became. His thinking centered obsessively around how he could have done this, or should have done that, all the possible strategies that would have allowed him to maintain control over his drug deals, his friends, his criminal associates, his girlfriend and prevent getting busted. It was a life that had gone out of his control and from whose resulting chaos he had surrendered and then run away.

"Fuck, fuck, fuck, fuck, fuck!", he screamed.

Pam stiffened and her eyes went wide with fright.

He stood upright, grabbed the cushion and threw it into the fire. She pulled it out before it began to burn and he glared at her.

"What are you trying to do to me? You don't think I was tortured enough by all that shit, now I gotta relive it too?"

He stomped off toward the car. Pam called after him that the practice was like that sometimes in the beginning, but that it was worth the effort and the discomfort.

"The only way out is through," she said

When he came back from the car she noticed that he seemed suddenly a lot calmer.

He hiked with her and they ate at a nice restaurant in the valley, but he seemed a little detached and then wanted to go back to the apartment a few days earlier than they had planned. She told him in the car on way back to Ridgeway that she had decided to go back to her parents in New Jersey for a while, but that she could always come back.

"But you're going to have to decide what you want, Rupert. It's a choice and you can't have both. I love you. I need you strong, healthy, healed emotionally and spiritually from everything we went through. That drug ... its so clear to me now. We're like the walking wounded, susceptible, vulnerable, and we have within us the seeds of our own healing. But its tough. Its a tough road, and that drug ... it offers such complete cessation from all the pain, but, you know, a big price. It doesn't work as well after a while and you need more and more and you chase that sweet cessation right down into hell."

She turned in the seat of Rupert's Escalade crying, her face streaked with tears and faced him gesturing dramatically, her palms raised heavenward in either resignation or supplication he wasn't sure which.

"I love you, Rupert, but I can't stay with you anymore. Stop using and I come flying back to you again. I promise I will, sweetie. I promise."

He snorted a little dope just before they got in the car to drive back to Ridgeway and he was feeling fine, not stoned but really, really, comfortable. He didn't want to talk and he didn't want to engage with another human being whose needs and conflicts always required such futile and messy negotiation. He just wanted to sit there in the Escalade and groove along to the gently vibrating roadway and listen to a little Revolver era Beatles on the magnificent stereo. But Pam wanted to relate and shit although when they got back to his place he had little to no idea what the fuck she had been talking about for the last hour.

She packed up her car and he convinced her to stay for dinner before the trip home. He sat her in front of the TV and said he'd take care of everything. He had some frozen skirt steaks pre-marinated from the Whole Food's around the corner, a vegetable salad and chunks of fresh mozzarella di bufala he served on a toasted, crusty, wholewheat baguette.

They ate and she enjoyed the meal and was about to compliment him and maybe even reward him with a little impromptu, going away love making, but he was watching her so intently and she was suddenly feeling so woozy. She was scared and stood up. The dark spots swimming in her vision made her sit back down again fast. She started to raise her arms in protest and wanted to shout to Rupert, but her mouth was all rubbery and wouldn't work right. She no longer had the strength to sit upright on the couch and couldn't feel her arms enough to prop herself up and prevent falling into that vortex of dizziness and blackness that she fought and then couldn't do anything but succumb to. The dark spots converged in her vision until there was only blackness.

When she woke she was in the bedroom tied to the headboard and footboard of his bed with strips of a torn up sheet. Rupert had his back to her and was hunched over intent on whatever he was holding. He turned around when she tried to say his name with her still rubbery mouth and she saw it was the box that held his dope and his works. She was terrified. He looked at her inquisitively, his expression surprisingly calm even gentle for someone who had just drugged and tied her up.

"I can't let you leave me, Pam, don't you understand that? This is best, you'll see. I know you're scared, but listen, I want you to love this great thing that I love. That's all. I don't want to hurt you. Dope is the great thing in my life that allows me to tolerate everything else. For people like us maybe, you know, it's just irresistible. Stop fighting it. I need you to do this with me. Don't abandon me now, Pam."

He seemed suddenly angry and she whimpered. Her fear had a calming effect on him.

"I need this and so do you and we can handle it. That's the problem with junkies you know, the drug controls them. But listen, we're smart enough to control it."

She hadn't regained full motor control and pulled weakly at her restraints. She shook her head from side to side and her eyes were wild and flitted around and around in their sockets, but she could not seem to fix on him. She was not going to be able to get away.

He was smiling as he pulled the drug up into the syringe. He tied her off and pushed the needle into the vein in her arm.

"A big dose and then, you know, maintenance. It'll be all right, hon, you'll see. Think of it as medicinal. A medicine for our relationship, and to make this wicked world bearable."

He pushed down the plunger and the drug was pushed into her circulatory system. Her eyes lost focus and he smiled knowing what that rush felt like. Her body went suddenly limp and the drug began to depress her respiration and started to shut down cardiac function. She turned blue and the arm he was holding was cold and clammy.

Her pupils had constricted to pinpoints. He dropped her arm in shock and her head lolled back on the pillow and then dropped to an unnatural angle on her chest. He felt her neck for a pulse, but could not find one.

He sat on the bed for a long time staring at her. Slumped and lifeless looking, her body didn't appear completely human anymore. She looked to Rupert like a thing and not a person. It was fascinating in a way. Her Pamness seemed to have drained away until it was just a memory that resided only with him. It felt like what he had known as Pam no longer had anything to do with this object draped across his sheets.

But she did not die, and Rupert, no longer concerned with someone he didn't think had any further use in his life, did not notice. Afterwards, when she had fully recovered, she remembered only the blackness and nothing else. She had stood on the edge of the abyss and looked over the edge. It was impetus for all of what was to come. She had nearly been annihilated. That was what it felt like to her. It was like her entire life and all her experiences had been reduced to mere collateral damage caused by Rupert's sick, sick, sick acting out. Everything in her was repelled and outraged by this. He wasn't going to walk away without facing retribution for what he had done. And the thought of him remaining free, spreading suffering like some kind of pestilence, haunted her and would not let her be.

Chapter Four

He closed the door to his bedroom and slept on the couch. In the morning he called Matias who had sold him the heroin. He assumed that Matias, if not an actual Cartel member, was at least connected. They met on the street that night outside Rupert's apartment because Matias did not talk business on the phone under any conditions. Rupert drew out the general outlines of his predicament, but claimed it was for a friend who had gotten himself in trouble with a prostitute he had gotten high with and who OD'd. What he needed was disposal of remains, disposal of a car and personal items and the cleanup of fingerprints, DNA and anything else that could be traced back to the prostitute.

"Yes bro, we can do this for you easy. No problem. Your troubles disappear completely and you never have to worry again. But it cost you big, bro. And you got to have money up front and no questions about nothing. You understand? This part is very important. You pay, step back, and let us do our thing with no contact with the service providers at all. They see you, they talk to you, and you going to end up in the car with the body in the land of the disappeared. Yes? You can do this?"

Matias didn't even pretend to believe the story of Rupert's fictional friend. Rupert agreed to the terms and met Matias later at the Little Troby-Clarion River Rail Trailhead. He gave him 15K in 100-dollar bills, the keys to his apartment and the keys to Pam's car. It was Thursday and Matias told him to get lost and come back on Sunday. Rupert had transferred his drugs, cash and paraphernalia to the hidden compartment in the Escalade. He was looking forward to a doper's lost weekend in a good hotel a few cities over.

"When you come back your troubles will be over, bro. No worries."

"A weight has been lifted off my shoulders," Rupert said. "I feel that I am in a new phase of my life, new vistas, new goals and all kinds of possibilities. Sometimes you just have to let the old way of doing things and the old way of thinking about things drop away."

"Yes, yes, my friend, I see this now. A new life for you. Or at least a new girlfriend."

Rupert frowned and Matias raised his hands with his palms facing Rupert, his fingers spread wide.

"Enough! Listen, we will talk again." Matias said, "I have a feeling we will be doing much business together in the future, *meu amigo,*" And while walking back to his Explorer said it again, muffled, sarcastic, but audible enough for Rupert to hear, *"meu amigo."*

Rupert climbed up into the Escalade and headed out on the road. He felt unfettered and excited. Accidents happen. He had been trying to do something something hard for other people to understand, perhaps risky, but ultimately the best for both of them. He wasn't concerned that other people would be unable to see it. Now he needed the Cartel to take care of all the loose ends and complications that might incriminate him because, besides Eastern European and Latin American dictators, the Cartel seemed to have the greatest ability to make people who had been walking around one day, completely and utterly disappear the next. It was a good choice. He knew his limitations. He still felt independent and self sufficient, like a lone wolf, even though he occasionally needed the resources that someone like Matias could offer. Rupert was someone who did not need to play by the rules of a society that had no right to judge someone like him. He was not a mediocrity and that was who rules were for.

Late that evening Matias received an urgent text from his clean up crew within minutes of their arriving at Rupert's apartment.

"Unexpected developments, you come quick."

He parked two blocks away and came up the backstairs and into the kitchen. His guys opened the bedroom door and gestured for him to enter. Pam was sitting on the side of the bed drinking some water and coughing a little. It had been almost twenty-four hours since Rupert had shot her up and for most of that time she was as close to death as a human being could be and still come back to the land of the living.

Matias looked at his guys.

"We not no executioners," one said. "We do the clean up crew stuff, yes. Sometimes messy, but, you know, we don kill nobodies."

They were all nodding and looking at him and definitely not doing what they had been sent there to do.

Pam looked at Matias and said haltingly but clearly, "I will make a good deal with you. You'll see. You take care of me now and I'll pay you whatever Rupert is paying you. I mean it," she said and tried to stand.

She gagged and coughed uncontrollably, then threw up a thick yellow bile on the front of her shirt. Matias laid her down on the bed again.

"OK. You pay and I take good care of you, yes? Rupert don't have to know nothing."

He got a little more water into her and one of his guys went to get his car and waited at the corner with his lights off. Matias ended up carrying Pam down the back stairs and out into the street. His guy pulled up the car quickly and quietly and they loaded her in the back seat prone but belted in somehow and drove off. Matias told his crew to proceed as usual, cleaning everything and disappearing all of Pam's belongings. This time however, the vanishing act, which was always as irrevocable and as absolute as if that person had never existed, would not include a body.

He drove to a safe house the Cartel kept in a little rural industrial town halfway back to the New Jersey border on Rt. 80. He called in the nurse practitioner he used for his crew. She took care of the normal injuries endemic to their business, bullet wounds, stabbings, beat downs resulting in concussions and broken bones. She hooked up an IV, but said it was too late for Narcan or other detoxifying drugs. The drug would be fully out of Pam's system within three days. Her body had shut down almost to the point of death and had been terribly traumatized. She needed rest and to allow plenty of time for a slow recovery.

Pam was more exhausted and felt more desolate than she had ever been in her life. Back and forth she shifted unbearably between fury and despair. The fury was ignited by a certainty that she had been the only woman in the world to have ever fallen in love with someone utterly incapable of love. And when her indignation waned and its energy drained away to despair, it smothered her. She had the certainty that only she could have been enough of a loser to fall for someone and be blind to the fact they lacked the ability to love another person they way some people lacked a kidney or a limb.

As she hydrated and began to clear the poisons from her system her head also cleared. Rupert's words to her just before he shot her up came back if not word for word than certainly in terms of intent. He nearly killed her because he wanted company in his drug addiction. The sheer sociopathy of that desire sickened her. He had drugged her food and tied her to his bed like the abducted girls in Taken. It gave her a new lens through which to view a lover she had never really known. His charm and his wit had hidden a toxic, even an evil narcissism, and he was loose in a world that he could bullshit as easily as he had bullshitted her.

It was a period of taking stock. She needed to assess her own life and then decide what it was she wanted to do about someone as dangerous as Rupert. How far out on a limb did she want to go, how much did she want to risk. She felt she had been entwined in his madness and surely her gullibility and her own drug use had acted to some degree in enabling the monster. A determination was now set in motion inside of her. Initially she was furious with Rupert's betrayal, but the more she understood him the more a calm, even cold calculation set in. She was going to clean up the mess her life had become and the first order of business was Rupert.

Her grandparents had left her a sizable trust fund which she had come into possession of only in the last few years. Her parents had tried to take control of it knowing about her drug use and suspecting even before the bust that Rupert was the origin. When they couldn't find a legal way to accomplish this they tried to have her declared mentally incompetent and get her institutionalized. She never forgave them and they, horrified by their suspicions of her hardcore drug use, now also doubted the morality of what they had attempted to do. They had been told by her psychologist who risked prosecution by even contacting them, that if they did not intervene they should be prepared to bury her. It was a terrible double bind. Their failed attempt at institutionalizing their daughter left them utterly guilt-ridden and later unable to make decisions about even the most black and white realities of their relationship with Pam. It made them easily manipulated by the very worst impulses of their daughter.

Rupert, over a year or two, convinced her, little by little, to withdraw half of the trust fund and put all the cash in a safety deposit box in his Credit Union. He wanted to be able to use the money to make large purchases of drugs and did not want forensic accountants to be able to follow the money. He never got around to using any of the cash, but now it gave her the resources to fund an off-the-grid, anonymous new life. She undertook this mission feeling that it was really about protecting other people from the threat and the evil of Rupert. His narcissism made him insatiable. He was a carnivore that devoured everything he encountered. But she knew what he was and she had the power to do something about it. As far as her family and everyone who knew her, she had been disappeared, as suddenly, completely and irrevocably as an adversary of a drug Cartel or the hapless opponent of an Argentinian style military Junta.

Rupert was going to celebrate this new chapter in his life with a stoned weekend and indulge without restraint in the thing he loved best in this world. The drug gave him a feeling of euphoric wellbeing and an almost unassailable sense of safety and self sufficiency. These had been states that had been quite elusive throughout most of his life. In fact, there was only one person he could remember whose relationship with him contained anything resembling what heroin gave him. But he had paid a big price for what the rest of humanity seemed to get for free.

He remembered his grandmother Renata, a force of nature who drunk or sober bulldozed her way through life and was more Mother to him than grandparent. He remembered her intelligence and personal power and how in so many ways he had always wanted to be like his Grandma Ren. His memories were sharp and it was almost as though she was materializing now right in front of him at a point in his life when he needed her the most.

Rupert's grandmother was a German Jew whose red hair and fair complexion allowed her before the war, to pass as an Aryan in the household staff of her father's employer. After Kristallnacht her parents had fled first to Poland, and then with the German expansion into Austria and Poland went on to Holland. The idea was that once they had settled and Hitler's expansionism was satisfied by swallowing Poland and the frontiers of what they imagined were a few other "lesser" nations, that they would send for their daughter. She never heard from them again and she survived the war working as a domestic in the household of her father's former boss. She was twelve years old at the start of the war.

After the family she worked for were killed, and the house was destroyed along with the rest of Hamburg in the firestorm caused by Allied bombing, Rupert's Grandmother had been left homeless. Fortuitously, the family had sent her out of the city before the bombing after a Nazi official began asking some troubling questions about her family's origins. She rushed back to Hamburg and was left sifting through the ruins of the city for shelter and sustenance along with most of the rest of the surviving German civilian population. She told her children that although she was a Jew, she was horror struck to see what looked like the entire German nation on foot and migrating en masse from devastated village to burnt-out city living in the rubble of a surreal apocalyptic scenario.

"Like something you could never imagine even with a whole life to try to dream up such things," she used to tell Rupert.

She lived in rags and in the shattered cellars of bombed out buildings. Rats the size of small dogs watched her from the periphery of the fire that she kept stoked all night to keep them away. She was raped by a group of boys who beat her and left her with both tuberculosis which swept through the destitute homeless like a plague, and syphilis. She was treated successfully only when the Allies took full control of Germany and she was transferred to the displaced persons camp that finally made the arrangements for her immigration to America.

When she came to America she was twenty. The GI's she met as she worked her way through the post-war bureaucracy invited her to their parties and she began the drinking that continued throughout the rest of her life with varying intensity. It peaked when Rupert was about the same age that she was when she wandered alone through the rubble of Germany.

She married an older man she had never met just before the marriage ceremony. She had certainly never loved him, but he was a lawyer and a member of the Orthodox Synagogue in Newark, New Jersey that Renata belonged to. The Synagogue was committed to increasing birth rates among Holocaust survivors and were particularly interested in helping European Jewish orphans like Renata. Its efforts consisted mainly in pressuring refugees to submit to arranged marriages. The chief Rabbi was a war refugee himself from a shtetl just outside of Vilnius and his old world ideas could not comprehend American dating, romantic love and the idea of individual choice in making fundamental life decisions.

In Germany, her Judaism was somewhat superficial and her categorization by others as a Jew was forced on her by Nazi anti-Semitism more than by any cultural or ethnic attributes. Once safely in America, after enduring some of the worst atrocities in all human history, she needed the black and white realities of a conservative world view to climb out of the trauma, doubt and despair that enveloped her. The Seagram's 7 she began drinking with her morning coffee and continued throughout all her conscious hours also helped.

The marriage produced two children; Rupert's mother and a son, who after coming of age disappeared and was never heard from by any family member ever again. Rupert's mother, Eliana, was dominated by Renata in a relationship where she was little more than an appendage of Renata's, or perhaps more accurately a convenience, whose life purpose was only to further the aims and the projects of her mother. Renata hadn't allowed her daughter to marry until she was in her middle thirties claiming the need of her assistance in running the family's Newark Law Office.

When Eliana gave birth to Rupert, Renata promptly divorced her husband and moved in with her daughter and her daughter's husband, dominating that household the way she had dominated her husband's law office and her own home. Rupert remembered her holding court in the dining room while doing the family business. She sat at the head of the table with Rupert's father and mother along either side listening subserviently to her latest decrees, one of her knees bouncing furiously fueled by a lifetime of accumulated anxiety.

Rupert hated his mother for her passivity and throughout his life hardly deigned to even talk to her. It was a relationship his grandmother exploited and found amusing. Renata was a force of nature that ran over and plowed under any obstacle, human or otherwise, that stood in her way. Living with her was to never know what her reaction would be to even the most innocent interaction. Rage erupted as easily as love, but Rupert treasured those times as a young boy when they would spoon while watching TV, his back curled into her stomach and chest and feeling at least for the moment that the world was benign and that throughout his life he would be rewarded by a universe that made sense and gave good things to those who made the effort. These were the feelings he felt again for the first time since her death when he began to use dope. The only thing in the world that was at all like the feeling of well-being he had wrapped in her strong, authoritarian arms was putting a needle in his vein and succumbing to the drug he had found to replace her.

Chapter Five

Monday morning on his way back to Ridgeway, after an extremely stoned weekend he had spent mostly in the room of his hotel, Rupert turned his iPhone back on and his phone mail was full. He wondered how many calls he had missed. Pam's parents had left at least ten messages. They had expected her home the previous Friday evening. Their tone was at first concerned and friendly requesting what they said they knew would be his anxious help, and then in ensuing messages becoming upset, voices tense with growing suspicion, and finally accusatory, frantic and overtly threatening. The last call was a request from the Ridgeway Sheriff's Office notifying Rupert that a missing persons bulletin had been issued for Pamela Scheider last seen in the company of Rupert Levinsky. The department requested his presence at their office at his earliest opportunity to assist in their investigation.

When he got back to the apartment and checked in with the investigators it was a month from hell. He went from primary information source, to person of interest, to suspect in the first two weeks. He ran into what he assumed was Pam's parent's private detective on the street outside the restaurant Rupert frequented for dinner at the end of the month. The bastard knocked him down and told him that although the investigation wasn't turning anything up and that he would probably walk, that he would pay, and he would pay big time.

"They told me about the drugs, you know. And how you got their daughter hooked on your shit and took her away from them. I think that you're probably the type of guy who thinks other people aren't, you know, real or something. Like you're the only guy going whose life really counts and everybody else is along for the ride. Just there to meet your needs, yeah? So ... it's like fine to hurt them. It's fine to get rid of them when their presence in your life is no longer convenient, because it doesn't really matter. Yeah? Any of this ring true to you, Rupert?"

Rupert looked up and began to push himself up off the sidewalk. "Fuck you," he mumbled, but maybe just a bit louder than he intended. He had to say something. He was angry and it just came out, but he was also afraid of retaliation from a guy who seemed kind of violent for a detective.

The detective kicked Rupert hard in his chest because he had heard him and also to give a little taste of what was coming. It left Rupert gasping for breath and curled up on the sidewalk in a town where he was now despised based on what were only allegations, without any evidence at all. When he tried to regain his feet he was so out of breath that he fainted and rolled out into the street. Cars were stopping, but when they saw that it was only their very own small town, celebrity monster, they honked, flashed their lights at him, opened windows and yelled profanities. "Ha, you got yours didn't you, fat bitch," - before finally swerving around him and spinning their tires as they accelerated away.

Rupert staggered to his feet and folded his arms across his chest protectively. He was furious and there was that clenched feeling in his gut he always got whenever he was in conflict. It was the desperate feeling that his whole world was endangered. It was the fear that all his projects were going to crash and burn, which ignorant pieces of shit like the entire town of fucking Ridgeway couldn't even understand. He wanted to kick in the doors of the car parked next to him and smash out all its windows. He walked toward the car and his rage began to subside when a poison flower of an idea began to blossom in his mind. There was gonna be payback for this. He wasn't going to take it. All the bastards that had treated him like a pariah since Pam's disappearance were gonna get theirs. Just wait and see if he didn't come out on top. He belonged on top. Fuck the DEA, fuck Ridgeway and fuck Pam's parents and anyone who had it in for him.

On his way back to Ridgeway he had buried the remaining dope and his works in a double bagged garbage bag in the woods beside the State Park knowing he would be investigated as soon as he crossed the city limits. When he returned to his apartment he was clean. He had been using regularly enough to feel the negative effects of suddenly being forced into abstinence. The physical effects were cramps and some morning retching, but he could handle it. What he was having trouble with was the anxiety that rebounded and surged after cessation of his "medicine."

The Ridgeway cops went through his belongings and car and he had to get a hotel room for a day while they searched his apartment. Despite a microscopic investigation of every centimeter of his living space, true to Matias' word, not a shred of physical evidence indicating foul play was found. The circumstantial evidence consisted only of Pam's presence in Ridgeway with Rupert and now the fact that she was gone. She came and she went, no one had seen any fighting, harsh words, or seen anything in their relationship that suggested vengeance, exploitation, or aberrant, dangerous sexual practices. In short, although he was shunned by the community as a monster, Rupert was free and clear.

The one thing that bothered him was his association with the three dirt bags he had approached a few months before in order to cop. They had been his intro to Matias and they knew about his predilection for heroin. But perhaps there was an opportunity here as well. Here was the possibility of payback. He could strike back at a town that had turned against him and also tie up a few loose ends. It was the opportunity to kill two birds with one stone.

He found it hard to believe, but just as E had said, there were companies on the Web advertising sales of fentanyl to foreign buyers. E had done some homework on fentanyl when it looked like they needed an "additive" to spike up an adulterated batch of heroin.

Rupert invented the name of a pharmaceutical company, GoodLife Pharma, He laughed when he considered the use for which he intended the shipment. When he texted a company in China they responded within an hour and by someone who wrote and spoke excellent English. They didn't need any additional paperwork other than an order form with the company's letterhead and contact info and could ship within 24 hours. Rupert ordered enough 3-methylfentanyl, four times more powerful than ordinary fentanyl, to kill half of Ridgeway. He had them send it to a post office box he opened in the next town over and it arrived in a week.

He didn't want to kill half of Ridgeway, but there were certainly three dirtbags in Ridgeway that the world could do without. When he left, he didn't want to leave behind anyone with compromising information about his predilections or his associations. He still had a lot of the dope he had bought from Matias. When he drove out to where it was buried he was tempted to allot a bit for personal use as well. He was surprised that his focus was so intense that he found the discipline to resist and brought back just enough to do what he was planning.

He bought some baking soda, a mask and good plastic hospital gloves. He wore his windbreaker with the collar up and zipped firmly to his chin. He had heard stories about the unbelievable potency of fentanyl. Within an hour he had ten bags of fentanyl laced heroin, carefully sealed and stamped with his GoodLife logo. There was enough 3-methylfentanyl in each bag to kill four men. The problem now was how to distribute to the right people. He had a shitload of the fentanyl left which he put in a pharmaceutical grade vial wrapped up in a plastic bag and sealed with duct tape and he took it out to where he buried his dope. He'd collect everything on his way out of town at the right time.

He knew what to do. All three dirtbags hung out together and with a bunch of other pieces of shit that the good citizens of Ridgeway could stand to lose. Two birds with one stone he thought - tie up loose ends and and take a little revenge on Ridgeway itself by eliminating some of the disreputable but still beloved sons of the community.

He tucked the heroin into his wallet along with eight-hundred dollars in hundred-dollar bills, but removed his credit cards, license and documents. He was sure that when he was robbed the discovery of heroin and cash would make the bastards overlook a somewhat depleted wallet.

That night he went to the dirt bag bar and let himself be seen drinking heavily. He sat next to a row of calathea planted in a long trough-like basin and all night he surreptitiously dumped most of his drinks in there. The dirtbags came in around eleven and immediately spied him sitting by himself. They made the rounds with other groups of friends, but he could tell they were talking about him. Rupert theatrically had a loud, drunken argument with the bartender who he accused of giving him the fish-eye. He went to the bathroom and made sure to knock into a few tables and elbow roughly past people. He could see the dirt bags smiling out of the corner of his eye, amused at how easily Rupert was setting himself up to be taken. One of them finally walked over.

"Mr. Levinsky," he announced standing by Rupert's chair with his elbow on the bar, "You've made quite a name for yourself in our little town. You seem to be having a good time tonight, but all by yourself. Don't you want any company on a Saturday night? I guess the Ridgeway ladies might be a little concerned about being alone with you right now, but listen, I'm not, so let me sit down and buy you a drink. OK?"

Rupert was holding his Seagram's 7 and 7 in front of him, swiveling his body back and forth and letting his big belly slop the drink over the sides and into his lap. He leaned over as if to speak to chief dirtbag confidentially and spilled his drink into the guy's lap.

"Ahh," Rupert said and started laughing. "I guess fucking not. You better run along home now and change motherfucker. Looks like you peed your damn pants."

Rupert slammed the glass down on the bar and pulled out his wallet. He rifled through the bills letting the money be seen and left a twenty on the counter for the bartender.

"Don't be stealing that now after I leave," he said to chief dirtbag. "OK? I know you freaking guys don't like to let any opportunity go by in this backwoods town. Not much opportunities out here for "gangsters" like you. Right? Am I right?" Rupert hooted and giggled and put his hand over his mouth drunkenly as if to stuff the words back down his throat.

He knew he was going to have to take a beating for all of this. But it was worth it. It was worth it. It was well worth it.

He pushed open the door to the bar still doing his drunk act and bumping into the frame and stumbling over the sill. He made it about a block down the sidewalk before he heard them running up behind him. They pulled him into a dark lot beside the bar and chief dirtbag hooked him hard to the side and followed by a straight hard shot to the abdomen. He doubled up and was happy to remember later the torrent of vomit he unleashed on their legs and shoes. They pushed him to the ground, went through his pockets, and were delighted to find along with the money ten bags of heroin. Within seconds they scurried out of the lot tossing his empty wallet onto a pile of scrap.

Rupert regained his feet clutching his belly and side and smiled.

Chapter Six

By morning, five errant sons of the good people in Ridgeway, Pennsylvania had overdosed on heroin. Two had died together and although they only snorted Rupert's concoction, it killed them as dead as if they had injected it into their veins. Three others were found alone, the needles still in their arms, having split the bounty and gone their separate ways to get high by themselves. The fentanyl was so potent that they hadn't even been able to push all of the drug out into their veins before losing consciousness and then dying. None of the media reports mentioned the other five bags that Rupert had prepared. Chemical analysis had been done on the drug still in the needle and revealed the excess fentanyl. Of course the media sensationalized the deaths immediately, suggesting a mass killing of the five whose past lent credence to their assertion that it had to do with a drug deal gone bad.

Which was actually true Rupert thought, and laughed, taking pleasure in his achievement as though he had put together a winning ad campaign or some other kind of business success. Perhaps the other five bags were in circulation in the dirt bag community and would soon yield more fruitful results.

Over the next week, two more dirtbags died in the next town over and whoever had ownership of the last three bags probably decided to get rid of them rather than risk causing any other deaths. Rupert felt triumphant. Disruption had come into his life to take him down and he had dealt with it and won. What people did not realize was that he was a force like natural selection, like predation itself. Eat or be eaten made things work on so many levels and he was its chief devotee and enabler.

Rupert stuck around Ridgeway long enough to savor the town's grief and go to the funerals whose crowded attendance suggested an emotional investment in these five lives that had never materialized in any practical way while they were alive. In the town park where an ecumenical outdoor service was held for all who wanted to attend, he walked around the periphery of the large crowd encircling the caskets. Halfway through the service he'd had enough and walked back to the parking lot where he left the Escalade. Before he could get to his car a black Explorer, the type favored by politicians and law enforcement, pulled up. When the window powered down it was Matias' grinning face that was looking at him. Rupert waited for him to speak and Matias just looked at him and then slowly raised a fist with his thumb up. The three or four shadowy occupants of Matias' SUV burst into raucous laughter and he slowly pulled away.

That night Rupert loaded up the Escalade, left the last month's rent in cash on his kitchen table, picked up his dope where he had buried it out by the park, and headed out on the road. He had a general idea of heading west and then in order to be evasive just in case, go north and double back east. Perhaps not necessary, but it made him feel safer to take some precautions especially after Matias' appearance. He hadn't known how to take that thumbs up by Matias, and the chorus of what he could only interpret as mocking laughter. Was that the Cartel's kind of sardonic approval, or was he now at risk from what he had hoped would be a valuable future resource? He could take care of a bunch of street junkies but Matias was hands off. He had the influence and fire power Rupert only dreamed of.

He wasn't sure how far west he would go and ended up in Cedar Rapids, Iowa. He stayed a couple of days in a surprisingly good downtown hotel, got high, watched movies and ate at a nice restaurant inside the hotel. After the second day he drove up to Minneapolis and from there planned to drive across the top of the country and look for longer term lodgings in New Hampshire.

He wasn't sure why New Hampshire stuck in his mind other than the camping trip he had taken with his dad in the White Mountains when they climbed Mount Washington. He remembered telling

Werner Scheiner in great detail about the three-hour hike to the summit and how the July eighty-five degree temperature at the base had given way to a gusty forty degrees at summit. He and his dad had been so cold and exhausted by the hike up that they hitchhiked back down. They got a ride with an out-of-shape family that found their hike up the mountain a feat of almost miraculous endurance.

"You should have just driven your car up in the first place," said Scheiner laughing hysterically at what he thought was moronically self evident.

Rupert always took his insinuations personally, but let's face it, with Scheiner it was meant to be a slap in the face, a humiliation, an insult that was just one of a hundred thousand to take you down a peg.

In Minneapolis he checked into a downtown hotel near the clubs and restaurants and went clubbing that night. He was lonely, he was horny, and although he didn't specifically miss Pam, he had in mind to find someone like her. It was a late spring night and every kid in Minneapolis was out, half in the clubs and half in the street. The street had become as much of a party scene as the clubs themselves.

He skirted a couple of groups of kids before seeing a bunch with a few obviously single girls, huddled together, laughing, teasing each other with that lewd, sassy way a lot of college age girls had that he liked. He stood off to the side and watched them for a while. One of them was slim and muscular like Pam had been. She was teased the most and had a somewhat passive, scandalized reaction to it all. She was attempting to be a good sport, but obviously needed to be validated by the other girls. It was alluring and reminded Rupert of Pam when she was a Freshman at Drew. He remembered how that sincerity and sensitivity he liked so much always drove her into the most adorable and naive overstepping with people. It was her nature to become entangled and to feel instantly guilty for any misunderstandings that developed, which was perfect for someone with inclinations like his.

This girl wasn't a clone, but in all the ways that counted she was a member of the Pam tribe. Rupert skirted her group of friends and sidled up to her from behind.

"Ohh, they tease you a lot don't they?" he asked.

She turned to face him anxious that even though they had never met he should understand what the real intent of her friends was, which might not be readily apparent.

"They love me," she said. "They can't help teasing me because they know they can and I always react the same fucking way which they love." She looked down sheepishly when she said this and shook her head slowly from side to side, just like his former Pam.

Rupert hadn't expected her to use fucking. In fact, he would have thought that it was a word that she would never use. He kind of jerked back and opened his eyes wide and she laughed and he was smitten.

"Hey, who are you anyway?" she said laughing as she pushed his shoulder and tugged at his shirt.

Rupert saw she was interested in him and that there was now some connection that he could build on.

"What's your name, honey?" he asked.

"Pam," she said and he turned to her and smiled.

"Of course it is," he said. "Listen, do you like to get high?"

He took her into the Alibi at the Exchange and they walked to the very back of the club in the corner by some stacked up banquet tables and chairs on huge dollies. He offered her just the merest taste and she snorted it off the top of his fist and he emptied quite a bit more on his hand for himself.

She liked it. It was a light buzz to be sure, but she liked it and was still energetic enough to drag Rupert out onto the dance floor where the Electronic Dance Music, the strobe lights in perfect sync with the synthesized beats and his good dope made Rupert forgot who he was, what he was and where he was. He liked it a lot also. Outside of the pleasures of just plain dope, it was an intense experience and after half an hour he was exhausted and the new Pam had to drag him over to a table in the back and pour some hydrating agents into him. She ordered beer and between the dope, the dancing and the alcohol Rupert was soon bent over the table where suddenly he retched and a torrent of vomit gushed across the table toward Pam drenching the front of her dress and some splatter actually dotting her forehead and dripping down her face. She was speechless.

Rupert groaned and because he was so stoned tried to wipe the vomit off the table with a stiff arm as though all that was necessary was a bit of a cleanup and they could go right back to the activities of the evening.

"You come back my hotel, right?" he slurred and mumbled. "C'mon wif me. Yeah? I got works. I show you what to get high is all about. K, sweetie?"

Pam was beyond interpreting the garbled noise that issued from his hideous, befouled mouth. She didn't even look at him and after perhaps the luckiest but certainly the most disgusting series of events in her young life, she stood and bolted out of the club.

Rupert was instantly surrounded by four bouncers with towels and spray bottles of disinfecting agents. They sprayed him liberally and wiped him down and wrapped the towels around him so they could manhandle him to the front door and push him out into the street. He was lying motionless where a boot to the lower back had propelled him face first on the sidewalk and they felt it wise to call 911 before they went back into the club. By the time the EMT's came there was only a damp spot where Rupert's ample body had been lying.

Chapter Seven

Pam was athletic and fit now that she was out from under the malign influence of Rupert. She had lost thirty pounds since her days with him, but he was a six-foot-three, two-hundred-and-sixty-pound man. The most functional and deadly defense skills in the world like mixed martial arts, krav maga or systema were not going to give her any advantage if she physically confronted Rupert. She could punch him, she could kick him and as long as she stayed outside of his reach could probably hurt him to some modest degree. But as soon as he rushed her and enveloped her in that huge, mushy, but really quite strong body, well, it was probably all over. She needed firearms and the skills to properly use firearms if she was going to take this guy down.

She rented a bungalow in Mendham, New Jersey on a property with eighty, largely forested acres. Her place was situated down a private, dirt road out of sight from the main house and her privacy was almost complete. No one seemed inclined to conduct any business out in her part of the estate. She was in training mode and this place was perfect for the preparation and the skills she needed to develop. The owner had set up a crude shooting range deep in the woods and when he saw her canvas shotgun case on moving day he encouraged her to use the range anytime she wanted. The property was also a great place to run, having old, dirt roads that wound throughout its expanse, and she could lift weights at a nearby Y.

She had bought a car and a new wardrobe. She furnished her three room bungalow out of the IKEA catalogue on the web, but until they delivered, she slept in a sleeping bag on a yoga mat in her empty rooms. It made her feel tough and resourceful, like one of those female warriors in the dystopian TV series she currently favored.

She cut and dyed her hair, wore glasses instead of her contacts and stayed the hell out of Morristown where her parents lived. No one was looking for her and no one even expected that she was among the living. She felt secure now and was ready to go to war. She would conduct her campaign intelligently and exact as much of a terrible and painful price for Rupert's many sins as was possible. She was going to win. Rupert would not get away with how he had exploited and almost killed her. She was going to get this fucking guy for what he had done to her and what he would do to others if someone like her did not step up to do what needed to be done.

She got in touch with a former friend of Rupert's, who had a bitter falling out with him over Rupert's drug use and dealing. Mikael had been a member of the IDF's Special Forces and worked providing personal security for Wall Street heavy hitters He was a straight arrow with that particularly intense Israeli sense of righteous indignation and justice. She suspected he had always been attracted to her and she confided in him and he was happy to advise and give her instruction for all she wanted to accomplish. But she was surprised when after all she had accomplished living this anonymized, off the grid life elicited little in the way of surprise from Mikael.

"No big deal," he said with a smile and an Israeli's acceptance of all the surprising twists and turns life can throw at you. "We do what we gotta do, yes? I don't judge nobody's decisions." he said and was smiling and made Pam feel that she was not the only person to ever undertake something like this. That realization settled her down and made her feel more practical about the whole enterprise.

He bought her a 9mm semi-automatic Sig Sauer, "less recoil and shorter barrel for a woman," he said. He insisted she have a short barreled tactical Mossberg shotgun with a foldable stock that could be fired from the hip with a pistol grip, or have the stock unfolded and placed against the shoulder. Then he took an old, Italian target rifle with a tripod from his trunk and handed it to her.

"You can borrow this and learn to shoot accurately. If I give you real sniper rifle now and you miss target, well, no one in Mendham is safe," He looked at her with a straight face and then burst into roaring, laughter pounding the top of his fender with the side of his fist. "Those rounds will deflect off rocks and trees and, you know, the range is unbelievable. People will be dropping in the shopping center waiting for a latte,"

These Israelis are an altogether different breed she thought.

She shot everyday, three times a week with Mikael, and the rest of the time deep in the woods by herself. The owner of the place, a bit of an eccentric, was happy to leave her alone. She searched on-line for info on how to locate people, eavesdrop on their current internet activity and take them down, digitally as well as in the real world. Mikael was quite informative, but the best info she found was from the right-wing lunatics on 8chan. She established an online identity, made friends with a few prolific posters and received instruction in such things as doxing and all the other nefarious strategies people used to destroy other people.

Mikael insisted she learn to break holds and strike vulnerable areas like the trachea, eyes and groin, so that if she was physically restrained she would be able to strike, drop and roll, and come up firing her Sig Sauer. They worked together for a long time and the one thing he taught her, which influenced her perhaps the most profoundly, was, when it was appropriate, to psychologically commit to violence fully without remorse as a legitimate even moral way to bring her world back to order.

"This," he said, "was what made plans like yours possible. You must be ruthless and hard. You straight in the head and you find a whole new realm of abilities you never even knew you had."

Six months after Ridgeway and Rupert was living in Jackson, New Hampshire in a small mountain resort town in the White Mountains, selling dope to mountain dirtbags a bag at a time but not killing anybody. It was enough to keep him going. He also subbed for the local high school, teaching business classes to a bunch of kids whose only goal was to get the hell out of Jackson, New Hampshire and head for Brooklyn, New York City or Portland. His relationship with Matias made possible all the dope supply he would ever need. Matias' cartel had associates in most states, but Rupert still had to travel a couple of hours down to Manchester to score from his associates and he resented it.

His own use had spiked after Minneapolis and then subsided. He snorted occasionally, but did not think he had an addiction. In the meantime, like most of the kids in New Hampshire he had developed a taste for weed. The weed in Jackson was very good although quite expensive. It was a high end resort town with tourists coming in and out of town during all seasons. They had the usual refined tastes of people of their social class as far as cuisine and intoxicants, the intoxicants consisting mainly of expensive wines and only the most discriminating choices of weed. Rupert gradually moved his drug business into this more lucrative direction. It consisted of personal delivery of small volumes of extremely high grade and expensive product with a high profit margin.

Rupert approached his high end weed dealing business like a wine sommelier. He was an articulate and educated purveyor of choice and sumptuous wares. He could describe in detail the subjective qualities of the psychotropics he sold, and the pharmacology of why each strain differed in its effects. His language had the literary qualities of fine wine and food writing which his customers loved and quickly built him a sizable clientele based on word of mouth. They could not wait to introduce him to their friends and set him up at some tasting parties modeled after the wine tasting parties they had all enjoyed. It was a sizable investment for Rupert, but perhaps one of the highest yielding investments he had ever undertaken. It was even better then keys of coke and the talents of Los Fuerte to disseminate product.

He generally set out his buds and divided a white linen table into two sections: Sativa and Indica. He assumed that his Jackson customers were mainly an Indica crowd looking for sedating even relaxing highs and leaving the Sativa fireworks to the young people although he had a couple of Sativa strains. The buds were lovely to look at and fragrant to smell and after a short presentation he would stand by his table with all of his wares carefully labelled and conduct his audience small group by small group through a tactile, olfactory, and finally a taste tour of his product.

"The science of cannabis cultivation," he said, always referring to cannabis with his customers instead of calling it weed, "has progressed in sophistication and technology, and like the wine industry has combined with the artistry of decades of cannabis lovers to create something special, something quite remarkable. After all, cannabis is finally just another way humans have devised, like wine, like fine cuisine, and even art, to enjoy the full array of our human senses."

His customers looked at him with respect, even gratitude, thankful for substantiation of what they themselves already believed about their own recreational drug use, but did not have the eloquence to provide a rationale for. Rupert knew that with this crowd all you needed to win them over was to provide lots of bullshit justifications for what they already believed was their own innate superiority.

At the fifth of these cannabis tasting presentations, he was standing by his table and giving some of his more inquisitive customers bong hits, "one to a customer, unfortunately just a taste," he reminded them. A guy in good shape, carrying maybe a little more muscle than even a guy in good shape normally carries — which made it surprisingly difficult to assess his age — put a glass of wine into Rupert's hand while he had turned away to answer a question. Rupert was surprised and flinching slightly turned quickly to see who it was that had presumed any such desire on his part. Indefinite age was just part of what bothered Rupert about the guy. Rupert didn't like anything hard to read about other people, or anyone presuming anything about him. And part of his first reaction, although he didn't know why, was that here was a challenge, here was some potential danger. The guy's skin quality was thin, tight although slightly crepey at the neck. His hair was silvery and fine which gave him a patrician look and Rupert guessed he was probably in his seventies. Rupert stood without saying anything and waited for him to say something.

"That is a terrific peasant Chianti from a northern Italian village that my people immigrated to America from 100 years ago. The same family has probably been making it for 400 years. I took a plane into Milan, rented a car and drove an hour and half into the mountains to find that town. My wife and I had dinner at an outdoor cafe that we had to hike up to on walking paths that wound between ramshackle family houses built into the steep hillside. No roads for modern vehicles there, but I had perhaps the finest meal of my life on a terrace overlooking a lake with the friendly and inquisitive townspeople. It was capped by this."

He raised his glass to tap against Rupert's and both took a synchronous sip. He looked at Rupert expectantly. The wine had a deep, fruity flavor much like the cabernet that Pam favored. Rupert was not much of a wine drinker and knew little about wine, but liked this very much.

"Very good," he said with a lot of emphasis on very. His new friend smiled from ear to ear.

"Robert," he said to introduce himself. He switched his wine glass to his left hand and shook Rupert's firmly. "Retired. At least that's what ICare/BeautyCare tells me, until of course the new management team gets themselves in over their heads and I have to ride in and save everything... which has happened over the last ten years exactly three times and with three different executive teams."

The guy had a disarming smile. It was not the facial expression of a braggart or a rich, pompous ass, which his last statement made Rupert suspicious of. He offered Robert a small bong and reached for a pinch of his best Sativa, the J1. Robert put a hand on his wrist and shook his head. He smiled and held up his wine glass to Rupert and said, "The only intoxicants, in fact, the only drugs I use. I came with my wife who very occasionally likes a bit of weed, but we are not users by any means. Our friends insisted we come, I suppose more for sociability than possible sales for you. Sorry."

Rupert saw that Robert had charm and a natural sort of friendliness that disarmed people. But Rupert sensed something in his watchful, intensely observant attention and wondered if his social skills were tools cultivated mostly for corporate success and did not represent a natural beneficence or a genuine desire to be with other people.

"ICare/BeautyCare? You've always aspired to corporate executive officer status?"

"I was an English Major originally who got a low lottery number and sent to Vietnam at the tail end of that whole mess. After basic I volunteered for Special Forces. I was lucky enough to be exposed to a skill set that came in very handy much later. I went to law school when I got home after finding out what the practical realities of being a well read English Major that nobody wanted to employ was all about."

"You never practiced?"

"Ohhh, I practiced all right. Spent a few years as Assistant Prosecutor in Paterson, New Jersey and then a few years in private practice as a defense attorney specializing in rich kids who lose their way in life, if you get my meaning."

"Corporate executive, ICare/BeautyCare?"

"One of my clients was the daughter of an ICare/BeautyCare exec who got busted with a ton of drugs. I saved her. I saved her and she's still to this day a bratty, Paris Hilton type wasting her life and her father's money," Robert said, laughing a little. "I wanted out of defending people like her and her dad got me on his management team. Let's just say that he liked my style primarily because I didn't let anything get in the way of accomplishing my goals. After ICare/BeautyCare I got interested in the law again. I specialize in taking cases that the cops, detectives, and the courts have all failed at, but that with my background, a person like me might be the only way for my clients to achieve satisfaction."

Rupert eyed Robert uneasily. He put the rest of his wine down on the linen table and began collecting his weed and equipment. He swung his case up onto the table and caught the wine glass with its edge sending a spray of impossible to acquire in America, Italian Chianti spraying across the front of Robert's khakis.

Robert looked down at his pants and smiled. "It's all right. I understand. I make you nervous and I might as well tell you at this point that I really came here to relay a simple message," he brushed some of the wine droplets with a napkin he had picked up from the table.

Rupert looked at him and was thinking about his Glock velcroed up behind the wheel well in his RV.

"E. and Werner Scheiner. You remember them, yes?"

Rupert tried to say something, but Robert interrupted.

"I thought so. Thought you wouldn't have to worry about them for good long while yet, huh? Well, they have a new trial. There were errors in that first trial. Procedural mistakes in interrogation and evidence collection. Prosecutors figured they had it so sewed up with your testimony that they didn't have to pay attention to the details. I'm here to let you know that we expect to get them off. They're gonna walk and it will be soon."

Something halfway between a gasp and a moan escaped from Rupert's throat.

"They sent me up here because they felt you should know. And to tell you that the next time you see me it will be under very different and more dangerous conditions." He paused, "For you!"

Robert stepped up and stuck his index finger in Rupert's chest with his thumb cocked as though his hand was a pistol, "Put on your best game, pal. That's the way I like it."

Robert smiled and Rupert just looked at him. He didn't move and kept staring until Robert finally snorted and walked away.

"See you again soon," Robert said

Chapter Eight

He thought seriously about getting the hell out of Jackson, but didn't want to give up the weed business. It had the potential to make him lots of money. What he wanted to do was to go to his client's primary residences and establish networks of distribution among them and their wealthy friends who lived in major American cities. His wealthy clients didn't seem to have homes Rupert mused, they had "primary residences."

He'd set some of his Jackson contacts up in those cities as sort of glorified drug dealing delivery men. They all said they wanted to get the hell out of New Hampshire anyway and here was the perfect opportunity for a bunch of underachieving, overly medicated, rich kids. But he would be the one who established the networks and dealt with the clients. He'd be the one who would supply the weed. He'd establish control by having them do delivery and nothing but delivery, set them up with their own apartments with bank accounts he pumped money into. It would be all based on volume of delivery. All other details Rupert and a middle man who doubled as an enforcer would handle, especially monetary transactions and communications with clients. His guys would be mute, deferential delivery men and that was all. To insure the mute part might require a bit of discipline, but he didn't think that it was anything he couldn't handle.

All of this required coordination, enough bodies to keep the network viable and keeping abreast of all developments either unusual or routine on a regular basis. That might be the easy part though. After all, in today's world his primary tool would be his iPhone.

Robert had upset him, but he wasn't ready to bail on Jackson and the town was too small for anonymity. He couldn't change his name on rental agreements and all the other discoverable documentation one needed in life; there just wasn't any viable way he could hide out here. And anyway, after the delivery of his message/threat to Rupert the guy seemed to completely disappear. He had some time to prepare himself before Scheiner and E. finished their legal stuff and then make their plans as to how they would deal with Rupert.

He contacted Matias and Soprano's style arranged a sit-down in Manchester. He told him he had new plans for the biggest drug network he had ever attempted and needed supply but also protection. He figured it was in Matias' interest to brain storm with him about protection perhaps even eliminating the causes of his current discomfort. A couple of those Sicario's made famous in media and film working on his behalf and his problems could well be over. How much could it possibly cost anyhow? Whatever it was it would be worth it at this point. He desired to have his life back, to have no obstacles and to make his way as other men did. He told Matias about this guy Robert who had threatened him in Jackson and how he worked for his two former partners and gave Matias a summary of his history with E and Scheiner.

"These guys are coming after me. Not now, but soon. I'll have to do something about it."

Matias sat across from him in a French restaurant in Manchester and sipped his expensive wine and laughed and laughed at Rupert's revenge and self protection fantasies.

"Sicarios Bro? What the hell do you know about Sicarios? These are people a guy like you has no business knowing. Believe me. They're not a service. It's not like getting your house painted. It's an army and they're like the Special Forces. You don't want to deal with these people, bro. They gonna eat you up and spit you out and then there's nothing left. No more Rupert! No nothing."

Matias was leaning forward and suddenly his grin disappeared and was replaced by a grimace. He raised his right hand and pointed at Rupert.

"You better listen good to me, bro. This ain't like you see on fucking Netflix, this some serious shit."

"Yes, yes, I'm sure they're some bad boys, right? But, you know, they offer an expertise and I have issues that they have solutions for. Yes? Business, Matias. It's just business."

"You gonna get yourself dead with that shit, man. You go through with this and I don't want to even know you. But you know, except for that, listen, I get you some good self defense. We hook you up with the best security devices and you gonna be all right. Nobody gonna step up on you when you got Uzi, magazine fed, semi-automatic shotgun and a good handgun. Maybe you move out of town. Something more defensible. Let me speak with my security people. We get you the best, OK?"

Matias rose and folded his napkin and placed it next to his partially eaten Confit de Canard. The waiter ran over sensing unhappiness and possible insult to the restaurant's reputation.

"Sir?" he asked with as much deference as was possible in just the utterance of one word.

Matias didn't even look at him. He put his hand out as if he were turning away a dog with an overactive interest in his crotch.

"Rupert, I hope you listen to me, man. This is something I know like I know my brothers and sisters or my parents. I know these people. You don't even want to make people like this aware of your existence. You understand me?"

Rupert was already thinking about a million other things regarding his new business.

"Ok, Matias. I gotcha. Don't worry, you'll hear from me soon."

Rupert contacted his client from New York City who had a Manhattan apartment and knew everyone in the theatre and dance world and loved good weed. He did a repeat of his Jackson cannabis tasting party and charmed the pants off everyone who attended. He knew he'd go over big. He turned on the 100-watt smile and didn't even need to prepare. Better if he just winged it. They could not get enough of his overcooked, flowery prose which sounded like a mixture of Beer Advocate, ("notes of pear and tangerine with a slightly astringent finish"), and Bon Appetit.

Over the next couple of weeks he set up a route for his delivery guy and got him an apartment in Brooklyn. He hadn't yet hired his middleman/heavy but had a couple of guys in mind from his hometown in New Jersey.

He had developed a ring of acquaintances among the townie twenty somethings. Like Ridgeway, for all their talk about heading East or West the day after graduation, many of the adult children in Jackson seemed to have a hard time in breaking the bonds with their hometown and venturing out into independence and adulthood. They were still there leading quasi grownup lives, living at home in "basement apartments," working at low level jobs, saddled by large college loans, depressed, whining, and taking lots of drugs. From the beginning of his arrival in Jackson, Rupert had taken pains to cultivate them as allies. He wasn't sure exactly how they would fit into his plans, but sowed fertile soil with them by selling them good drugs for near his cost and letting them taste some of his outstanding products.

They loved him. They loved him like the jerk-off wealthy tourists he had enchanted with his gourmet cannabis tasting crap. All he had to do is turn on the smile and turn on the bullshit. It was the easiest thing in the world for him. When he saw those gullible, beguiled faces fixated on him and every word of his nonsense, well, he was tapped into something inexhaustible at that point. He could understand what drove those politicians on and on through so much shit. It was almost as euphoric as dope.

The twenty-something townies kept him abreast of anything new, different or unusual in the town. They were his KGB and glad to work with anyone who helped float the drug use that made life in Jackson tolerable for them. Their surveillance gave him a sense of security, a sense that E, Werner Scheiner, and this new guy Robert were going to have a tough time surprising him. He carried a go-bag with cash and a new handgun in his Escalade hidden where he had hidden his dope. Matias had come through with a shotgun, a 45 caliber Glock for the car and one for the house, and security cams and alarms for the cottage he rented out in the woods on the edge of town. It was all hooked up and motion detectors constantly alerted his devices. It was all he could do. He had done the best he was capable of so fuck it. Now he was going to turn his full attention to building his new business.

He had a guy in mind to be his go between. He wanted to test drive the New York network for perhaps the Spring and Summer and see what problems came up and what the best way to solve them were. After that he'd approach some of his other contacts for setting up in Boston and maybe DC. This was going to be the best thing he had ever done and he wasn't going to let , Scheiner and E stand in his way.

Then he got a text from his KGB. There was some guy in town asking questions about Rupert and no one had ever seen him before.

"Talk him up and see what's what," Rupert texted back. He didn't want to sound overly concerned yet wanted his guys to approach it seriously. Let's see what these fuckers come up with, he said to himself. I keep my distance and maybe it will seem to this guy like a bunch of clowns from the town just asking stupid questions, but not anyone with a connection to Rupert.

The KGB said the guy was driving a BMW sedan with Jersey plates. Cody said they had lunch together at the Country Cafe, the main meeting place for Jackson townies and all-season denizens. When the guy sat next to him at the counter, Cody wondered aloud why a tourist would come to a place like the Country Cafe while right down the street was a Starbucks, a Panera Bread and even some fast-food places.

"I never go to franchises," the guy said. "Brett Somners," he boomed and extended his hand. "I make it a point to always check out the places the town folks go. They know what's good, they don't steer you wrong." He laughed and it was the reflexive, insincere laugh of a salesman, or maybe a guy with ulterior motives.

Cody asked him how small town life in New England might differ from the Tri State area, especially West Caldwell, New Jersey where Brett said he was from. He asked him what he did in New Jersey and where he spent his time. It was small talk on Cody's part, but it gave him some context from which he hoped he could glean more information than direct questions.

And then, finally, as Brett offered to pick up the check for the two of them he mentioned a friend from New Jersey he heard had taken up residence in town. He was passing through on his way to Freeport, Maine looking to do some business with L. L. Bean, but had heard that Rupert was here so made a detour.

"Do you know him? A bit of an overweight, big guy with one of those aristocratic, 18th century names. Rupert, if you can believe any parent would burden their kid with a name like that. Anybody know the guy?"

Cody shook his head and seemed mystified. "Woulda remembered a name like that," he said.

Cody stopped by Rupert's cottage and gave him a thorough report on all that had transpired between him and Brett. He gave him the details of Brett's appearance, a description of his BMW, the license plate, and everything he could think of that might be germane. These were details he had picked up watching CSI. It was his idea of what a real investigation was all about.

"Thank you," Rupert said. "You've helped me out, Cody," Rupert put his hand on his shoulder. "I've got plans for a guy like you, but do me this favor. Keep me appraised of this guy's movements. And ... listen, get me advanced warning if he starts heading my way. OK? Don't worry, I don't forget. I'll take good care of you."

Cody, excited by Rupert's appreciation and the seeming promise for future advancement with Rupert's projects nodded, bustled to the door wanting now to look as energetic and even aggressive as possible. "I gotcha, Rupert, I got your back, man," and walked/ran to his car slamming it into reverse and disappearing down the woodsy lane Rupert lived on.

Rupert sighed.

The vibratory alert on his iPhone woke him late that night. Rupert was a light sleeper and swung his feet to the floor and reached for the loaded shotgun he had lying just under the edge of his bed. The alarm was from motion detector 2#, the one he had scanning the 50s style carport on the side of the bungalow and where he parked the Escalade. He checked the cam on the side of the house, but other than a shadow that passed across the Escalade so quickly he could not make out a shape, he saw nothing. His pants were on the chair next to the bed and he put them on and slipped into his cross trainers without tying them. He didn't turn on any lights and silently crept to the side of the window on the south side of the house where the carport was. He picked up his handgun on the way through the kitchen and shoved it into the back of his pants. He kept it in his kitchen utensils drawer with the knives and the forks believing it was safest to spread his weaponry throughout the house.

He tipped a single blind and scanned the carport and then went to the front of the house in order to scan the front lawn. He repeated this on all four corners of the house and seeing nothing and hearing nothing, thought about how he might slip outside into the woods that bordered the bungalow and try to work his way around to a good vantage point to watch any attempted entries into the house.

The bungalow had a boiler which was oil fired and had the ability to be heated by coal as well as oil. The previous owner, evidently a bit of a prepper, was frustrated by the gas and oil crisis in the 70s and had bought it just in case of catastrophic energy shortages. There was a coal room on the opposite side of the cottage from the carport. It hadn't been used in years and had a coal chute with a port that locked from the inside. It was just big enough for Rupert to slip through and hustle into the woods that ringed the property.

The yard was small maybe 250 feet by 300 feet. In ten minutes of stealthy creeping, once tripping over a boulder probably excavated a million years ago when digging the foundation of the house, and once groaning audibly when he walked straight into the half broken off branch of a birch damaged in a winter storm, he managed to ring the property. He ended up to the right of the house in a little pine grove by the gravel lane. He sat on the trunk of a fallen tree and waited. If it was a guy sent by E and Scheiner, or better yet two guys, Rupert was going to make a dramatic statement. He wasn't just going to call the police or run these guys off, he was going to take these motherfuckers out big time. The shotgun was enough to do quite a bit of nasty damage if you shot someone in the fuckin' head. When he called the cops he'd wail and moan about how scared he was and that all he could think to do is shoot and shoot, he was just so scared for his life.

Rupert was thinking that maybe he'd be left the fuck alone after that. Show that there was a price for fucking with him. All he had to do is sit here, which he could do all night if he had to and let these guys cook their own goose as his grandmother used to say.

He was smiling to himself pleased with this fantasy of vengeance when he felt the barrel of a handgun slam into the back of his head and force his chin down. He dropped the shotgun and his handgun was yanked out of the back of his pants.

"Whatever they're gonna pay you I'll double," Rupert said.

He was pleading for his life within the first five seconds and the guy hadn't even said anything to him yet. The guy kicked him in the lower back and he flew off the trunk of the tree he was sitting on and ended up on his knees.

"Hands clasped behind your head."

He felt the muzzle of the gun whack him again in the back of his head and then was held at the base of his skull. Despite himself he had a mental image of his brains exploding through the front of what used to be his face. Rupert closed his eyes and began to whimper and moan. He felt a hot stream of urine flood down his thigh. In the cool night air it didn't take long for his soaked pants to press cold against his skin.

Chapter Nine

"I think you're probably the type of guy who thinks other people aren't, you know, real or something. Like you're the only mother fucker going whose life really counts and everybody else is along for the ride. Just there for your convenience. Yeah? So it's to hurt them, it's to get rid of them when their presence in your life is no longer expedient. Because it just doesn't really matter. Any of this ring true to you, Rupert?"

Rupert moaned. What he was hearing he had heard before and his memory which was buffering and freezing like an old laptop, finally fixed on the streets of Ridgeway and Pam's parent's detective. Although he stunk of urine, and was on his knees, and just moments before was whimpering and envisioning having his brains blown out, Rupert seemed to somehow regroup.

"Whatever they are paying you I will double," he said slowly, pronouncing each word with care.

"You remember me, don't you, Rupert?" asked his assailant.

Rupert remembered. He remembered being knocked down to the sidewalk in downtown Ridgeway and humiliated in front of everyone who probably hated him anyway and were hanging around just to see what level of degradation he would be brought to. He was reliving his past. This was the thug detective who'd done that to him after Pam's death.

"My clients aren't going to just let their daughter's murder go. It took awhile to track you down, but you always get people talking about you, don't you? Hard to hide a personality and a BMI as big as yours."

Rupert began a new line of defense insisting that Pam had been a

70

stone junkie since college and that this fact had been unknown to her parents. He had been trying to force her into rehab when she just took off. Rupert had no idea where she went, perhaps he had been too aggressive, but he loved her and...

The detective blew out a hard, short breath of indignation and derision and clubbed Rupert in the side of the head with the butt of his pistol knocking him face down into the dirt. He stood over Rupert, flipped him over by kicking him in the side and pushed the muzzle hard into Rupert's nose. He then lifted his shirt and showed the wire recording their conversation. He switched off the recorder.

"They want me to scare the piss out of you and get you to confess. I think that it's too good for the likes of you. I think I'm just gonna shoot you in the head with your own gun and say you tried to shoot me when I came to question you about Pam. Yeah, Pam's parent's have been through so much. I mean, they know you killed her. They don't have any misconceptions about that. They're good people you know. Well, ... I suppose a piece of shit like you doesn't know."

He reached around and pulled Rupert's Glock out of his own waistband and put his gun back in the shoulder holster inside his jacket.

"This'll make a nice sized hole in Rupert," he said and pointed it at Rupert's belly.

"First a gut wound just to hurt you really bad, then I blow your fucking head off."

"Nooo," Rupert sobbed and tried to cover the ample territory of his stomach with his hands. "Nooo, please ... whatever you want, whatever you want, please."

The detective's last words were, "I feel just like fucking Dirty Harry," as he was clubbed in the side of the head by a tree branch and three townies fell on him and quickly relieved him of all weaponry. One by one the townies regained their feet and looked down at the detective who wasn't moving. The side of his head was literally caved in and he was bleeding profusely from the mouth.

Cody prodded him in the chest with the toe of his boot but to no avail. They bent down and and Rupert pulled himself up into a crouching position still clutching his gut. They looked carefully at his open and sightless eyes. Rupert saw the same absence he had seen in Pam on the day she OD'ed.

"Oh shit," one of them said.

Before dawn they dragged the detective behind Rupert's cottage, found his keys, found his car and drove it around the back of the house so that it was hidden from the road.

"We did a drive by 'cause I saw how serious you were about this guy and then we saw this shit going down."

"I can take care of it," Rupert told his townies gesturing at the car in which they had deposited the detective's body, "but you guys are with me now. You know what I'm talking about? Like on TV ... you're my guys. Anybody says anything to anybody, no matter how innocently, and they end up in the same place this guy is going. It's going to cost me big time, so what you do for me in the future will make up for what I have to do now. I mean, I didn't ask anybody to bash this guy's brains out. This is something you took on yourselves. But ok, just so you remember, you're part of my crew now and we're all in this together."

Rupert looked at each one. They were sitting on plastic lawn chairs in the back yard looking at the detective's car in which in the back seat, covered by an old tarp, lay the detective's body. The sun began to break through the trees and the back yard was lit with golden light.

"We saved your life," Cody said.

"And I'm grateful for that and we are going to make a ton of money together, OK? But this is serious shit and we have to do this the right way. The right way is for you guys to do things my way. Remember. Not a word to anyone. I don't even want to hear you guys talking about this night among yourselves. You slip and you die. You got that? You're gonna be questioned about this guy's disappearance ... especially you Cody, but you know nothing. You had one encounter with him and that was it. The less you say the better. Don't get all elaborate in explaining anything. The more you say, the guiltier they know you are."

"Well ... what I say is that its about time to change those pants, Rupert," said Cody laughing and holding his nose, "Gettin' a little rank there, aren't ya?"

Rupert looked around at his three clowns and he knew he would have to rule goofballs like them by fear. He wasn't yet sure about Cody. He had a little more on the ball than the others, which could be good, or it could be bad. They stood around him in a semi circle and he asked each one if he could count on them. One by one they murmured their consent and sealed their pact with the devil.

He didn't want to use his phone to have Matias meet him again at the restaurant in Manchester, so just sent him a date/time and a YouTube *Sopranos* clip showing Tony and Johnny Sacks at Satriale's.

"You're lucky, bro. I've had some extended business in Boston. The Organization has enlarged my responsibilities. I'm upper management now, bro. Can you fucking believe it? My territory is like Boston, New York, DC and I got to manage several different crews, but outside of my regular routes I don't travel easily for anybody these days. The Organization wants me to spend my time on only the most profitable enterprises. You understand? Big time shit. I'll take care of you, Rupert because you were with me when I was coming up, but you got to be more practical about when you call me in. We're not business advisors or fucking management analysis, bro. And I got a good idea about what's coming. Anything, I think, that has to do with you and the way you conduct business is gonna involve dead people."

Rupert did not like the inference. But he needed this guy and the services he could offer. Right now he needed to disappear a car and a body and watching *CSI* and *The Sopranos* hadn't given him any ideas about how to do this properly. He needed the real thing not some script writer's idea of how it went down.

"I need the service you provided for me in Ridgeway," he said simply.

Matias was nodding and smiling. "Yeah," he said. "I knew that shit was coming. Rupert, you got to learn how to conduct business without killing everybody."

"Look who's talking."

Rupert told his clowns to stay the hell away from the bungalow and then took a three day jaunt to Kennebunkport in Maine. He ate a lot of seafood, having a particular weakness for New England fried clams and lobster, and went to a blues festival on a pier in the middle of town. He followed around some of the local girls from bar to bar, trying to look harmless, but only succeeding in looking peculiar to girls at least ten years younger than he. They blew him off fast even when he pulled out his stash of exotic intoxicants and attempted to go into his cannabis tasting spiel.

Instead, he decided to indulge in some good wine and some great restaurants. When he got back to Jackson everything was just as it was before the detective appeared. It was like the guy never existed.

Matias had not wanted to sell Rupert small to moderate amounts of a wide variety of weed strains. Rupert tried to convince him that this was the weed business of the future modeling itself on what would become available to consumers once weed was fully legalized and not just decriminalized. He made the case that a black market that emphasized price and high-end product could survive even legalization considering how inflated prices would be. Every state in the Union had it in mind to pay off their state pension plans and perhaps even do a little infrastructure repair through taxing the hell out of recreational weed sales. The underground weed business would not have to pay a tax that was liable to be at least 15%. It was quite an advantage competitively. The black market was going to have to change, but it could survive.

"I don't think this is the business for us," Matias said. "We're not gonna wanna be labor intensive enough to do business the way you describe it. We just want to come in, dump a ton of narcotics on

U.S. soil and walk away with a ton of money. But Rupert, like I said, I'll see what I can do to set you up. Maybe not with us, but you know, I got friends, I got associates. I help you out, bro."

They had met again to talk about supply and Matias had also brought Rupert the quarter ounce of heroin he requested.

"Bro, you using a lot? Got to be careful. You use too much and it's bad for business."

Rupert told him he was selling a bit of dope on the side. He liked a taste now and then, but he was under control. Matias could count on that.

Matias leaned forward smiling broadly, "And you can always call me up for a clean up. We take care of that good for you, bro. That's a service I think Rupert always gonna find indispensable."

Chapter Ten

Curiously, no one ever followed up on the detective's disappearance. The name he had given Cody when he first appeared in Jackson was, surprisingly, his real name and when Rupert did a search on Google a *Star Ledger* article came up at the top of the page and explained everything. Brett Somners had been a cop, specifically a detective, in Essex County. He worked directly with the Prosecutor's Office investigating organized crime in northern New Jersey. He was accused of taking money from the Mob and testified against a couple of low-level associates in order to keep himself out of jail. Although he was pushed out of law enforcement, his detective agency business became quite lucrative. His previous history as a man who liked to play both sides of the fence made him just seem resourceful in the eyes of the public. But when he disappeared, everyone wrote it off as payback that had at last come due because of his testimony against the Mob Associates.

Rupert figured as far as Somner's appearance in Jackson that he was either acting as an independent agent, or Pam's parents had sent him up to do a little more than just scare the hell out of Rupert and get a confession. Most likely they sent him up to exact vengeance and not justice, despite what Somners had said to him and now were afraid to follow up on events that they feared might implicate them. The order of business was probably to get a confession first, and then execute Rupert and make it look like self defense. In truth, the detective hadn't had the patience to go through the full rigamarole. He just wanted to jump right to the good part.

Her parents had always treated Rupert with contempt. He could imagine them sitting in the old man's study, Pam's father meticulously working out the details of his murder with Somners and enjoying imagining Rupert's terror and suffering at every step.

"Well, surprise, surprise," he said to himself, "the best laid plans, huh? Send me more mercenaries and get the same fucking result."

He enjoyed thinking about how that scenario might play out and went over it again and again in his mind.

Pam knew a couple of things: Rupert was in Jackson, New Hampshire and her mom and dad were minus one detective. Rupert had been seen in Manhattan by some of their old friends, who, scandalized by Rupert's bust and his betrayal of E and Werner Scheiner, had then gossiped to Mikael who had been part one of Rupert's pre-drug friends.

She had her 8Chan buddies to thank for helping her locate Rupert and hack into her parent's iPhones where she learned about Somners. And she had Mikael to thank for staying in touch with her and doing anything he could to help her project.

She thought she would take a little trip north. She had two goals really. She wanted to see if any evidence could be had as to the disappearance of her parent's detective and if that failed to see if she could shake up the drug business that Rupert was no doubt involved in, or even have him targeted by local law enforcement. She wasn't going to walk up to the guy and blow his fucking brains out although that was a lovely fantasy. She'd harass him a little, stay hidden, make his life miserable and see what was what. Did he have friends? Was he getting high? Did he have a girl friend? Was he endangering the public welfare? Was he a threat to women, children and small animals?

She was laughing, but not because she found anything truly funny. It was black humor and she had to control this tendency of hers. It was really bitterness, wasn't it? And it could turn so easily to anger. That would interfere with her being able to keep her head straight and slowly drain away her energy and resolve. This is what she had learned from Mikael and she would keep it close to her heart.

She got a motel room in North Conway and drove into Jackson

with her big, dark sunglasses, her new hair, her thirty-pound weight loss and she felt safe and sufficiently camouflaged. She was just another tourist in a Subaru Forester, probably wealthy, probably spoiled, innocuous and looking for a good time. Under her, in a pouch sewn into the bottom of her car seat was the Sig Sauer. Along either side of the wheel wells, hidden beneath and against the plastic molding was the tactical Mossberg, 5 + 1, loaded with slugs and on the other side a small sniper rifle with a suppressor for noise and muzzle flash, and a tripod. She felt ready although she didn't envision using any artillery first time out. She was there more for information gathering, but you never knew for sure. She felt good.

She drove down Main Street late morning and there of course was that bastard's Escalade parked in front the Country Cafe. She was stopped at a light alongside the Café's parking lot and the back of his car was pulled up to the edge of the street. Suddenly, Rupert was getting out of the driver's side with his back to her, but then turned and looked down through her windshield the parking lot being slightly raised above the roadway. He stared at her. She stared back and he furrowed his brow quizzically and looked ready to approach when his phone call tones started playing And Your Bird Can Sing. He looked away and brought the phone to his ear. Pam pulled away and drove further down Main Street until she was out of sight of the restaurant and pulled over and was shaking and crying. First encounters are not easy she was thinking to herself. It's tough, but she would persevere, she knew she would. Her strength was not to overwhelm by greater force necessarily, it was to outlast and to out-think, and to finally turn the tables on this monster by putting him in a jail cell or putting him in the ground.

Rupert's business prospered, but rather than extending into the other east coast cities, Rupert and company worked up a stable of delivery boys in NYC. He wouldn't have been able to handle maintaining control of business if it had been too geographically spread out iPhone or no iPhone. This however was manageable and he got to spend some time in the City on a regular basis which he enjoyed.

Devin, the kid from Jackson he had set up in Brooklyn, began meeting a million other kids his age who worked as bike messengers in Manhattan. He had soon recruited a small stable of high-end personal cannabis delivery agents. They had their own bikes. They had their own apartments, all they wanted was the money. That he could provide, on time, plentifully, and in cash. For this he had their loyalty. Like everybody else in this world, as long as the money was good they loved him.

Cody, Alain and Alexander were indispensable to the new business acting as conduits for the drug supply and going over the Manhattan routes for the delivery boys. Rupert canceled his plans to hire a right-hand man from his hometown. These guys seemed like they would do. Rupert and his three Jackson guys spent a lot of time on the strict expectations they had of the delivery kids. Everything was done by bicycle and in a standardized uniform of black Under Armour tights, Under Armour gym top and Under Armour backpack. Communications of any type beside greetings, goodbyes, answers to business questions which were encouraged to be as terse as possible, usually consisting only of an assurance that management would be alerted, were prohibited with a promise of termination for even first time infractions.

It was Cody who shepherded Alain and Alexander to NYC and back and kept an orderly and professional orientation towards business uppermost in their minds and behavior. He had exceeded Rupert's expectations by about a million miles and seemed motivated to make lots of cash. Ordinarily, this sort of self interest was about the only personal trait in others that Rupert trusted. But Rupert couldn't shake the feeling that Cody was a part of the business that Rupert didn't have total control over. He was a bit of a loose end and Rupert figured a watch and wait policy was probably best. After all, it was Cody who had been seen establishing contact publicly with the detective. It was Cody who could tie Rupert to the guy by admitting that Rupert had asked him to pump Somners for information. And it was Cody who knew the details of the Detective's death which could easily enough be blamed solely on Rupert. No one had come in search of missing persons, and the prevalent theory seemed to hold that Somners was taken out by the mob associates he ratted out, but that didn't mean that everything couldn't change in the future.

Rupert took his boys out to a Jackson club to celebrate getting the business up and running and hiring on two new delivery guys and getting them set up and functioning. The business was going to be in the black much sooner than he had expected and much of it due to the clowns, who, when it came down to it, were willing to follow Cody's leadership which seemed to make all the difference.

He had arranged for a catered dinner in a private back room and a night of free drinks, music and dancing and whatever. The boys brought their girls. Rupert pledged to himself to no longer refer to his boys as clowns as long, of course, as things were going well.

Cody brought a young woman he was seeing who Rupert hadn't met yet.

"The big cheese," she said to Rupert the first time she met him. She was sassy and used old-fashioned slang and lines from Bogie and James Cagney movies. He liked her immediately.

"I'm the guy who doles out what makes it all worthwhile, if that's what you mean," he said.

She looked him up and down in her bright red "fuck me" high heels and said, "Yeah, you look like the guy who makes it all happen. Yeah, Rupert? Are you that guy?"

She was laughing a little, confident and flirty, but not in the little girl mode that a lot of her Jackson girlfriends shifted into whenever they were around men. She was one of those women who made a beeline for the men and did not seem to gravitate to other women for companionship. She was what he thought could be described as a man's women. She had slightly angular facial features and a long and lean body. not classically beautiful, but very attractive and very bright.

"You're fun, maybe we'll talk a little later?" Rupert asked.

Cody looked annoyed with her and then a little worried at Rupert's obvious interest. He grabbed her hand and tried to escort her across the room, but she spun around toward Rupert. When she turned, after Cody tried to redirect her away, she tossed a mane of long burgundy curls over her back shoulder and her eyes bore into Rupert's with intensity but also with humor. She put her other hand on top of his which was resting on a chair back.

"If you want me, just whistle," she said and puckered her lips.

He looked at her blankly taken a little off guard in front of Cody.

"You know how to whistle, don't you?"

It was silly and yet the sexiest thing anybody had said to him in a long, long time.

"Leila!" Cody yelled and tugged at her arm hard and they disappeared into a jumble of bodies. He could hear her angry protestations as they worked their way through the crowd including her reference to him as a little prick and a loser. The rest of her denunciations were garbled by the crowd in the main room. Rupert turned to Alain standing next to him with widened eyes.

"She seems a little much for old Cody, don't you think?"

"She's probably too much for anybody, at least anybody that I'm friends with, but Cody loves her. She treats him like shit, but Cody totally loves her and that all he knows," Alain said.

Rupert saw her in passing a few times during the evening and she seemed bored and impatient. He had kept his distance and she made no attempt to close the space between them, but she looked back at Rupert brazenly each time he saw her. Whether her directness with Rupert was because she was angry with Cody or was desire for Rupert was impossible to tell. He suspected that emotions might overlap in Leila in a jumble that made it hard for even her to know what it was she was feeling from moment to moment.

He thought about her often in the ensuing weeks even as his business began blossoming and events conspired to go his way.

Matias had come through with exactly what Rupert needed, an introduction to a consortium of weed growers whose libertarian philosophies kept them off the grid and uninterested in working with any businesses preparing to do what would be in the future legal weed sales. They were evidently critical of any standards the State might force growers to agree to in terms of potency and variety of psychotropic effects, and of course protested vehemently the top heavy taxation that would take what they felt was a gift of nature and make it a luxury item.

It was some of the finest product he had ever seen and they had the strains his customers were looking for in addition to a few innovative products for which he was sure he could create demand. Since his volume was not extremely high he found it easy to send his boys out for pick up to Sussex County, New Jersey where there was an old, abandoned airfield supposedly being converted into growing and manufacturing facilities for the production of CBD and the raising of organic produce, but secretly grew lots of weed. The consortium had converted the old airplane hangers to modern grow facilities. The water and electrical demands their 24/7 grow-light, temp controlled, hot house production labs used were easily explained by what they had set up to cultivate in the fields and in the labs devoted to CBD. Business was welcome in small towns in Sussex who hadn't received the tax revenues that Home Depot and Walmart were bringing to Newton. Any business was welcome, especially if they utilized some of the abandoned property in the town like the airfield. The consortium was left pretty much alone, which was much to their liking.

Rupert sent Cody down to New Jersey for pickup a couple of days earlier than he was expected. When Cody got there he was told that they couldn't possibly put together his order before the date they had given Rupert. With other customers and other business obligations it would take them at least a day and a half. Cody called Rupert who suggested a hotel in Parsippany.

"Watch movies, eat good food and take it easy, buddy," he said.

"You deserve a little down time. Don't worry, the company will pick up all expenses."

Rupert called Leila and they met two towns over in order to avoid any undue public scrutiny at a restored 18th century stone mill that had been converted into a restaurant. A well known chef who tired of the New York five star scene had set up a rustic restaurant in a town no one had ever heard of and like an ethnomusicologist of food, she studied the the cuisine of the ethnic communities in Northern New England as well as their countries of origin. She was interested primarily in the original European population and recreated many of the dishes of early Northeastern America before there had been assimilation into a broader American culture. She served lots of game, truffles and root vegetables, and had a stone oven authentically recreated from the designs of ovens hundreds of years old that produced loaves of Anadama and crusty European ryes.

Leila looked stunning. She was funny and sexy and they had a meal that both could not stop talking about, a marinated venison with organic, locally grown squash mixed with roasted, caramelized Brussel sprout halves and tossed with a light, flowery olive oil and cheddar flakes.

Rupert, a Jewish kid from North Jersey, had never had venison and was surprised by how tender the medallions were. Leila had asked to order for them both and he went along with her wishes, but expected something tough and gamey which he prepared for by drinking lots of wine. The wine seemed to only make his dinner that much better.

"This is wonderful," he said after his first forkful.

Leila smiled, happy she had pleased him. "Wait until you try the vegetables."

By the end of the evening they had drunk almost two bottles of wine and Rupert was feeling quite happy. But he wasn't drunk. Happy with his restaurant choice, happy with his company, and happy with his plans to take Leila home and make love to this vivacious, energetic, fascinating woman. He hadn't felt like this in many years and was in fact surprised after all that had taken place that something like this could still happen to him. He had sent Cody to New Jersey and out of the way, but was already wondering how this was all going to work in the future.

On the way out of the restaurant and just before they parted he walked with her over to where she had parked on the opposite end of the parking lot. He kissed her delicious wine flavored mouth and lingered on her plump lips. He was startled to hear her name being called and broke off the kiss. A girlfriend of Leila's from Jackson was standing a little too close to where they were entwined. She stood stiffly and her hands fluttered in the air indignantly just below her chin and her upraised sneering mouth.

"OMG!" she shrieked. "Cody's not here, I'm guessing."

Leila looked at her haughtily and looked to the left and then to the right.

"Mmm," she said. "I guess that's right, what the fuck is it to you?" Leila turned and without another word got into her car and drove off.

The friend looked at Rupert. "I just hate the way she is always gonna do whatever the hell she wants to do, no matter how it impacts other people. You know what I mean? You know people like that?"

It was distasteful this kind of display Rupert thought. It seemed motivated by jealousy. Rupert understood money and power, but didn't really understand this. He pushed past her not really interested anymore in her or whatever it was she was going to do. He got into the Escalade impatient to meet Leila at his cottage and didn't want to make her wait too long.

He knew what it was he wanted. He wasn't going to let anything interfere. He was feeling things he thought were long dead, feelings he had written off as sentimentality. Now, Leila had opened a door on a part of his life he had turned away from, and he could not wait to walk through.

Chapter Eleven

She stayed for a couple of days and when Cody arrived with the product from New Jersey, for which Rupert had built a distribution and storage office in what had formerly been the coal chute, Cody would hardly talk to him. When asked direct questions, he answered monosyllabically. Rupert supposed that Leila's nosy friend had given him a heads up.

Leila appeared in the middle of their unloading, ignored Cody and kissed Rupert goodbye, Cody was suddenly gone. Poof, like he had disappeared in a puff of smoke. They heard Cody's truck in the driveway, spinning its tires in the dirt and gravel and then blasting down the street.

Leila shrugged. "Win some, lose some," she said.

"Sore Loser," said Rupert and they laughed together.

The next morning a sullen Cody appeared at the door summoned by a text from Rupert. Rupert invited him in and they sat in his kitchen and drank coffee and had, as Rupert termed it, a "sit down."

"I was hurt, man. I mean, I've done such a good job for you and got all your ducks in a row with the guys and we're making money now. Now this. I mean this is the time you choose to treat me like a bitch? I don't get it. I mean, everything was working out so good and now you done me like this. How can you do it, Rupert? You know I loved her. Why do you hurt me like this?"

Rupert felt his face flush, but he answered calmly.

"Sometimes you just have to accept that things aren't going to work out the way you want. You can see what she wants. Maybe you'll just have to accept that. I certainly didn't set out to take her away from you. It just happened."

Cody jumped up and and leaned over the table. "When I heard

that you two were seeing each other I was so mad. I was just fucking furious. I'm thinking, I saved this fucker's life and see what I get. Well, I can just turn this shit around any time I want. An anonymous phone call to New Jersey. The boys and I unanimous and tight as far as our story, and you're toast. No more Leila, no more nothing for Rupert, but a six by eight in a fucking SuperMax!"

Rupert walked around the table and sat Cody back down. He got him another cup of coffee and rather then addressing Cody's threat began talking in detail about all they had accomplished together. They were on the cusp, right at the beginning of making some real money. Rupert in all honesty owed a great deal to Cody's hard work and he would need him in the coming years. But she was done with him. Cody and Leila were done. He'd have to accept that, and Rupert was gonna make Cody a ton of money in the future, but he'd just have to let this thing go.

"OK, Cody?" He put a hand on Cody's shoulder and looked him in the eyes. "Can I count on you, man?"

Cody was still sullen. He walked to the front door slowly as though still deliberating with himself. At the door he turned and looked Rupert in the eye.

"I don't like it. I don't like it at all. But yes, you can count on me, man."

Rupert took a dramatic pause and said, "I'm glad, Cody. I'm very glad to hear that." He patted the back of his shoulder and then almost as an after thought said, "Hey listen, I've had a lot happen to me over the last few years some of which you know and some you don't. And there's something that's been a real pleasure for me ... allowed me to get away from the pressure, you know, take a little vacation from it all and get a rest. Weed doesn't really do it. Dope does. It's just chipping for me and you have to use some discipline, but that is about the best high I've ever experienced. So, what do you think? Try it. Just a little taste. You can snort it, but just a pinch so you can still drive and shit. K?"

Cody was intrigued perhaps more by Rupert's obvious

enthusiasm than anything else. Rupert fetched his dope box. He had removed his works in the bedroom, and let Cody see what was left of the first quarter ounce that Matias had sold him. He gave Cody, true to his word, just a pinch, but enough to give him a taste of that golden world that Rupert loved so dearly.

Cody snorted it off the smooth cover of Rupert's box. His eyelids lowered, his body sagged a little and Rupert brought him into the living room to sit. Cody didn't say much at first and then after a time stood and said, "Yeah, yeah. That's good. That's some good shit. I can sure see why you like that so much. OK ... well, let me go. I got shit to do, and whoa ..." He held on to the edge of the sofa for a few seconds. "Yeah, yeah, that's a good drug. How about us, we good?"

"Yeah," Rupert said. "We good."

Rupert watched as Cody got into his car, started it up and pulled out into the wooded lane. Not too bad, but this was Cody at about quarter speed. All in all, probably safer for the world at large.

A week later Rupert was called into Manhattan to do another of his cannabis presentations for the friends of a new customer. He asked Cody to assist and told him he'd like him to get acquainted with what it was he was doing to create customers and networks and that perhaps he could move into full partnership with him. Cody was surprised and flattered. This was something he had never expected. They'd do the show, as Rupert referred to it, and stay overnight in Manhattan and then head north the following morning. They didn't get back to the hotel till late. A few customers had been pumping Rupert mercilessly for technical info on the strains and how they were raised, and for info on the Consortium. He refused to divulge the location and they took to haggling with him interminably on pricing. They were quick to use the tools of their trade — it was almost entirely a roomful of lawyers and wall street bros — to try to negotiate down to a price that would have left Rupert pretty much just a delivery boy. Rupert bobbed and weaved and at the end of the evening had a business that was growing and despite the lawyers' best attempts, profitable. Rupert and Cody were tired but keyed up and Rupert pulled out his dope box and asked Cody if he'd like to indulge.

"Maybe another taste, huh?"

Cody agreed and they snorted some dope and then Rupert snorted a bit more. Cody was already nodding in a deep, plush chair in front of the TV. Come morning that was where Rupert found him. He was hard to rouse and Rupert had to guide him into the bathroom and into a shower. Afterwards, Cody seemed fully awake and ready to get back to Jackson.

"Was it good last night, Cody?"

"Oh yeah, it was good. Man, you got that shit down for all those wealthy motherfuckers. You got the language, you got the style they love. I just gotta watch you do that magic some more."

"No, man. I mean the dope. You like that stuff, Cody?"

Cody smiled and rolled his eyes back into his head. "Yeah, Rupert. I like that stuff."

Back in Jackson, Cody lightened up and was even able to talk civilly to Leila when he saw her at Rupert's bungalow. Gradually, civil discourse moved on to a more natural even a friendly tone.

Leila moved in with Rupert. She had been staying with him every weekend and taken over one of his closets. She brought over enough plates, tableware, cleaning devices and products to remove the last vestiges of feral bachelorhood from Rupert's place. Finally, a higher percentage of her stuff was at his bungalow than her apartment and they decided it was time for consolidation.

This woman added a spice and a flavor to Rupert's life he just hadn't had before. He thought about all the different time periods in his life, before the troubles, and when he had lived with Pam in the McMansion in New Jersey and realized something was now different. He was happy. She wasn't compliant and actively seeking to always meet his needs; in fact, she was pretty high maintenance, but she, he had to admit it, thrilled him. She was exciting and sexy and always interesting to be with. He realized his life seemed immeasurably richer with her. He hadn't thought he would ever get back to this place again, where things were going well and he was actually excited about rather than dreading the future. There was just the one thing that kept bothering him. It was like a taint, or a scratch in the lens through which he was looking at a beautiful pastoral scene. It was Cody's threat concerning that anonymous call to New Jersey and his claim about how unanimous he and the other clowns would be claiming their innocence in any wrong doing.

He kept thinking about Cody's outburst. It implied that there had been some prior strategizing between the three. Everybody had their contingency plans, but in this case, especially in light of the money making operation that was in place, which could just as easily be run without Rupert, it was dangerous.

He expressed nothing but calm and even professional respect with the three clowns, but on the inside Cody's threat bothered him more and more. What would it take for these guys to change their minds? What would it take for Cody to become disenchanted again and decide that he had indeed been fucked big time, or, that the king was ripe for overthrow and his kingdom just too lucrative to let this chance pass. Even goofballs can rise to the occasion when they realize that the only opportunity their sad lives are going to throw their way is passing in front of them and it was now or never.

There was all of that, and his mind went round and round with it, and, there was something else unbidden and unwelcome that kept intruding in his thoughts. It tarnished everything, made what he loved most in Leila seem somehow used and tawdry. He simply could not stand the idea of Cody touching Leila, of Cody kissing Leila, or worst of all Cody fucking Leila. He was repulsed and disgusted when he thought about their intimacy. At first it was something he could bury. But it grew. It got bigger and more pervasive until he had the feeling that his life would not really be his own until this Cody issue was settled. The taint was Cody himself and to remove the taint required the removal of Cody.

And then he heard through the grapevine that old Cody was trying to go out on his own. He had approached Laurent who was

Rupert's contact at The Consortium about doing some business. He had approached him warily through the CBD side of the business and spent some time making Laurent think that the CBD was his only business interest. Finally, Cody leveled with him, asked Laurent for a pledge of confidentiality and told him about some customers he met in his business with Rupert and wanted to cultivate "his own thing."

"Please," he said emphatically, "I don't know for sure what Rupert would do if he heard, but I damn well know he wouldn't like it."

Laurent said to let him think about it and he'd get back to him in a few days. He immediately called Rupert who wasn't angry, wasn't disappointed. It merely substantiated what he had always known on some level he would have to do.

The means to resolve his "problem" fell into his lap seemingly out of the blue, and he smiled when once again events conspired to go his way, the way they always seemed to do. Cody asked Rupert if he could buy some of his stash. He promised it was for an occasional high that he said he would snort and not "mainline." Rupert wanted to laugh out loud, but wanted to appear to Cody blasé about it and told him for the good of his business and the stress levels of his most valuable right hand man he would sell him a couple of bags at a time and no more. Rupert wanted to make sure he was only chipping and staying free of addiction, which was something Rupert knew a lot about and could protect Cody from developing.

"OK, man," said Cody looking a little annoyed, but thanking Rupert for his concern. "Look, I want to be upfront with you about everything I do especially when it affects you."

"All right," Rupert said wondering what the fuck this guy was on to now.

"Friday night Leila and I are going to meet for a drink. But no worries, no worries, no last ditch make up efforts on my part. I want a feeling of resolution and closure to our relationship. Just want to explain myself, I mean I ended up looking like a real jerk off after all that shit went down. And that's it. I say my piece and Leila and I are now friends and working together productively on the Rupert Team."

Cody was grinning his overly sincere I ain't shittin' you, brother grin.

"And then I thought I'd go home and get high on some of your good dope," he added and laughed.

"Well, Ok ... I guess I'm glad to hear you're cool with my relationship with Leila and you always seem to be thinking about the business so yeah, stop by Friday morning and I've got a couple of bags for you. You know, I need to weigh it out and uhh, you know, make it right for you."

"How much, man. I have no idea how much this shit sells for."

"You don't have to worry about that. Believe me, it's my pleasure. Bonus," he said when Cody began to protest, "for all your good work."

Cody paused for a beat and looked at Rupert. This was going the way he wanted, but with Rupert you still had to be always careful. He didn't want to end up like that fucking detective.

"Well thanks, man. Look, you're always taking care of me. I guess I just want you to know how much I appreciate it and I'll always do a good job for you, man. Yeah, you taking good, good care of me and you can be sure that I will always turn that around and do right by you. OK? Cool?"

"See you Friday morning," Rupert said.

Chapter Twelve

He was a totally unexpected ally. She knew he was connected to a ruthless Cartel and yet when she was recovering from her heroin overdose he was gentle, even kind to her. And then she started getting, seemingly from out of the blue, and from an ostensibly anonymous source addressed to an anonymous recipient, email updates about Rupert's activities. She knew it was Matias, but it was a one-way communication and although she replied she never got an answer. She received sporadic updates as though they were intelligence agency bulletins to all agents and the subject line read, all in caps, sounding like something from a James Bond movie: FOR YOUR EYES ONLY!!!

The first email copied and pasted the newspaper blurb about the deaths and then encouraged a course of action that fit right in with what she also felt she should do. Establish a relationship with a Jackson detective anonymously, perhaps much the same way Matias had done with her, and give them the necessary information to start connecting the dots. Tell them that Rupert was a psycho drug user/drug dealer who killed Cody and Leila, and that there was a history she could give them that would substantiate this and give them enough circumstantial evidence to get this threat to all that is decent off the damn streets. She'd include the name of the New Jersey Prosecutor who handled Rupert's drug bust case, and the detective who headed up the investigation in Pennsylvania of Rupert's missing girlfriend. This was clearly a pattern of criminality that led inexorably to his latest horror.

She read the newspaper account Matias sent at least ten times and grieved for the two who hadn't been lucky enough to escape the monster the way that she had:

"Two dead in apparent drug overdose in Jackson County. Cody

Ableson and Leila Oliveira, died as the result of an overdose of heroin Friday night in an apartment in downtown Jackson that belonged to Ableson. The drug had been cut with fentanyl, an opiate often added to heroin to increase potency and volume. Fentanyl has a potency sometimes as great as 50 times that of heroin. After a preliminary investigation a police spokesman said that their toxicology lab's tests revealed that the drugs the two had ingested contained enough fentanyl to kill ten people. They had been seen earlier in the evening at Rick's, a popular downtown bar, and left at about 11:00 p.m. evidently on their way to Ableson's apartment where they ingested the fatal combination of drugs."

The other townie breakfast place, the one that Rupert never frequented, was abuzz about the overdoses and everyone there either had gone to school with the two victims or had children who had. They were all sure that Cody and Leila were in fact victims rather than just users and that their deaths had to be intentional and planned. This judgement seemed to be shared by the town police because of the amount of fentanyl in the drugs they said. The cops had perhaps let a little too much slip to their fellow citizens over their morning coffee and eggs. The townies knew Rupert and they knew the dynamics of the relationship between the three of them. They had suspected Cody and Rupert's business dealings for some time.

It seemed that all Pam had to do was to sit attentively at the counter while eating and listen. They all seemed to have known each other almost all of their lives and if she sat quietly and tipped well she became like wallpaper and the town gave up all it knew and all it suspected. Her hatred for Rupert grew and grew and it was all she could do to squelch the desire to grab the shotgun, knock on his door and blast a watermelon-sized hole in Rupert's fat belly.

Rupert heard the news Saturday morning on the small TV he liked to have on in the kitchen while he drank his morning coffee. He had tried to get in touch with Leila the previous evening to see how her drink with Cody had gone and her phone just rang and rang and finally her voicemail was loaded up and would not take his messages. He hadn't known what to think. He honestly believed however, that a romantic rapprochement with Cody was not in the realm of possibility so finally went to sleep around 12:00 expecting that when he woke up, Leila would be sleeping beside him. Perhaps Cody had gone straight home and snorted the dope Rupert had given him. She may have gotten news about his death and spent the night in the hospital, hysterical, maybe even sedated. Anyway, Rupert would sort it all out in the morning. No one to his knowledge had any idea about Cody's recent interest in dope, or that he and Rupert had gotten high together. He was clear on that account, and he slept soundly.

When he heard the news on the TV that morning, he moaned and felt such utter despair that the room spun and he had to grip the edge of the counter to prevent dropping to the floor. He spilled his hot coffee on his bare feet and hardly felt it. And then he did drop, striking his head on a kitchen chair on the way down and gashing open the skin on his forehead. Spurting blood seeped around his face and bubbled against his mouth when his breath blew into the thickening pool.

That is how the police found him. Their interrogation of Rick's patrons had revealed Leila's "recent cohabitation with Levinsky." Repeated knocking had not brought anyone to the door of Rupert's cottage and one of the cops circled the house and saw Rupert's prone form through the sliding glass door of the kitchen. They called 911 and broke in. He didn't really come fully around until he was in the hospital and the staff had staunched the bleeding, hydrated him and sewed up his head. The police were in the room as soon as he had asked what the hell had happened.

He played it completely straight. He told them that Leila had formerly been involved with Cody and that she had broken up with him in order to pursue a relationship with Rupert. They had wanted to have a private talk to provide closure for their relationship and

Rupert had been in complete favor of this. She hadn't come home that night and did not answer Rupert's repeated calls. That was all he knew. He had gone to sleep a little disturbed, but figured everything would sort out in the morning.

Before the cops took him home they quizzed him extensively about his drug history and the bust in New Jersey that had ended with his freedom and his friends' imprisonment. His record in New Jersey had been largely buried to the point of other investigating law enforcement departments not being able to gain full access to the case. Rupert told the Jackson cops that he had acted as an informant, had no personal criminal involvement in the case, and that was all he was at liberty to reveal.

They interrogated him again about his own drug usage and the usage of Cody and Leila. They insinuated that Cody and Leila had perhaps restarted their romantic relationship and that Rupert making this discovery had sought revenge.

"Enough fentanyl to kill ten men," said the Detective suggesting foul play by quoting what the larger media had picked up from the local Jackson station.

They told Rupert that they had contacted the Ridgeway, Pennsylvania Police who told them that there was still no evidence linking Rupert to Pam's disappearance. But the Jackson detective implied that even if there were nothing substantial enough to be used as evidence, it implicated Rupert by the mere prevalence of criminal events in and around his life. Rupert was outraged by this insinuation and shouted in a rant that this was why citizens did not testify readily for the fucking cops or help with their investigations. They were always ready to prosecute on the slimmest of hearsay evidence. The cops told him that they might have further questions, and they suggested he stay in town and be available for their continuing investigation.

He had intended to launch into a longer denunciation of the cops, of the town and a past he felt was rife with law enforcement who were biased against him, but felt himself unaccountably deflate

95

and run out of steam. Leila was gone. He remembered looking into Pam's eyes in his Ridgeway apartment and seeing that utter vacancy and when he thought now of Leila he felt a similar sort of absence. With Leila, he felt he had outrun his history and that she would be the love of his life. This was evidently not to be.

Poor, poor, girl, he thought. Caught up in something that had nothing at all to do with her. That sassy, sexy, vital girl gone. A spirit gone out of the world that had revitalized Rupert, that had reacquainted him with all the juice and all the vitality that makes life worth living. He swung his feet over the edge of the hospital gurney and the nurse took his arm to help him up. Rupert felt himself overcome by a terrible feeling of emptiness. His vision went black at the edges and he felt cold. Instead of standing he pitched forward and did a header into the stand holding his IV liquids.

The cops had him under the arms and were roughly pulling him to his feet despite the nurse's protestations. When they had him upright his head cleared and he shook them off. He sat momentarily on the gurney and they got him some orange juice and took his blood pressure.

"A false start, Mr. Levinsky, but I'm sure you'll regain full strength and be able to pursue your activities with all the energy you've displayed in the past. And we'll be watching, Mr. Levinsky, watching you pursue all your future activities. We'll be watching very closely."

Rupert looked at him blankly losing interest with these guys who obviously had nothing and were just trying to shake him up. Shake him up and make him say something he shouldn't or run home and do something he shouldn't. Yet he wondered how these small town cops had put together so much so quickly.

Cody was dead. Leila was dead and he was going to have to abandon the best business idea he had ever had. There was a certain amount of background information the cops had and he wondered who they had questioned to get it. Alain and Alexander, the two goofballs who worked for him under Cody were still too involved in illegal stuff themselves to inform on him. Perhaps they tried to take the heat off of themselves by supplying that background info. Or, perhaps it was friends that the two goofballs had confided in. Rupert didn't know. He didn't think that was where the danger was. He had evidence to dispose of and a business to close. And he needed to get the hell out of town. Jackson suddenly seemed dangerous and lying in wait to take him down. He needed to cut himself off from this place, but needed to take his time. Sudden departures unless they involved going completely off grid and underground were an admission. He'd talk to Matias about that option, but would probably have to wait it out for at least awhile.

He was right to get rid of Cody. That was a loose end which would have continued to unravel over time. He could look at Leila's death as collateral damage, but then it hit him. It hit him like his grandmother slapping him hard in the back of the head which she did with some regularity whenever he did anything wrong. She laughed and laughed and his mother frowned, but his own mother never said a thing to protect him.

"Stupid-head!" grandma said. "American empty-head full of TV and comic books and sports and commercials. You don't know how the world can turn everything you took for granted on its head. Everything you thought was safe from the harsh realities my generation had to face, forces that make you live everyday of your life with dread; these are the things you thought were ancient history with no more ability to rear up and take away your comfortable, safe, bourgeois life. Yah? You never know when the ground will open underneath you and all the things you depended on for insulation and protection will not save you."

You never know when the ground will open underneath you, Rupert said to himself. He had dared to love again and it was swiftly and irrevocably taken away from him. A terrible place this world he said to himself again paraphrasing his grandmother. Strange and terrible.

Cody brought it on himself. Cody forced him to take action. That was undeniable, yet he never thought Leila would end up being a casualty in what he had had to do to take care of Cody. What else could he possibly have done? He felt that with Leila's death some force beyond life and death had singled him out. It was like a Shakespearean tragedy where all his elaborate strategies which had been employed to bring order to this disordered world only served to make him lose what he loved the most.

Rupert was going to have to up his game and play it as ruthlessly as befit the nature of the world as it really was. His path had been full of traps and pitfalls and deceptions, but he had the ability to jump over or otherwise elude them. Rupert had the resources and the resilience. He was not like other men.

Chapter Thirteen

The Jackson Police had nothing. The Ridgeway Police had nothing. And the DEA as far as his bust and then the trial in New Jersey were concerned, never wanted to hear his name again. He was good, but not in Jackson. He suspected an unprecedented level of scrutiny and it would probably not let up. After hearing of Cody's death and Rupert's abandonment of business as usual, Alain and Alexander had left Jackson for Brooklyn and were attempting to take over the business. They had no access to The Consortium however because Matias' referral was something of an exclusive invitation. When the product was not up to Rupert's former quality, and the selection of specialty strains his wealthy clients favored were either inconsistently available or worse yet faked with a lesser product, they quickly lost most of his former customers. Probably good candidates to become bike messengers in Manhattan like the delivery men they had hired. It was something that without his direction they were much more suited for. Not bad kids necessarily, but in need of a guiding light like him.

When he projected the authority that came naturally to him, without interference, then people did what they were supposed to do and stuff worked. Fuck with Rupert and everything started to degrade and there would be hell to pay. It was something like entropy in physics, Rupert being the necessary agent to prevent a human tendency toward disorder. He knew it sounded crazy, but his experience was what had borne this out to him again and again. He had always had this gut feeling about himself, but he had let other people influence him. Rupert was not going to let himself be compromised any longer.

Slowly the Jackson Police lost interest in him and he knew it was time to leave. He gave half of what he had left from the quarter

Matias had originally sold him sans fentanyl to one of his dirt-baggier contacts. The guy stole the Escalade for him and abandoned it two weeks after Rupert left town in a deep mountain ravine. It had burst into flames when it plunged off the road and into a rock outcropping thirty feet down and burnt to pretty much a frame, an engine and a trans and not much more. After his first quiet year in Jackson he had re-registered it to himself and put in for the paper work to have the title changed from his father's ownership to his name. There wasn't anyone else in the family to contest his getting the insurance money, and his company paid off promptly.

The Escalade had become too associated with Rupert himself, yet he was sorry to see it go. He had removed everything from it first except for a few nonessential personal items in order to give credence to the robbery ploy. His Glock, his dope and the irreplaceable and much prized complete Beatles discography on CD were the most essential of the removals. Heading out of Jackson in a rented Honda CRV he had his favorite album going full blast and was singing along at the top of his lungs.

He had what he needed from the cottage, the rest he had donated to the diverse array of druggie councilmen, street thugs and dopers, and various other hangers-on whose alliances he had cultivated over the last few years of his residence in Jackson, New Hampshire. He had also added to his cash supply from the New York business, so giving away most of the product he had stored, which had been meant for wealthy clients in New York City, had been a loss that hadn't been too tough to eat. Some of the most expensive strains he hid with his dope and works in the false compartments he had created in his presentation case. He was snorting a little more dope than he had in the recent past though and seemed to have lost his taste for weed.

He turned in the rental in Connecticut and bought a loaded up new CRV with cash. He didn't think that it was a car that would be associated with him and it was comfortable with plenty of places for hiding stuff he did not want found. He was headed back to New

Jersey, to Morris County specifically, and he wanted to see if he could resolve all problems with former associates or anyone else who might cloud an otherwise rosy Rupert future. He was ready for negotiation or war, his opponents could decide which it would be. Rupert was just so sick of feeling that he could be ambushed by who knows what or whom, at any time, at any place. He was going to take care of these problems once and for all. He wasn't going to just sit around and let events happen without his participation.

"Participation." He said it to himself and savored the word. It was his new way of describing this new part of his life and how he intended to shape it. It wasn't meant cooperatively. It had nothing to do with compromise; life was a shitstorm and he was in and ready to fight. When things started to happen he was going to make sure that his interests were properly represented, no matter what it took to insure that. He swam with the currents, but when he saw his opportunities he took them. Everyone was sitting at the banquet table and he for one was not going to let the good stuff pass him by.

He rented a small cottage in Indian Lakes in Rockaway. It was where he had grown up and was a half hour north of where Pam had lived. The house in Indian Lakes was shielded from the street by a thick wall of rhododendron perhaps growing wild since the days when the community's property had been owned by the Indian Lakes Fish and Game Club, a 19th century group of New York City robber barons who built themselves an English Hunting Lodge, now a club house, just beyond first beach. The remains of a stone wall and an old stone bridge over a stream which was overflow from the lake, could still be seen in the woods like ancient ruins indicating a previous indigenous people leading arcane and mysterious lives. At one time the wall had probably ringed the sunken gardens and sloping lawns around the club house. Indian Lakes had made a fascinating transition from playground for Wasp aristocracy to a sanctuary for the children of Holocaust survivors. The sunken gardens which evidently marked the foundation of the first manor house built on the property by Whitman Meadows had been converted by the current Property Owner's Association into shuffle board courts, and the great lawn in front of the club house now contained a band shell upon which the sons and daughters of POA members reprised ragged renditions of *Fiddler on the Roof* and *South Pacific*. The POA theatre director evidently refused to direct anything written after the 1960s, bowing to the loudly voiced preferences of the Saftas and Babushkas in the community.

When he was very young he had always referred to his Grandmother as Oma Ren and for him it was a title more than a name. He would have been afraid to refer to her informally, and there was no warmth or affection in his addressing her, or in her response. His friend's grandparents when called Bubbe and Savta beamed back at their grandchildren as though the pleasure of being addressed by grandchildren in itself made up for a lifetime of hardship and trauma. Their reactions fascinated him and yet he never understood these relationships completely. It was as though his friends were cherished by virtue of their mere existence and not by the merit of what they did.

He knew the dynamics of his family were different than the other families where he lived. His life at home was subservient to Oma Ren from the time he woke in the morning until about ten each night when their roles completely reversed. She was so drunk by this time, drinking he didn't know how many coffee cups full of the Seagram's and Seven-Up she favored, that he had to put her to bed. First, she would careen around the living room knocking over lamps and threatening to charge and trample the TV which she seemed to take a particular displeasure with. He had to learn to direct that unhappy energy toward her bedroom and especially away from the kitchen where if given the opportunity she would pull out all the drawers in search of knives and other destructive utensils for purposes he could only guess.

He had to drag her into the bedroom, undress her, put on her bed clothes, and then often recapture her as she attempted to roll off the bed and crawl back to the living room and her Seagram's. He put the pillows under her head and pulled her covers up to her chest. And then at least a few times a month she would rouse and seeing his face floating above hers cradle it in her hands and begin sobbing uncontrollably. It always happened in the same way.

"Poppa, *mein* poppa," she cried. "Why?" and she would begin to cry harder. "Why did you and momma leave me?"

He was so horrified the first time this happened that he froze and literally could not speak. She demanded an answer and all he could do is stutter, " I ... I ... cah, cah, can't bbb be your Poppa. I ... I..."

She slapped him and beat her fists against his chest.

"You deserted me and left me with the Nazis! They wanted only to kill me and I had to pretend I was one of them. Why! I was an orphan. I had no one to love me," she screamed.

He let this go on until she tired, turned over and fell into a troubled sleep punctuated by sudden full body jerks and whimpering and shouts in German. After a number of these episodes he learned to pull a chair over to the side of her bed and hold one of her hands while stroking her forehead.

"I'm here now, darling," he said.

She protested saying, "No, no, you and Momma ran away. You ran away ..."

"Shhh," Rupert said over and over and stroked her hair, her forehead and the sides of her face. "I am here now. Now it is time to sleep. You can sleep peacefully and you will know that I'm here and that you are safe and all is good."

This reversal of roles was deeply unsettling to him. At all other times the roles of his subservient father and mother and dictatorial Grandmother seemed to be unalterable for all eternity. And yet each evening it was as though what was set in stone suddenly became as malleable as clay. What he learned from this period in his life was that the universe was a dangerous place and that people were deeply and intractably unreliable. And yet, for all this, Oma Ren's drunkenness, her solipsistic need for other's submission, he looked back on this time as formative in giving him the tools with which he now navigated his life. She had taught him that the only intelligent behavior for a human being was predation and the only sensible place to be was at the top of the food chain. If all is disorder and dangerous, then domination and control was the only logical way of relating to a world such as the one he found himself in.

Chapter Fourteen

He had a first name and a work history. He figured Robert to be in his seventies which meant he probably got his B.A. in the 1960s. If he had worked for a few years before law school he probably finished school in the 70s. He hadn't mentioned which law school he had gone to in their brief conversation at Rupert's cannabis sales party in Jackson. Rupert thought he might have better luck searching the net for pictures of the Assistant Prosecutors in Passaic County in the late 70s and 80s, and in that way get a full name and the ability to begin tracking him down. And although he couldn't get the website to cough up the names of Assistant Prosecutors from that era, there was a picture of lawyers who worked in the Prosecutor's office. It was a charity event that had taken place at William Paterson University and there was a picture of the group sitting in bleachers with Robert smiling and holding a drink while standing next to the first row. It was a younger, thinner version with an earnest perhaps idealistic grin, but it was definitely the man sent by E and Scheiner, the man who had threatened him in New Hampshire.

His name was Robert D'Altorio. In half an hour Rupert had a career history, an address, phone number, family members and email address. D'Altorio had found him in Jackson and probably knew he was back in New Jersey. This guy scared him. He seemed formidable in a way his other opponents did not. For the purposes of professional or social advantage he had developed an easy facility in projecting a persona and an agenda which were not his true persona and agenda, and all with an air of relaxed self assurance. It was a sign of resourcefulness and wide ranging skills in service of a ruthless intelligence. For Rupert, ruthlessness did not have the pejorative qualities people thought. It was realism. People like D'Altorio, who could pursue their goals without emotion and a focus which lesser lights misunderstood as cruelty, were the most dangerous. He wasn't sure in what capacity he was operating for E and Scheiner. He suspected however, that it was a lot more than messenger and legal representation. Robert D'Altorio was a fixer, a guy who did whatever it took to make problems for his clients go away.

Now that he had a full name, lots of articles were coming up in Rupert's searches. He made some phone calls to D'Altorio' former associates pretending to be a journalist. They told him stories much richer in detail and implications than the events Robert had sketched out in New Hampshire. In 1975 he was an Assistant Prosecutor for Passaic County working mainly on narcotics prosecutions. Several of the detectives on the Paterson Narcotics Task Force, whose cases he had prosecuted, were dissatisfied with recent plea bargains he had made. They wanted him to accompany them on raids to some of the most drug infested, gang controlled wards in the city. These were areas where the police feared to go and where all civic authority had been lost. It was almost as though parts of Paterson had seceded from U.S. jurisdiction. The idea was that a close familiarity with how these raids went down and the reality of these procedures and not what was written in some procedural manual without a realistic understanding or even concern for what the cops were encountering, would result in more successful prosecutions. The cops wanted to get everyone "on the same page" by giving the prosecutors a little dose of reality.

The cops put him in a bullet proof vest and told him to just follow their lead. That was about all the instruction he got until he pulled out the service handgun he had been given when sworn into office and the cops promptly took it away from him and started laughing.

"That's just what we need in a shit show like this - friendly fire from a fucking amateur!"

D'Altorio protested that he had been Special Forces and a Vietnam Vet, but no one was listening.

Robert was put at the end of the line of officers who assaulted the front door of a tenement which was practically the only building standing on a block that looked more like a war zone than an American city. The rest of the cops circled the building and synchronously entered through all doors and the basement cellar door. The bad guys seeing the depth of the police presence began surrendering and filing out into a large hall at the front of the building where they were told to lie face down and put their hands behind their backs. Robert followed closely behind the cop in front of him and when the cop suddenly had his legs swept out from under him by a perp just starting to kneel on the floor, Robert was also knocked over by the overweight and flailing cop. The guy on the floor was grabbing for the cop's assault rifle when Robert fell heavily into them knocking the rifle out of the cop's and the perp's grasp and sending it skittering across the floor. The perp made a grab for the 9mm Beretta in the cop's holster and all of them were scrambling on the floor in a jumble. The cop was on his belly, the perp pushing himself up on his hands and leaning over him and attempting to get control of the weapon. Robert, lying sideways between the two, was able to scissor around the guy's head with his legs and flip him over, pulling away from the cop and sending the Beretta sliding into Robert's side. He reached around and grabbed it and sat up banging the perp's head off the floor by driving down with his legs and pointed the pistol at his head.

Perhaps it was because he was out of practice, or the exertion of being knocked down and then wrestling the guy into submission, but at least for Robert the unthinkable happened and the Beretta went bang and the guy's brains and the top of his skull were suddenly sprayed across the cheap, dirty linoleum tile in the tenement's front hall.

The other cops rushed over and grabbed the cop's firearm out of Robert's hand and pulled him to his feet.

"Ohhh, my God no," he said, and then said again two more times and was groaning.

The other cops looked at him and smirked. "We gotta bring this guy out with us more often," one said and the guys standing around Robert started laughing.

In Vietnam he had been part of a kidnapping and assassination unit operating in the rural regions of South Vietnam. With his unit he had ambushed and destroyed several Viet Cong units operating in their region and had felt scared, challenged, but largely blameless in participating in what was after all warfare. But then his unit kidnapped a local Village Chieftain suspected of collaboration with the Viet Cong. His children were shrieking with grief as they dragged him into the Huey and his wife clung to the edge of the open door, screaming and clawing at the faces of her husband's captors. She did not let go until the helicopter was thirty feet off the ground and somebody smashed her hands with the butt of an M16. She fell to her death in the middle of the village pavilion and in front of her children. Robert's Detachment Commander, suspecting the Chieftain of coordinating ambushes against American Forces asked preliminary questions. When met with stoic silence he pushed the Chieftain to the edge of the door, placed the barrel of his Colt Commander against the back of his head and blew most of his brains out the front of his skull. The body was blown forward and out of the Huey. Robert, standing just to the man's side had his fatigues decorated with splotches of blood, brains and scalp, hair still attached. He fell backward into the Huey retching violently, much to the amusement and howling laughter of his unit.

Robert's PTSD manifested primarily as insomnia, nightmares, ED and a tendency to drink too much unless he maintained a lot of control. Generally, his efforts at a lot of control paid off in being seen as wrapped a little too tight but capable of high-functioning behavior. Occasionally, due to events, certain people or perhaps the conjunction of the planets, he lost it. Seeing his perp's greymatter on the linoleum floor and hearing the cop's laughter brought back his trauma. He spent weeks on leave holed up in his apartment except for quick trips to the VA to plead for tranquilizers and benzodiazepine.

After that he had no stomach for his work. The department Psychiatrist put him on paid leave for a month after he was found weeping in his office by his boss and he never went back. After a summer of casting around wondering what the hell to do with the rest of his life he was approached by a law firm in Short Hills. They appreciated his experience as Assistant Prosecutor assigned primarily to narcotics cases and wanted him to work from the other side to defend the wayward children of their wealthy clients. He did this for a couple of years until while defending the bratty, eighteen-year-old daughter of a Short Hills ICare/BeautyCare exec he had enough. He was trying to get through to her that the only way to avoid a possible decade long sentence was to plead out. She slumped back in her chair and crossed her bare legs.

"I don't think so, Mr. D'Altorio. I think you're gonna have to do better than that. I mean, you know, you were working in New Jersey shitholes for all those years with the most corrupt, racist legal system in the fucking country. Surely you can find a way to get me off. Yes?"

"I'm not sure exactly what you mean, Sarah. Perhaps you can spell it out with more detail?"

"The drugs, you know. I'm sure you can find some poor asshole on the streets of Paterson whose life would probably be better off in a prison than having to wander around that stinking city. Like, make him admit to it, right? We say it's his drugs and he raped me and threatened to kill my family and burn down our house unless I sold this shit for him. You guys did this stuff all the time. You can do it for me."

Robert stared at her. "You want me to frame somebody for you?"

"Yeah, yeah, of course. Look you do this for me and I won't fuck with you. That's how it works, right? I mean a young woman like me ... people take the stupid shit we say seriously. All I gotta do is say how you were like trying to grab me and talking a lot of sex shit to me and your lawyer days are over ... at the least. You could even go to fucking jail."

Robert walked out of the room without saying a thing. When he came back appearing to be contrite and asking her to perhaps tell him with more detail what she had in mind, he was wired. It didn't take much to get her to repeat the whole thing including the personal threat. He took this to her father who like his daughter didn't seem interested in the moral implications of his daughter's attempt to manipulate her counsel, but rather just what the quickest and fastest way out of this mess was.

The quickest way out was for Sarah's dad to facilitate D'Altorio's move out of the law firm he was working for whose ethics weren't any better than the ICare/BeautyCare exec's seventeen-year-old drug dealer daughter. He was hired to the upper management team for ICare/BeautyCare/Europe where he spent a couple of happy decades jetting back and forth between America and Western Europe in the company's Cessna Citation Longitude. He was the guy the company called in to ax underperforming departments and empty out the offices of small companies that had been acquired. The people he fired had worked for a family owned business all their lives and were now hitting the streets with a pittance of a severance, a week for every committed year they had worked for people who they thought of as family more than employers.

He had learned after all these years to bury his feelings deep in an unseen part of himself that even he could no longer find. He repeated corporate cliches like "first in, first out" to rationalize axing the middle-aged lifers with no prospects for future employment. In his clipped New Jersey way of speaking, his explanations of what he did always had enough irony to suggest he wasn't just a corporate automaton. He defended the worst excesses of corporate predatory capitalism like it was some sort of higher reality that when you finally grow up — the inference being that most of us don't grow up — you just must acquiesce to. That is if you are mature enough to live in reality as it actually is and not how you wish it was. His experiences in Vietnam, Passaic County and Short Hills had finally soured him to humanity and all its problems. At ICare/BeautyCare he had learned to capitalize on his cynicism and make it the source of a personal style that had a deceptive, worldly charm. He was a snake, cold blooded and dangerous, but beguiling to anyone who had something that he wanted.

He was pushed out of ICare/BeautyCare the same way he pushed out a hundred middle and upper management people around the world. A younger CEO had come in looking to get rid of anything and everything he thought archaic. Robert's view was that the CEO defined archaic as any knowledge gained through hard-won experience as compared with the "brilliant" armchair theorizing of the beneficiaries of nepotism like himself. After his dismissal Robert came back to New Jersey angry, depressed, looking to play the game by his own rules and no one else's.

Chapter Fifteen

When she got back to New Jersey she called Mikael immediately and they walked through the woods at her bungalow in Mendham and she filled him in on the events of the last few weeks.

"The more you drag this out, the more complex it becomes and the more possibilities you introduce for everything to just go to shit. Listen. You sit in the woods above his house. You got rifle with no flash and noise suppressor and when he comes out the fucking door, boom, boom, you put two rounds in the chest. High velocity rounds put a big hole in Rupert. Then you done. You give me weapons and I dispose where no one ever see them again. And that's that."

Mikael rubbed his hands together as if washing away some nasty business, which of course it was.

He looked down at her, "Yes? You understand this? Simple," he said and tapped his big index finger against her forehead, "You keep it simple, bubaleh! You can't control everything and its not all going to go your way."

She began to cry a little there in the New Jersey woods and it surprised him.

"You can do it, Pam. No fear. You shoot and you walk straight back through the woods, nobody see, and you go to where you park your car far away. Safe. You get away easy. I will look and make sure everything is good."

"No," she said. "That's not it. A quick death, without even facing the suffering he's caused? It's not just me ... we don't even know for sure how many he's killed. A quick death ... it's not enough."

"Ohhh, I see. This is another matter," he said and laughed and hugged her. "You really got a set on you. Balls."

She looked at him sideways, but grinned despite herself, "I don't know," she said, "It's not exactly vengeance you know, I need him to face what he's done, even if its just for a milli-second, and know he's paying the price for it."

Mikael sighed and they walked back to her place in silence.

"You want I should go out there? I find you best spot to sit and shoot from. I find you good path of retreat and escape. I will figure it all out. No drama, no danger, you shoot, boom, boom, this chapter in your life closed. Next chapter, better chapter, ready to be lived."

He bent down and kissed her lightly on the cheek, "This I will do for you because I care very much."

She shook her head and looked at the ground. "Need some space to think out what it is I really want to do, Mikael. Don't take it personally."

She kissed him back, but it wasn't on the cheek. Mikael folded his big body around her and he wasn't anything like Rupert at all. Mikael lifted her off the ground like she was a feather and pulled back from her kiss which had become more and more passionate the longer she held her lips on his. He was grinning broadly.

"I am always being attracted to you even when you are still with Rupert which I never understood. But now, after I help, after I take care of you, I think that I am falling for you, Pamela. I just think about you all the time."

He stayed the night and was tender and strong and a terrific lover in a way she had not known with another man.

"Don't worry," he said while leaving in the morning. "We will figure this thing out. Rupert will pay, we will make him pay."

"Ohhh," she said laughing, "and Pam and Mikael, they're a we now?"

The next email from Matias concerned D'Altorio, E and Scheiner. "Your competition," the email said. "You could withdraw and know that Rupert will pay for what he has done in the past when E and Scheiner get at him. Or," the email said in all caps and several exclamations marks, "YOU COULD BROADEN AND INCREASE THE NUMBER OF YOUR TARGETS!!!

She knew E and Scheiner and she had always hated Rupert's friends. They were despicable even when compared to Rupert. She remembered them all sitting in the living room in Green Pond, Werner pulling out his "special stash" as a prelude to talking business. He offered the first hit from his bong to Pam something about his manner making her feel wary.

"Is it strong?" she had asked not really favoring weed, her own inclinations being more oriented to dope or a little meth use.

"You'll like it," Scheiner assured her, "You have to take a big hit though. Nice high, but you gotta take a big hit or, you know, nothing, no buzz." He glanced sideways at E who was smiling encouragingly.

It was the last time she ever smoked weed. She spent a terrified night in her bedroom while the boys laughed and jeered downstairs. She paced from her bed and the TV to her bathroom, washing her face, looking at herself in the mirror, trying to reassure herself that this too would pass and she'd have a semblance of normality to return to. The weed was so strong it was more like 'shrooms then anything she had ever smoked before. Two deep hits at the insistence of that psychopath Scheiner and she was tripping her brains out. It was horrible and besides making some calls up the stairs, "Hey Pam, are you talking to the dolphins yet?" alluding to a Joe Rogan bit, they never actually even checked on her, or offered her a Xanax or anything.

That event was emblematic in the way she viewed Rupert's friends, sadistic bastards all. But let them go to war and she'd see what was left. The world would be a better place without any of these bastards surviving and then this D'Altorio, hired gun, amoral mercenary, he seemed cut from the same cloth.

He sat on a bench in a little park along the Rockaway River where it crossed Main Street, went under an old railroad trestle and flowed eastward toward Denville. It had been a place he liked to come to since he was a kid and was for him a safe place that always made him feel somehow restored and ready to reenter the fray.

Through the trees and beyond the bridge he could see the ancient loading dock of a warehouse he had worked at while in high school which must have dated back to the time of the Morris Canal. He wasn't sure if it was the boats from the canal or freight trains that offloaded there. Maybe both. He was thinking about Pam and the accident that took her life. He wished she could be here now with him.

He walked up to Main Street, walked across the bridge over the river and sat down at a table of the sidewalk cafe that must have opened in the last few years while he was gallivanting around the country. The waitress introduced herself and told Rupert not only the many food offerings, beverages and deserts she was serving, but also a brief history of the cafe and even the foodie multi-cultural philosophy of the Cafe with some allusions to Anthony Bourdain. He looked up from his menu, squinted in the late afternoon sun that was shining over her shoulder and stared, something capturing his attention about the shape of her chin and the way her lips curled up at the corners of her small mouth.

"What?" she said when she saw him staring at her.

"Don't you know me?" he asked finally.

"Should I? Are you so well known?"

"Rupert. Remember? From Stoney Brook and then Copeland elementary schools. Oh, man I was crushing on you in seventh grade. You were that cute little exchange student from Ireland everybody was talking about, but so shy that you hardly ever said a word to anyone. Ilene, right?"

She blushed and at least momentarily laid aside her foodie sales persona.

"Rupert. Sorry, I suppose its not so nice to say, but I really don't remember you."

"Remember *The Producers?* I played Max Bialystock ... it was my junior high claim to fame." Rupert laughed in that self deprecatory way he had when he wanted to incur favor.

Ilene looked at him, wheels turning, memories being sorted, "That was you? Oh, for God's sakes! You were hilarious. I mean, some of the acting skills had a way to go, but, you know, you were so funny. Oh God, I can't believe it's you, Rupert. I mean, we moved when I got into high school. Not far, just into the borough but it was enough to send me to another school and I didn't really keep up with everybody, but that was you, huh?"

"Yeah, that was me," he said with some obvious self satisfaction, "and listen if you're not doing anything tonight why don't we go out for dinner. It would be like the realization of a childhood dream for me."

He was smiling in that mischievous but courtly manner that he had developed, first with Pam and then Leila. He could tell it was having its desired effect. He knew he was overweight and bore a passing resemblance to Zero Mostel. It was probably why his seventh grade teacher picked him for the role as Bialystock, but women were generally more evolved creatures than men and charm could often overcome other drawbacks.

She agreed and they met at a little family run Thai place in Rockaway. He had a chili glazed pork chop that made his scalp sweat. She laughed and said she never understood what it was that people loved so about chilis. They talked about school and the people they had known and when he turned on the bright light of his attention and listened, punctuated by seemingly really interested questions, she ended up telling him so much more than she had told even the most important people in her life.

She told him about her father's alcoholism and his abusiveness and how living with him for her was like always walking on eggshells. It was like being in a state of constant vigilance. She never knew what it would be that would set him off. When he was dying, she was his caretaker. She loved her father. She had wanted to take care of him, but it had been an extremely conflicted time in her life.

"Maybe I will tell you about that at another time," she said.

Rupert had a sense of what that conversation might be about. He had a feeling about her at the restaurant, that this was someone with a challenging past and with a hurt in her that showed through quite a bit of the time despite her best attempts to mask it. He saw that relating to other people was more about validating herself in their eyes than perhaps anything else. He suspected that for Ilene life was a constant threat to her very right to even take up space on the planet.

"And how about you, Rupert? You seem to be someone who's been through a lot," she said finally as they were walking out to the parking lot after dinner. "What trials and tribulations have you had to overcome in your life?"

When she smiled, he smiled as well, but it was strained and she noticed.

"Well, I didn't mean to go any place that wasn't appreciated."

What he objected to most was her presumption. She didn't have any right to think she could presume anything about him. No one fucking did.

"You think my life has been one of trials and tribulations?" he asked.

"Just a way of speaking, its a challenge for all of us, isn't it? Life I mean."

"Let's get something straight," he said sharply and grabbed her arm just above the elbow maybe more firmly than he intended. "If I want you to know something about me, you ask and I will fucking tell you if I have the inclination." His face was close to hers and although he didn't raise his voice he was too close and it scared her. She saw her father suddenly and felt his hands on her. That sick feeling gripped her guts and she felt cold and knotted up and tight.

Ilene shrank back, Rupert still gripping her arm tightly. "OK, OK. Look ... sorry, I really didn't mean to intrude Rupert."

He let her go, but she was so petite, and he had been pulling her arm up and keeping her off balance, that when he released her she crumpled to the ground in the middle of the parking lot. Rupert stood to her side and stared, surprised that she fell and about ready to pick her up off the asphalt. A guy had been watching them a few cars over and stood by the side of his car waiting to see the outcome of their exchange. He then skipped around his vehicle, ran over and stood between Ilene, who was still on the ground and Rupert.

"That's enough, fat boy," he said and when Rupert didn't say anything the guy began to turn to help Ilene up.

With a speed and finesse surprising for a guy so big, Rupert knocked his feet out from under him and the guy fell heavily to the side on his back. Rupert stepped up and leaned over him. He had his Glock in his hand which he always carried now that he was back in the land of E and Scheiner. He put the barrel against the guy's forehead and pulled back the slide so the guy heard a round clicking up into the chamber.

"Don't ever make the mistake of talking to me like that again," he said in the flat, affectless voice he adopted when he wanted to sound sinister. "I will fucking kill you." He slipped the Glock back in the holster he had hidden in his waist band. "You understand me?"

The guy looked up at him frightened and humiliated. He looked back at the restaurant, but no one had seen the altercation.

"OK," he said. "Don't worry. The last thing I want to do is get involved in your shit."

He got up and Rupert smiled when he scampered away like a small, scared squirrel. Rupert looked over at Ilene who was still curled up on the asphalt in a knot of panic.

"Fuck it," he said to himself and without saying another word to her walked over to his car, got in and headed back to the house in Indian Lakes. I tried. *She seemed like an interesting girl, but there's some baggage there. Without a doubt."*

He was home. Rockaway and Indian Lakes were really home for him, but there was going to have to be a reconciliation with his past and it wasn't the kind they did daily on Dr. Phil. Rupert was waiting for D'Altorio to make the first chess move. Rupert did not doubt that D'Altorio knew Rupert was back, but wondered how this game should be played. His inclination was to let D'Altorio do something, perhaps make contact that Rupert could then evaluate and respond to. He had set up the security equipment he had gotten from Matias and had the shotgun and the Glocks. Rupert mulled it over for a couple of days and then realized that he was going to have to direct the action. Get to D'Altorio and then E and Scheiner and perhaps his life would open up again and he like the rest of humanity could afford to be careless, and relax the constant wearying vigilance and anxiety that had become his normal, everyday mode.

He was in the kitchen when the alert on his iPhone went off and he ducked in the corridor and ran for the bedroom where he kept his shotgun. He carried the Glock at all times now whether he was wearing pajamas or pants. He turned on the cam at the front of the house and there was Ilene, pensive, nervous, walking hesitantly toward the front door.

She stopped and he said "What do you want," brusquely, through the speaker on the cam above her head.

"Well, I want to say how sorry I am for causing that trouble."

She was crying and nodding, looking down at the mat in front of his door that said, Welcome Friend!

"I don't even know you and look, here I go trying to get you to tell me all the intimate details of your life. I don't know. I don't know why I do it, I just .... Look, Rupert, you have a right to your privacy, you know, anyway you want to play it. I promise ... absolutely, I won't bother you ... I just keep doing this over and over like my father said. He always said I was a little busy body, that I should listen and stop this incessant need to chatter and look here I am in front of your door and I'm doing it again" She cried more heavily now and put a hand out to balance herself against the wall of his house. Her head was down with her long hair hanging in her face. He thought she might fall. He opened the door and leaned the shotgun against the coat closet just as she began to slide down the wall. He caught her under the arms and carried her into the house.

"Don't worry, Ilene," he said as he laid her down on the sofa in the living room. She seemed exhausted and he just sat with her for a while.

"You want to talk?" he asked.

"My father said the worst thing a girl could be was a pushy little bitch who didn't know how to take no for an answer. My father was an old-fashioned man and rigid. I always thought he was an anachronism. He was from rural Ireland and seemed almost ludicrously antiquated. But damn if all of my life, you know, I was just always pushing away all the men I liked. I mean, they all just walked away from me because I was like too much, too soon, insisting on making romance out of little more than an acquaintanceship or trying to walk right into the most intimate parts of their life as though it was my right."

She was crying again and Rupert leaned forward and put his hand on her hand.

"I just ... I don't know. I just don't want to think that he was right," she said.

Chapter Sixteen

She ended up staying for a couple of days and Rupert couldn't help but feel that through a fortuitous series of circumstances he had gotten the relationship off on the right foot. She cooked him scrambled eggs, onions, spinach and kippers which he hadn't had since his Oma Ren cooked them when he was a kid. She cleaned his house and when came upon his weaponry and ammunition, placed everything under his bed in an orderly way, laid out to be easily reachable. She did not mention his firearms, or ask any questions about his need for such immediate accessibility.

She was passive, but also curiously active and creative and transformed submissiveness into a kind of caring cooperativeness. She was willing to go the extra mile for someone she cared about she said, but he knew what it really was. He had the upper hand because she was willing to defer to him in order to avoid the catastrophe of one more failed relationship in her life. Normally a woman like this would be so beneath his contempt that he wouldn't want anything to do with her. And yet Ilene was so bright and so sensual and like Leila added a richness to his life in terms of food and music and an understanding of the world and people that was different than his own, but whose depth he found interesting. He liked having her around, and he liked the way she deferred to him in all things, but with lots of funny, ironic commentary.

He tried to contact Matias using a texted request for a meeting that had been their way of communicating over the past few years. He got no answer and tried again. After a response that was not Matias and whose unfamiliar voice was irate and accused him of harassment, he figured that Matias had terminated the account and the number had been reassigned. He assumed that he should resign himself to the fact that Matias was no longer a resource for him.

Friday, Ilene hadn't stayed the night because she had to work late. She came over early the next morning because she loved to climb into bed with him and snuggle up to that large male body which always led to other activities which she also seemed to love, especially early in the morning.

He was roused by the alert on his iPhone and saw that cam #3 was showing an indistinct figure looking into the driver's side window of his car. He checked his motion detectors and cams on the phone, the eight different security devices he had that overlapped and ringed the property. They showed no incursions or even errant animals wandering too close to the house. He placed a hand on Ilene's shoulder to rouse her and placed his index finger over his lips when she looked up at him. He quickly threw on yesterday's clothes that he had piled up on the floor by the bed. He grabbed the Glock and headed for the back yard. He figured he'd work his way down to the street by walking through his neighbor's back yard and heading to his car along the far side of the neighbor's house.

As soon as he rounded his neighbor's forsythia which effectively screened him from the street, he saw the figure walking away from him past Rupert's car and toward an Audi parked a few hundred feet up the road.

"Hey," Rupert yelled and rather than turning, the guy ran for the Audi, wrenched open the door and scrambling in behind the wheel sped off down the street.

He had his car keys in the pants he had thrown on and ran for his car and took off after the guy. Families walking to the 9:15 Shabbat service at the Conservative Temple had to scurry off the road as the two cars sped through the narrow Indian Lakes streets made even narrower by cars parked on both sides of the road. He was heading for the entrance to the Lake and Rt. 80 where Rupert's CRV would not be able to keep up with the intruder's A-6. Suddenly, the guy pulled over and slammed on his brakes. Rupert almost piled up into his backend but managed to steer to the right and ended up at an angle parallel to the front of the Audi. Rupert was out of the car immediately, his Glock pointed at the ground at the end of a straight right arm as he ran.

When he looked through the windshield expecting to see D'Altorio or maybe even his two former partners in crime, he saw a face he did not recognize. The guy got out of the Audi leisurely, seemingly now at ease and smiling and walked toward Rupert who had slipped the Glock into his waistband and covered it with his shirt. He kept his hand on his belly over the Glock. It was accessible if needed.

"You scared the hell out of me back there. Sorry, man I haven't responded well to surprises since 9/11. You know? I was in the first tower. I mean I recovered and all but surprise me and I go right into panic mode. You know? You know what I mean?"

"You were in front of my house looking in my car window," Rupert said as he looked at the guy skeptically.

"Well, I was driving round the Lake and I saw the car. I had been thinking of buying one of those for my high school age daughter."

The guy was smiling in that ambiguous way that might mean he was throwing out some obvious bullshit that Rupert couldn't do anything about, or was simply amused by his own actions and the trouble that had resulted and now had a hilarious new story to tell at dinner parties.

"A guy like you, you're like the decoy aren't you? Throw a little confusion to the prey and maybe next time he's relaxed. Maybe next time he disregards his own intuitions. Yes? Is that fucking you, pal?"

Rupert waited and when no response was forthcoming said, "You tell D'Altorio and those bastards he's working for, E and Scheiner, that it's not gonna work. I got his number. I know the story. I'm just looking to resettle in the hometown without causing anybody any trouble, but if that can't be done, well I'm not gonna take any shit. I'll stand up for myself. No one is going to push me around at this point in my life."

The guy shrugged and turned and got back in the A6. He pulled back onto the road slowly and turned and looked at Rupert one more time. He raised his hand as if to wave with an open palm, and then folded his fingers one by one to make a tight fist. He grinned at Rupert, gunned the A6 and was down the road and out of sight in seconds.

Rupert told Ilene that there were people out there that wanted to do him harm, hence the security devices he kept checking and the self defense under the bed. She asked him no questions about the whys and the wherefores of how this had come about and who the perpetrators were and his relationship to them, but rather wanted to get acquainted with the cams and motion detectors he had arrayed around the house. She suggested that she download his security apps on her devices and that she have a way to alert him without using messaging or her phone if she were approached or saw something. Rupert gave her a run through of the security app and showed her where she could turn on Emergency Alerts and how even if the phone was off, it would begin blaring like the East German Police.

He expected more in the way of probes from D'Altorio. He sent Ilene out to do a couple of weeks worth of shopping so he could stay at home and like that morning's incident, let D'Altorio know that Rupert was covered, Rupert was ready, Rupert could see him coming from a mile away. D'Altorio wasn't going to surprise him, and he was going to respond tit for tat, whatever it took to shake this guy off his ass.

Rupert and Ilene had some very pleasant dinners at home. She bought a case of mixed wines, mostly Cabernet and Chiantis which were like a revelation to him. She was just a killer cook.

The following night he was eating a dinner she had left him. Ilene had to work a late shift bartending at her new gig at The Exchange in Rockaway, but had left him some fresh sole broiled in lemon, a bit of butter and garlic and stuffed with cheese and sautéed spinach. Rupert opened her Pinot Grigio and was enjoying himself between the wine and her excellent cooking. His end of the street in Indian

Lakes was sparsely populated and the only sounds he heard that evening other were some birds in the trees alongside his house and the faraway sound of cars, motorcycles, trucks starting up and shutting off and being driven on errands of anonymous purpose.

When a message suddenly went ping on his iPhone, it startled him and his forkful of fish fell back to his plate splattering a bit of sauce on his shirt. He dabbed at the yellow splatters across his belly with his napkin before looking at his phone which lay beside his wine glass.

"Surprise, Rupert," said his message. "Better check your alerts! Never know when somebody's creeping up on you!"

Immediately, when the message had pinged its way onto his screen his alerts showed activity. He pushed back his dinner and his chair and ran for the bedroom. He grabbed five preloaded 15 round magazines for the Glock and picked up the shotgun and a box of double-aught shells which he threw in a small canvas bag with the mags and headed for the basement stairs. The cellar was old, damp, the only light coming from a ground level basement window over his head. He slumped against the wall and slid down until he was sitting on the floor with the shotgun in his lap.

He sat there in the dark feeling as though whoever came down the stairs was an easy target for him and that at least he'd take a lot of these bastards out before they got him. Then he realized that all they had to do was set the house on fire and Rupert would be unable to escape and unable to exact a price for his own death. His phone was quiet and he checked it there in the dark. The cams showed no intruding figures huffing toward his house carrying AR-15s. The motion detectors had turned on the floodlights in the front and back but again all seemed quiet now.

He realized, there on the dirty floor, that there were other people in this world who could get the upper hand. He seemed to be dealing with one of them and the guy was testing him. Rupert felt like a bull in one of the Hemingway stories he had read in high school. The matador was progressively weakening him. A spear thrust to the flank and his will and energy were draining away with his blood.

He didn't know what to do. He had been flying by the seat of his pants trusting that events would fall into his lap the way they always had in the past. Whatever forces had caused things to go his way seemed to be now somehow absent. He groaned and remembered the abject hopelessness he had felt when the DEA had first arrested him and let him rot for three days in that horrible little windowless room while they interrogated him. This guy was making him feel like those fucking DEA agents had made him feel. He got squeezed, he got played, and now here it was all coming around again. Rupert sat there on the floor, going over and over a situation he had let get out of hand. How would he turn it around? Was it even possible? He sat until he heard the alert for his front walkway and saw Ilene on the cam running for the front door. She had obviously seen the alerts go off all at one time on the security app.

"Rupert," she was screaming before she even got to the door. "Rupert, Oh God please. Are you all right?"

He stood up quickly and dusted himself off. He wanted to get upstairs and get his firepower back under the bed before she went through the front door.

Chapter Seventeen

Yes. He was having a little fun with Rupert, but there was a method to his madness. Take a few pokes at him and show him the weaknesses of what he might have thought were his solid defenses and he'll doubt himself. That is a very good position for Robert D'Altorio to be in, to have an enemy whose anxiety about his ability to defend himself consumes him. It was like his negotiations with the Europeans when he worked for ICare/BeautyCare. You show those small timers the sheer folly of attempting to bargain with a giant, modern multinational. They are stuck in their small town, small-minded culture, thinking small because they do not grasp the modern predatory business world. They have no understanding that it is their worldview and business culture itself that will result inevitably in their being torn apart and devoured. Show them their potential weaknesses and everything goes more smoothly. He had that line from *Star Trek* emblazoned on T-Shirts for his Acquisitions Department: Resistance is futile. You will be assimilated!

His past experience definitely had some similarities to this current situation with Rupert. Not an exact fit, but Rupert's weakness was his sociopathy and a narcissistic personality disorder which manufactured delusion in order to keep afloat the idea of Rupert being always at the center of the world. It did not allow the cold, objective assessment of reality that D'Altorio felt was his strength. In warfare, one wants to be on the side that sees reality as it is in itself and not as a projection of the ego about how things could or should be; always, one wants to see how things actually are. This was D'Altorio's *Art of War* and everything else flowed quite simply from this one fundamental idea.

His employers at this point just wanted Rupert fucking dead and only wanted him to know who was killing him in the moments before he died. E. and Scheiner wanted D'Altorio to stretch out that scene as operatically as possible so that Rupert had an intense, unmitigated experience of being executed. D'Altorio had other ideas. Rupert was a gift, a chance given to him to make up for a life where an unfair burden of bullshit and mayhem had come his way.

When he worked for the Passaic County Prosecutor's Office he saw it as a commitment to a learning experience that would be a stepping stone, not to help rich people prevent their delinquent children for having to pay for their misdeeds, but as an invaluable experience for a committed future defense attorney. And once he had paid his dues and was in his own practice, he could be selective about his clients. His primary purpose would be to see justice served despite the usual obstacles to that process, namely, as he saw it, race, class, and ethnicity. He suspected his motivations were too cliched and sentimental being mostly inspired by Atticus Finch and Perry Mason. And a disordered world cheated him out of a vocation that was perhaps only a mirage anyway.

As a result of accidentally killing the drug dealer in Paterson, an incident whose psychological repercussions for him were so brutal because of its parallels with his Vietnam experience, he was forced to grow the hell up. He gave up his naiveté embracing ruthlessness as an authentic reaction to the realities of this world. It was this understanding he took into the business world and he ate up all the little fishes he could find. He never repudiated what he had done in business, even though in the real world he played absolute havoc with people's lives. He played by the rules as he was given them. And yet, adding to the whole mess this world was in took a toll on him. Rupert was an opportunity to at least in microcosm bring order back to a chaotic world and shake his fist in the face of God for creating a reality that should never have been. He was going to bring this guy to justice and make sure that every deed was pulled out of its dark corner and exposed to light.

He knew about the girl friend. He had guys talking to the staff at

The Exchange and guys in the hills above Rupert's house at the back of Indian Lakes. The woods were deep and rose at a slight grade and went back at least a few miles to Green Pond Road and Hibernia. A guy with binoculars in the woods and some crude but friendly interrogation at the subject's significant other's place of work and you've got quite a bit of information to work with. Bringing Rupert to justice did not necessarily involve avoiding collateral damage in D'Altorio's thinking. If he could use Ilene and she got hurt, well, she had made her choices in this life and Rupert was her worst.

In this line of business there are always parts of the operation that cannot be initially planned for. Anomalies materialize suddenly and unexpectedly. They can be a destructive challenge to those unable to adapt. Raffi, one of the guys with binoculars he had in the woods above Rupert's house saw a bright flash on the right side of the house where the owner had piled leaves and brush cleared from the back yard. Raffi was far enough behind Rupert's house where the security cameras did not penetrate. But he could clearly see the side of the house and the flash was intermittent and worked its way forward and seemingly underneath the branches and leaves. He squatted down and watched through his binoculars. The brush was in a direct line of sight to the front door. A big guy, dressed all in camo, stood and piled a few more branches in front of his position and then laid back down. As he reached for more cover his sleeve rode up his forearm and a large metallic watch reflected sunlight. A long barrel rifle lay on top of the brush and the intruder grasped it and lay back down in a tactical position with the rifle pointed toward the front door. Raffi called the boss.

"Someone who has the same designs on Rupert, eh? I mean who knows how many enemies he's picked up along the way. But this is a complication that could very well screw our plans all to hell. You wait. I'll park on the street and you come from the back and we'll flush him out like a fucking game bird. Let him catch sight of your movement, but don't give him a target. He's probably got a sniper's rifle and he's not gonna be able to get that thing around too easily and target you in all that brush before we can take him. Rupert is in Morristown. Just don't be seen by the neighbors."

Even as D'Altorio pulled up on the street he could see a figure retreating into the woods and running on an angle behind the neighbor's property. He figured he was heading for the dead end on Apache Trail which was a road that most deeply penetrated the woods behind Indian Lakes. It was about a half mile directly through the woods from where the guy was running. He could clearly see the rifle he was carrying and it made his intent obvious. The guy eluded D'Altorio's man and took off through the woods like a fucking gazelle. He did not give D'Altorio the impression of being an amateur.

D'Altorio got back in his Audi and floored it knowing he could beat the guy to Apache Trail. He parked a little more that three quarters of the way down the street and backed into the driveway of a house that looked unoccupied. He had a clear line of sight to where the road ended and a thick growth of prickly bushes bordered the woods. He saw a figure work its way around the stand, strip off the camo he had on over t-shirt and jeans, and carrying the clothes and his rifle scurry over to a Range Rover. The back hatch popped open as he approached and he dumped everything into the back and was blasting down the road past D'Altorio literally seconds after appearing through the trees.

He got the model of the car and the plates and the last friend he had in the Passaic County Prosecutor's Office ran the plate and he got a name, address and occupation. But his friend had plenty to say about Mikael Ablesmekov.

"IDF Special Forces Retired, works security for some of the top Wall Street power players, this guy is no joke. I don't know why you wanted me to look up a guy like this, but if he is a problem for you, you better get out from under whatever bullshit you're involved with now. You don't wanna come face to face with him."

D'Altorio drove out late that night to the address he had for

Ablesmekov. He found the car and sat and watched, peed in a fucking bottle, wished he had brought food and water and then in the morning finally saw his guy get in the Range Rover and drive out to Mendham/Bernardsville Road and head North. The Range Rover took a right on Cherry Lane, in Mendham, and D'Altorio drove past the turn slowly and watched in his rear view mirror. Ablesmekov turned right through a large stone gate which was just the second driveway in from Mendham/Bernardsville Road.

D'Altorio raced out to 24 and went right on Tempe Wick and then got on Cherry Lane from the other end. It was a narrow country lane winding its way through old farmland. All along its length had been built a remarkable mixture of country estates for the Morris County elite mixed in with more modest habitations probably predating the moneyed influx. At what looked to be the property line where his target had disappeared, he pulled his car off the lane and partway up a dirt road that was partially overgrown. He slipped a magazine into his Berretta and tucked it into his waist holster. When he had walked into the woods and was out of sight of the road he came into a clearing where neat rows of small pines had been planted in orderly rows. A path at the end of the field let to a green house behind which stood a prefab garage and shed full of, what looked like nursery tools.

He followed a dirt road which led out toward the main buildings on the estate. Ahead of him was a bungalow with a smaller SUV and the Range Rover parked in front. Two people stood beside the front door of the bungalow. He ducked behind some piled up fencing and got out his iPhone and attached the zoom camera lens. D'Altorio quickly snapped off a series of photos. It was Mikael and a woman he had never seen before. They embraced, she went back inside, and Mikael did a K turn and drove out toward the front gate. Happy with his good fortune, D'Altorio trudged back up through the woods and headed to Passaic to see his "friend" for a little face to face. He was going to have to do some serious bartering for the services he needed now.

D'Altorio started visiting The Exchange when Ilene was bartending. He stopped in a couple of times and ordered from her and tipped her generously and made a little small talk. Like many women whose relationships had an inequitable power balance she left herself subtly open to the interest of other men. He could see she was intrigued by him, stealing quick glances and arranging to do her clean up where he was drinking at the bar. He introduced himself the second time he came in. Giving her a false name and false history was sufficient protection from Rupert, at least for the moment, because she knew the guy Rupert told her was his enemy by description only and had probably never seen a picture of him. If he kept away from any parallelism in D'Altorio's life and this new persona he had become, he could do what he wanted. What he wanted was a pic of the two of them that he could shove in Rupert's face at least digitally. He meant it to be a provocation, a declaration that D'Altorio had the power to take away anything Rupert thought was his alone and that his activities were an open book. Nothing he did could guarantee his own safety. And who knows, along the way, perhaps she could be persuaded to shine a little light into the darkness which was Rupert.

"You're a very industrious worker, but so serious. You must be of German descent ... raised to work but have no fun, no fun ... never any fun." He smiled broadly making sure she understood he was teasing her.

She laughed in that way a woman sometimes does when she is caught out by an interesting man. She was laughing at herself, but also with the delight of being flirted with. She put on the thick Irish brogue of her mother.

"Ahh, you're the observant one now, aren't you? I can see that if I'm too talkative with the likes of you you'll be going on and blabbing about me to the whole bar."

"Such a pretty little thing," he said to her. "I hope that you are unattached, because I can see I'm going to be chasing you."

She smiled, a little warily, but there was pleasure for her in what he said.

"What's your name?" she asked.

"Dalton," he said. "Dalton Roberts."

He had met the owner of The Exchange and had arranged for The Exchange's media guy to come over and take a picture of the two of them. He specified privately to the owner that he wanted to sponsor an ad for The Exchange in the Rockaway Patch. He told the owner it was a private joke, but that he'd pay for the ad himself and it would contribute to the bar's friendly ambience.

"Free advertising," he said. "Can't beat free."

He got her to lean over the bar and told her to show the world the excellent customer service that was typical of The Exchange. She placed her hand on his shoulder and lined up her face with his, but he turned quickly as the picture was being taken and planted a kiss on her cheek. The look on his face was so loving, so adoring, that what would usually have been an innocuous photo looked like he intended so much more.

She pulled away upset, realizing how angry Rupert would become if he saw a picture like that.

"Oh, don't worry. I'm old and harmless," he said knowing she was upset about Rupert's possible reaction and not his kiss.

"Harmless are you? I'm beginning to doubt that."

D'Altorio subscribed Rupert's email account to the Rockaway Patch. He had gotten it from the Indian Lakes High School Alumni Facebook Group and was surprised at how easy social media made such things. He wanted Rupert to make this discovery on his own.

It didn't take very long to see that Rupert had in fact reacted to the picture of Ilene and "Dalton" at The Exchange. D'Altorio's early morning surveillance guy reported that when he drove past Rupert's house on his way to his post in the hills above Rupert's place, he saw the front door open, the house empty and realized Rupert had just up and pulled the hell out.

"Guess he didn't like being a sitting duck," D'Altorio's man said.

D'Altorio frowned at him, but it didn't really matter to him that Rupert was taking defensive action. It wouldn't be enough in the end. D'Altorio wanted to ratchet up Rupert's paranoia to the highest possible level even making him suspect that Ilene was a D'Altorio plant and that he was vulnerable on the inside as well as the outside.

In order to appease the Sussex County community where the Consortium had set up business, they had agreed to buy the old airport, and an adjoining tract of land. A real estate development company had planned to build vacation homes around a golf course imitating and perhaps competing with Trump's place in Bedminster and looking to appeal to wealthy retiring baby boomers. Unfortunately, the developers had planned to do this simultaneously in Wisconsin and New York State and had become seriously overextended. They abandoned the project after building a couple of model homes, a few holes of the golf course and clearing some of the pastureland that had been family dairy farms in the 60s. One of the models was hidden in a grove of old growth forest left standing around a river that wound its way through a small, shallow valley west of Stillwater.

The Consortium, anxious to do further business with Rupert, which he had indicated was also his intent, rented the place to him under his *nom de guerre,* Alfred Sheldrake. Only the Consortium CEO knew Rupert's identity. It was a comfortable and secure base of operations and he had soon rigged up his security technology with a few innovations suggested by The Consortiums tech guy. He had a bit of an early warning system with a few cams in the trees along the dirt lane which led to the house. It was a private road and did not go through to any public roads but ended in a cul-de-sac now so overgrown that it was really just a dead end.

The Consortium had taken good care of the property running management meetings and holding parties for the staff at the house. He was comfortable even though he really lived in only about three rooms of the three bedroom, three full bath vacation home. But he was getting a little stir crazy knocking around the place by himself.

Every time he looked at that picture of D'Altorio kissing Ilene, he envisioned what his revenge might look like. Often it was stepping up to D'Altorio in a public place and smiling in his face before blowing his fucking brains all over the three people behind him. Sometimes it involved a public denunciation punctuated by Rupert blowing D'Altorio's brains out. The common theme of course was a deader than dead D'Altorio with a smashed pumpkin for a head lying on the ground while being stepped around by horrified witnesses.

There were two things that he was mulling over obsessively: betrayal by Ilene, and D'Altorio marking another notch in the win column. But when he thought about it after a line of dope and a glass of the Cab Ilene had taught him to enjoy he began to doubt her complicity. It just didn't make sense in terms of what he had come to know about her psychologically and how she had fit into his life as precisely as a jigsaw puzzle piece. This was his gut talking, his intuition, and not his overactive mind that was always thinking and planning. She was his and he was going to take back the things that were his.

When he walked into The Exchange he was surprised at how familiar it all seemed to him. The decor had changed, even the room layout, but there a certain attempt to recreate 50s Americana, although perhaps with too much of a touch of irony for his taste. He remembered sitting around a table with E and Scheiner right by the low wall by the entrance, eating clams and drinking some of the worst beer the big American breweries had ever produced made only slightly more palatable by being on draft.

She saw him right away from her position behind the bar and gasped and dropped her towel as both hands shot up to cover her mouth. She hadn't seen or heard from him in a week and had given her fellow bartender the idea that there had been a break-up between Ilene and Rupert caused by the picture. When her co-worker heard her gasp and looked up to see her staring at Rupert, he hit the emergency button behind the bar and two burly security guys came trotting into the bar's main room in seconds. He pointed out Rupert to them and Ilene had begun to cry softly. When they grabbed his upper arms, she let out a piercing scream.

"Noo! Leave him the fuck alone!"

Chapter Eighteen

The bouncers seemed as surprised as he was and the three of them looked at each other for a few seconds before the the bouncers decided that there was really nothing here to enforce as far as breached rules or public disturbance.

"Best perhaps for all concerned," Rupert said to them as one let go of his arm where he had grabbed it just above the elbow. "I never know what I'm going to do in a situation like this. Man, sometimes I'm just capable of anything."

He smiled at them. The bouncers who had seen almost everything regarding the self delusion of the public, rolled their eyes and peeled off his sides like F16's quitting an intruder and headed back to the kitchen to flirt with the cook and get some handouts.

Their line of work sometimes conspired to have them run up against someone who was outside their usual ability to evaluate. These people were easy to underestimate. Better sometimes to just let it go and see what happens. Rupert smirked and shook his arms as though their touch had left detritus that had to be dislodged and shaken from him.

Just as well to be underestimated. There's always an advantage to that. For all their status as security professionals, he could have shot them both in the fucking head before either had a chance to even react. He pushed forward toward Ilene with only a slow expulsion of breath showing his dissatisfaction with having to deal with meathead security guys.

"Do you want to come with me, or what?" he said to Ilene.

Suddenly, D'Altorio, who Rupert hadn't seen when he first came in, charged from around the backside of the bar and headed straight for Rupert. Rupert's right hand instinctively reached for the Glock hidden on his left side under his loose fitting Khakis. Ilene saw him and ran up and while embracing him from behind blocked his access to the weapon.

"NO, no, no, no, Rupert. You do that and there's no future for us. You'll be in jail, honey."

She came around his side and was shaking her pretty, tear streaked face in his face. D'Altorio grabbed her from behind by her long ponytail and pulled her back so hard that she was thrown to the ground and into the legs of a couple at the bar.

Rupert lurched forward and threw an off balance hooking right hand while D'Altorio hopped over Ilene's legs and crouching, attempted to tackle Rupert by launching his shoulder into his midsection. Even off balance, Rupert's considerable mass put enough energy into the punch that when it connected with the side of D'Altorio's temple it sent him crashing backward into the bar where he slumped to the floor semi conscious.

The bouncers were back at the bar and grabbed Rupert under his arms almost lifting the big man off the floor. D'Altorio rolled over on his side and was on all fours. The bouncers yelled at him and demanded his name while still holding Rupert. D'Altorio jumped to his feet and sprinted for the front door.

Rupert struggled with the bouncers and screamed, "Get that bastard," and then yelled after D'Altorio, "I'll kill you you motherfucker, I'll fucking kill you," as D'Altorio shot through the entrance.

The owner of The Exchange had walked in at the point where D'Altorio had pulled Ilene down by her hair and gotten the gist of what was happening pretty fast. Rather then supporting his bartender he saw only a possible sticky web of romantic betrayals, violence and abuse. It was something he wanted his business to have no part of. He regretted consenting to let the picture of Ilene and D'Altorio be published. Who knew what would come of such things, better to avoid anything with even the scent of complicated human relationships.

He walked up to Rupert and said, "I let you go, you be a good boy, right? No one gets hurt? No one gets in trouble, but you stay the hell out of my bar. Yes? Is this possible for you?" He turned to Ilene and said, "You stay where you are and you'll tell me your side of the story next."

Rupert nodded and was released by his burly captors and stumbled toward the door. He stood outside on the Victorian style deck and looked up and down the street. There was no sign of that bastard D'Altorio. He felt for the Glock and pulled it out of his pants, pulled back the slide, let it release as a round pushed up into the chamber. He put it in his pocket and walked down the stairs and down the tree lined street. It was an old town and the streets were wide like boulevards in the 19th century. The night and the many trees thick with foliage obstructed the streetlights along the sidewalks and gave him enough shadow to remain unseen. The cars were parked bumper to bumper along the curb, allowing him to crouch behind them. He moved slowly down to Morris County Savings and then scurried across the street and snuck back slowly, stopping often to listen and watch.

A warning bell of anxiety was clanging in his chest. He just didn't feel that D'Altorio would cut and run. Especially after Rupert had clipped him like that. When he reached the intersection on the other side of The Exchange he reconsidered, stood under the streetlight and shook his head, disappointed in himself at overestimating his enemy. Across the street that same fucking Audi that Rupert chased out of the Lake not so long ago and that he really should have seen when he arrived, roared to life, spun its wheels until smoke began to pour off the back of the car, and launched itself at him like a sleek, black missile. As the car crossed the street, Rupert, often underestimated for his mobility and athleticism, dove to the right, rolled down the sidewalk and and into the fender of a parked SUV. He crouched, pulled the Glock and put three through the passenger window as the Audi sideswiped the streetlight and continued up over the lawn of a good citizen of Rockaway. D'Altorio gunned the engine and went through the hedges that fronted the side street, which was at a right angle to The Exchange. Hitting asphalt he accelerated up the street and out of sight.

Hearing the screaming engine and tires of the Audi and then the gunshots, people started streaming out of The Exchange to see what had happened. Rupert stayed low and pocketed the Glock. He waited until the crowd had left the deck and walked up the street en masse. He crept around the back of the SUV as they walked past him, stood and joined the crowd as just another curious on-looker. After a few moments he disappeared down Beach Street and found his car where he had parked it near the river in the parking lot of Saints Peter and Paul Orthodox Church. When he drove around the back of The Exchange looking for Ilene's car in the employee parking lot he saw her sitting alone on a bench under a tree with her face in her hands. He pulled his car up to her so slowly and quietly that when she looked up his face was practically a foot away.

"Oh Rupert," she said and dropped the armload of personal stuff she had in her lap.

She had obviously been let go and her face was red and teary. Rupert wanted to kiss those tears away.

"Where's your car, honey?"

"I got a ride from Ivy tonight," she said.

"You'd better come with me then," Rupert said smiling. "I got a new place way out in the northwest with the bears and the Republicans. You'll like it out there and I've been lonely as hell."

That wasn't what he wanted to happen at all. It ruined everything. It ruined his plans for the slow disintegration of Rupert's self-confidence despite his narcissism and D'Altorio's plans for creating an overpowering feeling of helplessness that left Rupert vulnerable. He wanted a program of carefully orchestrated, escalating pressure with everything he did dedicated to cracking Rupert wide open like a damn egg. Humpty Dumpty would have a great fall. But now this.

And yet, so much had just recently fallen into his hands. His friend in Passaic County's Prosecutor's Office got a match on their software for the photo of Mikael and the unidentified girl.

"When was this taken?" he asked D'Altorio. "You got the walking dead here for Christ's sakes. That's freaking Pam Scheider who went missing with no trace of her ever found after visiting her boyfriend out in Pennse. Poof. She fucking disappears and is presumed dead. Foul play on the highway home? Did the boyfriend get sick of her and take her out? Nobody knew. That one's in the unsolved file and will probably never work its way out of there."

"The boyfriend?" D'Altorio asked although he knew.

"Scumbag. Rupert Levinsky. You didn't hear about it? Ratted out all his buddies to keep his ass out of jail."

"Yeah, I know the story."

"Well maybe what you don't know is we had a visit from the Ridgeway, Pennsylvania Cops. They wanted us to open up the files on Rupert. They had an investigation cranking up after Pam's disappearance and some Rupert associates kept turning up dead. They told us the guy had Cartel contacts through a guy named Matias. Bad guys. Don't know which was worse, Rupert or Matias. 'Course in Matias' world being in the good graces of your superiors can be short-lived, if you catch my meaning. Word is in the department Rupert did some bad things up in Jackson, New Hampshire too. You hear about that guy Brett Somners who got kicked out of the Department? A guy who knows a guy said he's also a victim of Rupert. Somners told a buddy he was going up there to New Hampshire as a private detective working for Scheider's parents and that's it. Gone. Levinsky stayed up there in Jackson for a couple of years and then his girlfriend and his buddy OD and now he's outta there. This guy's like a one-man natural disaster. Wherever he goes suffering and death follow."

"Can you delete this file? I don't want anyone else suspecting she's alive. This one's mine. OK? You won't say anything about this? You never saw anything. Don't worry, this guy is gonna see justice one way or another."

D'Altorio's buddy nodded, "You got it. I don't really wanna

know nothing at this point in my career anyhow."

D'Altorio let E and Scheiner know that he was requesting a meeting. He did not want to be at cross purposes with them, but still had different goals then his employers. E and Scheiner hadn't let him know where they resided, still afraid of retaliation from the remnants of Los Fuerte or even who knows, the Jersey Mob, whose associate Rupert had given evidence against. It was guilt by association. They certainly hadn't given any evidence against anyone. Rupert had beat them all to the punch, and yet because he was one of them, they were complicit.

They met at a restaurant in Andover on a lake with the rear outdoor dining deck built out on a ledge of rock. The rocky shoreline looked more like Maine than Sussex County, New Jersey.

"Heh, heh, heh, there he is," said E in that nasally, gravelly affliction of a voice which was a product of his Brooklyn to New Jersey migration as much as his vocal cords.

Scheiner sat back in his chair in a state of easy and confident repose, his long legs crossed in front of him, affecting a Michael Corleone type of elegance and danger, and looked at E and then at D'Altorio with amusement. He didn't say anything.

They had ordered a bottle of wine and a glass was filled and awaited him where he supposed they wanted him to sit. He certainly wasn't going to drink anything these two served up.

"He's not dead," E said. "He's not fucking dead and we're not fucking happy."

He was long and skinny and whenever he smiled his nose and his lip curled up with such derision that it looked like a snarl.

Scheiner began a discourse that D'Altorio had heard several times before.

"He was our friend since high school and look what he did to us. We were businessmen trying to build up a North Jersey network and we cut him in on everything. Everything. But with one third the profit goes one third the risk. Bastard couldn't deal with that. He could deal with the Escalade and the big ass house up there on five

142

acres in Green Pond, but you know when the shit went sour the fat bastard fucked us. Without remorse. Without a second fucking thought. Just blubbered out as much shit as he could remember to the DEA and fucked us all."

Scheiner was winding up for a major retelling of the whole sordid story including his mistreatment in jail until he was befriended by the Neo Nazis who mistook his Germanic sounding name, Werner Scheiner, for heritage. He didn't tell them about his Jewish Grandfather who high tailed it out of Germany with his World War One, medals chased by the SS who didn't care whether he was a German veteran or not. Or how his grandfather joined the partisans and lived in the mountains of Eastern Europe picking off Nazi Officers with his Russian sniper rifle and blowing up supply trucks and trains for five long years full of hardship and blood during WWII.

"Let me do this my way," D'Altorio said to them and saw them both frown simultaneously like they were twins. "Let me ruin this guy, take everything away from him and leave him face to face with all he's done. Lots of ghosts. Pam, the boys in Pennse, Pam's parent's detective, evidently, his girlfriend up there in New Hampshire and that poor fuck Cody. There's a lot of people want justice from this guy."

"We don't care about any of that," said E. "I want to know that the guy that put me in fucking prison," and here his voice began rising and trembling, "has not gotten away with it. That he has not fucking gotten away with sending me to that shit hole for all those years and that he is gonna pay. That he is gonna fucking pay the ultimate price! He comes face to face with the barrel of a big Smith and Wesson that blows such a large hole in his fucking face that he doesn't even have a face. He doesn't have a face, he just has a bloody fucking hole where his face used to be."

E began to laugh. Hoarse and interrupted by fits of coughing, his heaving, skinny chest looked as though it would burst his ribs. He pulled some tissues from his pocket, blew his nose and hacked something nasty into them. D'Altorio looked away frowning.

Werner Scheiner stood and lit a cigarette. The bartender came running over and requested he limit his smoking to the outside deck. Scheiner waved him off and told him to kindly fuck off before he got angry.

"You kill him quick," he said to D'Altorio. "You kill him quick, or we'll get somebody who will. Only thing is, he'll kill you too."

Chapter Nineteen

When she remembered growing up in that house it upset her, but it wasn't because she was reliving traumatic memories. She wasn't sure that there had been anything like overt physical abuse, but there was certainly lots of self-interest among the males in her family. She had definitely been a victim of that.

She was the youngest of three other siblings who were all boys. All went on to follow in Da's footsteps in law enforcement. Growing up in a family of Irish cops was like living a 40s movie cliche. Two were FBI and Billy who was the homebody and the youngest next to her, became a Mt. Olive patrolman. Da had been the Chief of Police in Dover for it seemed like forever. She had been an English major at Rutgers. Her family indulged her in this, but clearly felt that no socially useful or practical consequences could result. As long as she took care of the domestic needs of the household she was given family permission to pursue whatever nonsense satisfied this thing so inexplicable to the rest of the males in the family; a female's need for self-fulfillment outside the family life.

She wasn't exposed to violence or abuse exactly. Well, except for that one period where she was her Da's caretaker during his cancer. He had, most likely, mistook her for her mother. That seemed to make the most sense, but he had roughly groped her breasts and tried to push her face down in his lap. There were periods during his treatment when he just wasn't himself. Even the doctor said so. There were all those drugs, but then the testosterone blockers kicked in and it didn't matter anymore.

She had always had the feeling that her life was not really her own. She was born into a domestic, caretaker role which her mother had rejected. Her mother abandoned the family and headed for a life in Atlanta and attempted to entice her only daughter to come

145

with her. In a mistake that Ilene was later to realize was perhaps one of the greatest of her life, she not only refused to go with her mother, but rejected her mother totally. She submitted to the demands of her father and brothers, and never saw her mother again.

It was only afterwards when she began to question almost everything she had let happen to her was she able to gain a useful outlook on her life. It was the context of all the different phases of your life that gave you perspective she had decided. She could look back and sense a kind of feeling-tone for each phase. That was the context she was thinking of. It was more of a body feeling and not an analytical process. Maybe what she had experienced was too much to think about and analyze. But she did have the ability to transition through the different phases of her life by feeling her way through. It was always like suddenly losing your taste for what had been fundamental in the way you lived your life before and finding only something very different could satisfy you now. That something often appeared out of nowhere and appeared quite undramatically and with a quiet voice. It was a guiding light. To try to bring it all into consciousness in a way she could articulate was impossible for her. It was like trying to piece together your house with the shards and splinters it had disintegrated into after a tornado. Her heart however urged her forward, gave her a path, meandering and bewildering though it was.

She knew Rupert thought that D'Altorio was probably watching her place and had wanted her to abandon everything and come to him with only the clothes she was wearing. It would be like she had disappeared from the earth and all that was left were some Ilene artifacts like clothes, a car, a few kitchen utensils. When she moved in with him in Sussex he seemed to have the money to largely replace everything she left behind and she texted her girlfriends to go into the apartment and take whatever.

She thought that this is what she wanted, but it left her feeling things she had not felt since Da had died and all her brothers scattered to the winds. They had started new families that seemed unconnected to the primal family and any connection on her part was mostly short holiday visits to unload gifts to nieces and nephews she hardly knew. She felt that her life had not been her own and that she was little more than something others shaped to their whim, like the boneless cat she had when she was a little girl. She remembered running into her parent's room with the cat draped over one shoulder.

"Look Da, look at this cat. She does whatever I want her to. She'll wrap herself around me and stay right where I put her."

She demonstrated by draping the cat over her shoulders and wearing her like a wealthy lady from the 40s movies she loved wore a fur wrap. The cat was utterly relaxed and utterly limp and purred ecstatically. She saw her mother sitting forlornly at the foot of the bed looking down at the floor and not at her daughter.

"Ahh, she'll do what you want, eh little one? Just like you. That's the way we like you, honey, unlike your mother. You, we are always sure, will do whatever is needed to take care of the family first."

He made a sound intended to be a laugh but sounded more like he was poked in the belly with a stick., He waved her away and closed the bedroom door. Behind the door he heard shouting and then the sound of her mother crying.

At the house in Sussex, nearly every day in the early evening, as the sun began to drop below the top of the rift and long shadows began their solemn procession across the backyard, a huge black bear wandered over from the woods and approached the steps of the deck. She watched from behind the glass French doors that looked out onto the deck. Once, seeing movement behind the glass, the bear climbed the steps to snuffle at the doors and assess them for potential pathways to food procurement. When she screamed, the bear also seemed alarmed and skipped off the deck and up the bank behind the lawn, scrambling toward the top of the rift.

"That's a good sign," Rupert said when she told him about the bear. "He hasn't lost his fear of people by hanging around the houses out here and eating garbage. Those are the dangerous ones, big, fat bears totally blasé about people and cars and dogs ... guy at The Consortium told me that he was walking his dog in Newton and a big fucking bear trotted up behind them and then ran past and down the middle of the street on a Sunday morning." Rupert laughed that booming laugh she liked.

"Sunday morning, can you imagine that?"

"Rupert, I don't know what to do with myself out here. I was hoping to sun in the back yard, but now I'm scared to death of getting mauled by the local wildlife."

Rupert laughed and although she had said it with humor she was bored out of her mind and his comment was unsettling.

"I got some guys from New Hampshire I used to work with and they're gonna grab your car in the middle of the night ... no one can tail these guys. We'll get it reregistered in Pennsylvania, get you some new plates and you're back on the road. You can go into Newton or head out to Stroudsburg. Go to the gym. Go to the library, just don't go down to Morris County until I figure this thing out."

She hugged him and felt bad about whining.

"We're gonna be all right, honey, I promise. After this we can go back to Rockaway, or get a place in Brooklyn ... whatever you want. Don't worry, I get these guys off my ass and the future is gonna be great for us." He put his large hand on her shoulder and she looked up. "K?" he asked.

But she was also upset that Rupert was getting high again and almost every night. He had progressed from snorting the drug to using the works he kept in his elaborate inlaid dope box. He told her he was only snorting and that it was "just a little bit of dope to take the edge off." Most nights in front of the TV he'd nod out and when she couldn't get him up she left him unconscious in the big arm chair after turning off the TV and the lights. She left on the hallway light so that when he roused himself usually at 3 or 4 a.m., he could find his way to the bedroom.

She thought about his stories about Oma Ren and her drinking and what she had put her Grandson through, but did not broach the subject with him, not saying a single word even as his use increased. He never let her see the ritual of preparation that he loved, cooking the dope and drawing it up slowly and deliciously into his syringe. He kept up the ruse about snorting, which he assured her was really nothing to worry about. He wasn't even sure you could even get addicted to dope by just snorting it.

When he offered her a taste and suggested that he'd like her to share this thing that was so pleasurable to him, she began crying. She shook her head in that adorable way she had as if she were not just saying no to him, but for all people and for whatever moral record was being kept. She cried harder when he continued to try to convince her and ran for the bedroom. He trotted after her and then gave up trying to get her to use and apologized.

"OK OK. You drink your Pinot Grigio and that's it. Listen, just don't begrudge me my pleasures. Don't judge me because of this thing. Maybe you don't understand it, but this is something I need and I know this drug. I know this drug well and love it and respect it. That's what makes me different than the junkies down at the Wall. I respect it."

He did not have infinite stores of money although his resources were still what he described to her as "considerable." He needed to earn and maintain a level of funds that insured his freedom from a wage slave's dependence on the "legal" economy. She was allowed to sit in when he sat down at their dining room table with the big boys from The Consortium. They wanted to eliminate some of the barriers between supplier and customer. The dealers they had been working with were high level and business-like in every way, but a lot of profit that could have been The Consortium's were siphoned off by these middlemen.

Rupert launched into his speech about real estate agents, artistic agents, all the professions where outsiders had insinuated themselves between product producers and services that directly turned product into revenue. The Consortium big cheese, Laurent, listened politely for a couple of minutes and then folding, his hands and leaning forward, pushed his forearms toward Rupert and interrupted.

"Rupert, we want to back you in your business as kind of a pilot program to see if this is for us. We'll supply you with runners and would like to work with you on all aspects of business. The benefit to you is considerable in terms of access to preferential product and special pricing. We want to earn back our investment costs, but beyond that everything is yours. If successful we reel you in and you become one of us. Becoming one of us has benefits which will become apparent to you over time."

Rupert didn't say anything for what seemed like an uncomfortable minute. Ilene realized he was surprised and at a loss for words. It was obviously something he hadn't accounted for in his planning for a new relationship with The Consortium. Ilene had never seen him react hesitantly before.

Rupert shook his head and laughed. "You hippie motherfuckers kill me, Laurent."

Ilene looked up in surprise and was about to say something when Rupert looked at her and put his index finger to his pursed lips.

"You got in this business to subvert the authority of our government regarding what substances we can and cannot put into our bodies and how we choose to make a living. You got into this as part of a Hippie/Libertarian protest against the status quo and now look. Y'all be sounding like the CEO of freaking Amazon or something." Rupert put his hands on top of his belly and laughed and laughed.

The Consortium members after a confused pause began laughing as well.

"Well, that's good." he said, "I like it," as The Consortium members leaned in and prepared to do business. "Because ruthlessness and maximum return on my investment is what I'm all about."

Chapter Twenty

Rupert texted his old clients in Manhattan who were happy to hear that he was back in the business. They wanted to discuss with someone they "knew" to be an authoritative source, the subtle and not so subtle qualities of high end weed as if they were talking about the acidity and tannin levels in wine. He was a sort of weed wine sommelier, shaman and neuropsychologist rolled into one articulate and charming package. His customers already had a variety of advisors who were responsible for their client's full enjoyment of all their activities. Personal Trainers, nutritionist/gourmet chefs, therapists, life coaches, interior designers - all whose employment by his clients was really the priority since each so-called expert carried status points useful for the kind of king of the hill or tug of war that passed for social interaction among this tribe.

Understanding the eccentricities of his customers was what Rupert depended on to differentiate himself from his competitors. When he was with his clients he listened and pumped up their self-indulgent theories and judgements, dressing them up in scientific and literary language. Smoking the best cannabis became a whole new arena for the rich to leave the stamp of their snobbery and elitism and elevate this ubiquitous and ancient human activity beyond the monetary reach of the masses. The delusions of the wealthy fit in perfectly with his business model.

The Consortium guys who came along for the ride to Manhattan quickly realized that Rupert's success was a matter of personal branding and not the business model of his high end weed delivery service. They were intrigued by how Rupert had made himself into a weed guru and weed therapist. Although he sold for absolute top price, he knew the psychology of his buyers and despite all the bullshit about Entheogens, Neurotheology and Terrence McKenna, what they really wanted was a weed hybrid that reproduced the effects of benzodiazepines and not DMT.

After Rupert's first foray into the city with The Consortium, and after they had reported back to the rest of the group, The Consortium pulled back and no longer wished to partner. They told Rupert that they'd make a financial adjustment to fund his first efforts but were no longer interested in pursuing this line of business realizing how dependent his business was on his own idiosyncratic and personal qualities. They were anxious however, to keep working with Rupert and considered him a special customer with prices and access to inventory that were put together just for him. The Consortium wanted him to continue doing some consulting for them. The business needed feedback from the field and someone who could objectively assess their business model and suggest changes they might make to take advantage of the preferences of their customer base. Rupert seemed to have an uncanny grasp of the psychology of people who liked drugs, even if it was just weed.

He was pleased with their recognition of his talents. He was pleased that his old customer base rushed back to him along with a bunch of their friends and that revenues were pouring back into the safe deposit boxes he kept at his credit union in Rockaway. He had no way to launder his profits, but paid for his expenses in cash and let the rest build and build. It was an easy matter to find the runners his two knuckleheads from New Hampshire had managed for him. After Cody and Leila's deaths he seemed to have a reputation with them that enforced discipline, and he liked this very much.

His customers wanted to put together their orders in private meetings with him that were more therapy/Spiritual Advisor sessions than drug deals and it gave him the opportunity to extract revenues he normally might not get. He did not rape them by any means, rather he was interested in customizing their individual usage of his products and directed them toward the best and of course the most expensive of his wares.

Pam Scheider and Mikael Ablesmekov were a complication that made D'Altorio's planning very difficult if not impossible, and additionally were competitors in the who gets payback against Rupert first contest. He would absolutely hate to be beat to the punch in taking down Rupert after all he had already done and the job's personal meaning for him. He was going to have to do something and the first thing he needed to do was to get a little more information. An alliance was not completely beyond the realm of possibility, but he wanted to scare the hell out of everybody first.

It was Mikael that really worried him. He parked the Audi in the woods on Cherry Lane, hidden by driving behind some of the denser brush and trees, and worked his way down to the nursery and then the road to Pam's bungalow. He was happy to see that Mikael's Range Rover was not there. He pulled the Berretta and circled the building furtively. He was peering in all her windows until he located her in the kitchen, washing dishes and looking out the window and up a gentle rolling meadow with old growth forest behind it. The front door was directly behind her. The kitchen opened to a living area that fronted the bungalow.

He walked back around the front of the house, kicked in the front door and had his Beretta out and was screaming at Pam to drop to the floor on her stomach and put her hands behind her back. He looped a white plastic strap around her wrists and slipped a black fabric bag over her head. He did this more to scare the hell out of her than for any kind of security purposes and pulled her roughly to her feet. She hadn't seen him as he came up behind her in the darkened living room. She was whimpering with fear and trembling and he told her to "shut the fuck up." He pushed her down so hard that she fell off the kitchen chair underneath her. He grabbed her under the armpits, hauled her off the floor and picked her up entirely into the air before depositing her on the straight back chair. He strapped her ankles and upper arms to the chair and smacked her once across the face with the flat of his palm.

She was crying hard, but stopped suddenly and screamed, "Are you working for Rupert?"

"No," was all he said.

She quieted a bit and then said evenly, "Well, who the fuck are you and what do you want from me?"

He walked around the kitchen, turned and saw a large bulletin board on the far wall of the living room that took up most of one wall. On it was a map and timeline of Rupert's movements since his trial and flight to Pennsylvania and then his escape to the Midwest and New Hampshire. Marked by pins with red flags were the locations where he had murdered his victims. Down one side of the map were print outs of emails from an anonymous source. These he read with interest.

"Who wrote the emails?" he demanded and she hung and shook her head. "You won't tell me? It won't be pleasant if I beat it out of you. And I will, I will have no problem with beating you half to death, believe me."

"I can't tell you because I don't know. Look at them for God's sakes. There's no damn attribution. They just started coming out of the blue. Someone who for whatever reason has similar motivations. Could be you for all I know."

D'Altorio snatched them off the board, folded them and stuffed them in the pouch that hung from his shoulder. He heard a car pull up to her door and took a step back behind her in the kitchen. He gripped the Beretta with both hands and leveled it toward the front entrance.

Mikael saw the broken frame where D'Altorio had kicked in the front door and called through the entrance, "You drop weapons and walk out with hands on top of head and I don't kill you," he said.

"Mikael, he's got a gun. In the kitchen behind the wall."

D'Altorio smacked her in the side of the head with the palmed gun, knocking her over and she thrashed against the chair on the floor trying to escape her bonds. Mikael rushed the kitchen firing as he advanced, the bullets penetrating the wall that partially separated the kitchen from the living room. D'Altorio dropped to the floor, crawled on his belly just as Mikael somersaulted into the kitchen. Before he could come up firing, D'Altorio had put two in his back. Mikael never regained his feet and D'Altorio stood, walked over to Mikael and shot him quickly twice through the head. This was someone he wanted out of the picture now. He saw some files and pictures on the sofa in the living room and dumped them all in his pouch. Pam was screaming, crying and thrashing on the floor trying to push herself over on her back. She screamed Mikael's name over and over and over and D'Altorio could still hear her even as he trotted up the dirt road past the nursery and through the woods to his car.

At home, Rupert hardly saw Ilene, his business in the city occupying almost all his time and demanding he spend at least a few days a week in a hotel in Manhattan. She was lonely and bored. A restlessness she couldn't shake compelled her to get out of the house and drive somewhat aimlessly around Stillwater and Blairstown. It was scenic, even beautiful, but she realized what she really needed were relationships with people. She needed to talk to people, see people, eat with people. She needed to be drawn back into a larger community of human interaction.

She enlarged the circle of territory she covered on her road trips. She had limited herself at first to Stroudsburg and Newton and then began some forays into western Morris County. She stopped at The Pub in Mendham and had lunch out for the first time in months. No Rockaway people here she was pretty sure of that, but midway through her turkey burger with onions, tomato, ranch dressing and peppers, a messy affair, but so good, she noticed a guy watching her from a booth on the other side of the bar. She was nervous, feeling that perhaps she had endangered Rupert and all his new plans that were going so well.

When he stood with his eyes fixed on her she was ready to run the hell out of the building. She looked down to gather her stuff and when she looked up he was standing in front of her table blocking the bench seat in her booth.

"A tragedy to see a beautiful woman eating alone," he said grinning.

He was sixty something, with the gym-built body of the freshly divorced. He was well dressed and well spoken and Ilene relaxed. This guy's desire was written all over his eager face.

"Well, why don't you sit and keep me company for a bit," she said. "I've been lonely. Married and committed to that marriage, but lonely and need someone to talk to and have a glass of wine with perhaps."

He began to sit with a concerned look on his face, but changed his mind, "I uhh ... well, listen I don't want to waste your time or mine. I mean, I'm really looking for a relationship and I think, you know, you just want to chat. I'm open to being social and all and taking it slow, but neither of us is getting any younger and you seem a little undecided about what the hell it is you want. Maybe you're like one of those people that wants to move on, but doesn't have the courage yet. Like you want it both ways. You don't want to take any chances but like the excitement of flirtation."

He was obnoxious. Ilene was losing patience.

"Why don't you just get the fuck out of here then, huh? I really don't need this shit. I'm just looking for a little quiet time before going back to my life. I don't want to be your fucking girlfriend or anything else so why don't you just go fuck yourself.

He walked across the bar and out the door in about two seconds. Ilene looked down at the table and smiled broadly. She surprised herself sometimes.

"Guess I said the wrong thing," she said to the waiter who she tipped well and paid with Rupert's cash. She pulled open the awkwardly heavy front door and walked unsteadily on the cobbled driveway, her arms out to her sides and shaking her head and laughing.

The next trip was further east into Morris County. She knew Rupert wouldn't want her to do it, but couldn't help herself, she was just so desperately lonely. She avoided Rockaway but couldn't help cruising up into Indian Lakes past the Club House and slowly driving past her friend Ivy Goldberg's house.

She parked a few houses down and walked up to Ivy's house as surreptitiously as possible. Ivy saw her on the street from her window, threw open her front door and started screaming "Ilene, Ilene" at a decibel level that was hard to imagine a tiny 105-pound woman could reach. They sat on her deck, drank iced coffee and caught up, although Ilene's version of catching up was a fiction she was forced to invent for one of her best friends. Ivy knew little about Rupert and Ilene had to lead her as far from the truth as possible. She hated, absolutely hated to perpetrate these falsehoods on a friend whose sisterhood and the sharing of the intimate venting of her emotional/psychological life she needed now more than at any other time in her life. It made her feel cut off from her real life. It was a feeling of fraud and decline that ran counter to some of the new things she was beginning to feel.

It was early evening when she left and even though she had not been able to be honest with her friend she had felt close to Ivy again and a sense of normalcy began to return to her. It was kind of a pre-Rupert normalcy and it created a forgetfulness about the circumstances of her current life. When she drove out of the Lake she was thinking about Ivy and her other friends and drove into Rockaway and then went left on Main Street and past The Exchange. When she realized that this might be dangerous territory and that there were too many people here that knew her she quickly turned left on Beach Street and headed back to Rt. 80 and Sussex County. No one had seemed to notice her or recognize her car.

Thinking about it later when she was safely back at the house in Sussex she had a sense of of colliding worlds. Her hidden, misanthropic, constrained world with Rupert and her old world which, if tainted by family and bad relationships was at least open to an intuition of what was most real and best for her.

"At least to be part of the swell and the contraction of life," she thought. Out here she was a doll on a shelf, an object that Rupert amused himself with and then put away."

She moped around the house in Sussex for a few days and finally feeling so depressed and lonely she could hardly get out of bed she decided she needed another visit with Ivy. Rupert had been in Manhattan all week. He wouldn't let her text or email anyone, so she hoped she might be as lucky as on her last visit and just cruise by and find Ivy at home.

It was helpful to stay mindful of her and Rupert's vulnerability by thinking of herself as a fugitive. She came into the lake the back way, by driving down Rt. 15 and then taking the exit by the mall. Instead of going right off the exit she went left and up into Mt. Hope. There was a back entrance into the Lake through a development and it led her out to just below 2nd Beach. She only had to drive around the lake toward the club house and she was at Ivy's, no drama and no one lying in wait to capture her driving an easily identifiable late model, red Jetta.

She drove down Ivy's narrow street made even narrower by almost all the residents parking on the road. It wound just above the shoreline of the lake with houses built into the hill on one side and across the road on the lake side were small wooden docks or tiny beaches which were usually just strips of sand between what was otherwise a rocky coastline. She liked this street and drove slowly savoring its peacefulness. Ahead she could see Ivy's house and the empty parking spot in front of it. She stopped in front and noticing no activity, did not want to take the chance of further investigation. When she pulled away she noticed a black Audi, which also started up and pulled out into the street.

Wasn't it a black Audi that Rupert said D'Altorio or his guys had? She wasn't sure.

When she drove past the club house and hung a left at the Pizza Place, the Audi took the turn as well. She turned onto Omaha Ave. with the idea of going out of the Lake the back way and onto Green Pond Road just below the entrance for 80 West. She approached the left turn for Sanders Road and saw two large black SUVs sitting at the intersection facing her. One was on Omaha, the other idling diagonal to it on Sanders. She looked in her rear-view mirror and saw that the Audi was right on her bumper. The SUVs started moving toward her looking to box her in with the Audi.

"Fuck you, fuck you, fuck you," she yelled. She wished she had Rupert's Glock. She'd shoot these bastards, she knew she could. She wondered where her fear had gone. She was furious.

She took a sharp left and drove over the lawn of the house nearest the intersection and between that house and its neighbor. The back yard was a fenced in pool area, but around the fence was enough cleared area for her to keep the Jetta moving forward. She drove behind the house and went right and down the grassy hill that bordered Sanders. The SUVs were tracking her progress from Omaha Ave. She slammed her foot down on the gas pedal and accelerated down Sanders and toward Green Pond. She'd drive to the Rockaway Police Station if she had to. She certainly wasn't going to lead the bastards back home.

When she hit the intersection with Green Pond desperately trying to brake enough to make the turn, the Audi was suddenly along her right side preventing her from going right toward Rockaway. Her tires locked up and she was spinning out of control against a red light at the end of Sanders. Cars were coming from the north and barely missing her. One drove off the road and and up onto a grassy bluff in front of a chemical company. She ended up turned completely around on Green Pond Road and she hit the gas with the SUVs now in the lane along her side and the Audi behind. Through the window of the closest SUV the driver motioned for her to pull over.

She screamed. "Leave me the fuck alone!" she cried, but couldn't get away from him. The other cars being just too powerful for her little 4-cylinder Jetta.

Past Hibernia on the left was a small pond and a left hand turn onto a dirt road that led to the back of Picatinny Arsenal. Her anger was gone and all she felt now was out of control terror. If she could make it into a Picatinny gate the soldiers who guarded the base would protect her. She gunned it up the dirt road and as soon as she was out of sight of Green Pond Road the two SUVs were on either side of the Jetta with the Audi right behind. The one on the right pulled slightly ahead and as the SUV on the left hit its brakes and slid behind them the lead SUV smashed into her fender and pushed her car over to the edge of the woods lifting her right front wheel until she feared the Jetta would flip over. She had to stop or be driven into the trees.

A guy jumped out of the side door with his gun drawn. He ripped her out of the car from the passenger side and her left shoe came off and her stomach was bruised by the parking brake. He slid a hood over her head and half dragged, half carried her to the SUV. Zip ties were cinched around her wrists and she was told to shut the fuck up and sit the fuck down. She leaned forward in her seat and she felt her forehead hit the seat in front. There wasn't anything more she could do. Her shoulders slumped and she started to slide down toward the floor until she was grabbed and pulled back roughly.

She cried. That was the one thing she could do and she felt it well up from deep in her gut and she couldn't stop until the bastard smacked her in the side of her head with an open palm.

"You'll do as your fucking told and maybe, just maybe this won't go so badly for you," he said. "Otherwise, you keep wailing and somebody's gonna find you on the side of the road with your brains blown out."

Chapter Twenty-One

"A red, Volkswagen Jetta with Pennsylvania plates was found abandoned on a dirt road behind Picatinny Arsenal in Rockaway Township, New Jersey. The car's front fender was heavily damaged as if it had been struck by another car and forced into the woods that border the road. The Jetta appears to have been registered to a fictitious name. Attempts to track down the owner or people with knowledge about the owner were not successful. Anyone with information about this incident is requested to please call Rockaway Township Police Headquarters."

The blurb was from the Daily Record Rockaway Police Blotter and was read by Alain and left on Rupert's phone mail. He was one of the guys from Jackson who he had asked to come down and steal Ilene's car. He had evidently stayed on in the area hoping to rejoin Rupert in business and perhaps convince him that he could take over Cody's position. Rupert heard the message on his way back from the City and had to pull over before making the turn onto Rt. 15. He sat, let this new information sink in and then pulled back onto 80 and went through the Delaware Water Gap and into Pennsylvania. Who knew what awaited him in Sussex County?

Of course, he knew who was responsible. D'Altorio grabbed her. But why Ilene? Did he honestly think he'd turn himself in for Ilene's release. Rupert sacrificed himself for no man ... or women. Was this part of his campaign to get Rupert off balance enough to be vulnerable? Perhaps he only kidnapped her in order to make her tell him where Rupert was. Yeah. Of course, that's what it was. Rupert thought D'Altorio might kill her now, his use for her being limited and his desire to avoid unnecessary attention intense. That would be a shame if Ilene ended up as collateral damage. She was a good kid and he liked her. He suspected that D'Altorio had finished playing chess and was now just looking to take Rupert out as quickly as possible.

He called his buddy Laurent from The Consortium who dressed his guys up like house painters and had them go into Rupert's place. They saw no surveillance and were able to surreptitiously extract his weaponry, dope, stray cash and most of his personal items including devices and even the fucking 80-inch Samsung with the elaborate sound system. They stored it all in one of the hangars they used to grow product. He had his guys drive by the house every few hours and although they saw no one, they found Rupert's outdoor security cams which he had hidden carefully in trees and on the roofs of out buildings, smashed and lying in pieces in plain sight.

Laurent hooked him up with a friend who had a cottage on an estate in Stroudsburg. Rupert reasoned that he couldn't keep cutting and running as he got discovered. He was going to have to finish it. Luckily, Ilene had no real information outside of where they lived together. She knew nothing about the new business or anything substantial about The Consortium. She had no knowledge of his accounts because he only gave her cash. The reality was that they could do what they wanted to her, she knew nothing more that could hurt him. It was up to Rupert now to hurt them. , Scheiner, E and D'Altorio were gonna have to go. This would be one of the great accomplishments of his life, satisfying, as only destroying your enemies' plans and removing their miserable existences from the face of the earth could be.

Laurent drove one of his trucks out to Stroudsburg with Rupert's stuff. They met at an old, abandoned warehouse that used to manufacture fitness equipment. In the parking lot Laurent helped him transfer his stuff to the truck Rupert got from a rental place downtown. There wasn't all that much. Rupert asked him if he had any contact with Matias and reminded Laurent that it had been Matias who had been Rupert's referral to The Consortium and that his last few attempts to contact Matias failed to get any response.

"Dead," said Laurent.

"No!" Rupert said, shocked, but not so much by Matias' tragic fate as the loss of this resource of resources.

"The Cartel suspected he was compromised by DEA or somebody. They took him at home in front of his wife and child. One sniper round through the front window. At least that's what I heard. Blew a big hole in his head with a 7.62 mm round."

Rupert just looked at him.

"The Cartel routinely hacks the devices of their top people. I mean, they supplied the phone, laptop and anything else Matias used. He really should have known. He was emailing someone anonymously and feeding them information about customers. The Cartel couldn't figure out what his intent was, but didn't spend a lot of time trying to figure it out. They can't have their people conducting personal vendettas, or their own business, and who knows who his next contact would have been."

Laurent put a cocked finger to his temple. "Boom. The recipient of the emails didn't evidently have any other info except on a guy the Cartel decided they didn't really give a shit about."

Rupert pulled down the door of his rental truck and jumped off the platform. "Gonna make things harder for me, but you know, nothing's impossible. I'm up to the challenge. You know the story. I told you when I had some guys hunting me. Amateurs, but dangerous if they get an opportunity because I make a mistake."

"You text in your orders, keep a little distance please, and we'll meet and take care of your business needs. I can hook you up with a guy that can get you military grade self defense. You let me know."

"Under normal circumstances I'd seek out some professionals. This is personal though. When it's done and these guys have been dealt with I can get back to full-time business mode. I'll need some equipment."

Rupert slid his hand into Laurent's and then slid his hand up to his forearm and gripped firmly.

"Thank you, man. I appreciate your help."

It was bullshit, but he needed fallback resources like what Matias had supplied for him. Laurent for the most part just wanted to smoke, research and sell his weed, but he seemed to have a wide network of connections. Who knew what Rupert would find himself needing in the future? Laurent was his new Matias. Not up to Matias' level but the best he could do for now.

She gave up the address of the house in Sussex easily. She was so scared that she could hardly stutter it out. They had tied her to a chair with the hood still over her head and she felt like she was spinning, spinning, spinning, being pulled ever downward and drowning in a whirlpool of forces she hadn't seen or understood.

"You tell us where he is and then you stay here for a couple of days ... don worry, we feed you, you sleep in clean place, nobody bother you. You don worry about nothing. You walk out of here and that's that. No more fucking Rupert to ruin your life and treat you like shit. You go the fuck home and live your life."

She told them. They were going to find out anyway. Her life had not prepared her to keep silent while somebody pulled her toenails out or beat her to a pulp. She stuttered out the location in Sussex and they pulled off her hood and untied her. She stood and they gave her some food. Pita, hummus, some kind of yogurt and cucumbers that was actually delicious. These Israelis were a brusque bunch and probably as ruthless as they come, but they ate well.

"Two days and I can go? What about my car?"

"You can't drive that no more," he said. "It's fucked."

"You'll fix it?"

Raffi erupted in laughter. After the normal amount of time for this kind of hilarity to begin to decline this guy was still going at it, now repeating her tentative question in a falsetto voice that sounded nothing like her and placing his hands against either side of his face and wagging his head.

"Oh, man, oh man," he said.

She looked at them somewhat shocked and then got angry.

"Look. I'm not involved in any of this. Why do I have to suffer?"

"Well, honeybun, you make your choices in this life. You spin the big wheel and where the little ball lands, well, we all must accept that. Right? You talk to the big boss about this fucking guy Rupert and the things he's done. Maybe you don know. But you ask him and then you can think about your choice and see if you still want to complain."

The door opened and D'Altorio stood in the door frame and scowled at her. She had known him as Dalton from the Exchange, but Rupert had given her a fair idea of who he actually was.

"As soon as he's gone, you will be released. Probably a couple of days and then - well look, you did something that benefits humanity. Ratting this bastard Rupert out I mean. This guy is like a biblical pestilence. Wherever he goes there's death, corruption, insanity. Feel good. You did the world a service," D'Altorio said.

He turned and left and the Israeli followed. Raffi pointed to a door in the back.

"You go in there. Bed. TV. Don worry, OK? You will be comfortable. I come back and bring you good food. What you like? Middle Eastern? You like Thai? No worries. Two days and it's all over. Believe me."

They brought her good food. They brought her magazines, but it wasn't two days. After four days she knew he'd escaped. She didn't know how she felt about Rupert's fate any longer, but she was getting more and more anxious about her own. Raffi treated her well, D'Altorio came and sat with her at a meal and pumped her for the people Rupert would go to to hide him or even mount a counter offensive.

She knew something about a Latino friend from Pennsylvania who was gang related or mob related. Something like that.

"Some guy he was trying to get in touch with. I never got the whole story. Rupert talked about this guy as someone very valuable to him though. Him and guys he knew from New Hampshire. Yeah. They came down and stole my car for me."

"Good old Rupert stayed true to form. He didn't tell you very much, did he? How'd you guys end up in Sussex anyway?"

"I don't know. I just know that it was, you know, out of the way ... rural ... nobody around to poke into his business. I know his business is in Manhattan, but that's it really."

"So," D'Altorio said, "the guy I really worried about was his Latino friend from Pennsylvania, but now no problems. My guy in Paterson tells me that there's been a shake up in management in the Cartel that supplied Rupert. Rupert's guy is fucking dead and his Cartel buddies could care less about some gringos from New Jersey, who don't sell dope or engage in anything that might be competitive with their business endeavors. And that's what's going to happen to Rupert. And as soon as he's safely dead, then and only then will we let you go. OK? You understand me? Settle in. Don't make trouble and soon Rupert will be the former Rupert and you can begin your life again."

He looked at her, hard. "You understand? This has been coming for a long time and now the bill is due and no more grace time can be given. The world can't tolerate a guy like Rupert forever."

"And you? What are you supposed to be? Justice? Karma? The superhero who brings the wicked world back to order?"

"Yeah, all that and more."

Chapter Twenty-Two

Pam kept screaming Mikael's name until she was so hoarse that she couldn't scream any longer. Finally, Larry, who owned the property and her rental, seeing the door to the bungalow wide open all afternoon and after investigating and seeing the frame shattered, looked in and found her on the floor bound and hooded. He pulled the hood from her head and snipped the zip ties. Pam looked at Mikael dead on the floor, looked at Larry and cried and cried, unable to speak. Larry put a blanket over Mikael and took out his phone to call 911.

"No, no, no," Pam croaked.

"I, uh ... have to call," he said and paused to consider how he could overcome her protest and simply said again, "I have to call."

Pam frantically threw as much of her stuff into the back of the Subaru as possible. She grabbed her Sig, which she had been keeping under her mattress, and her devices. She didn't say another word to Larry and drove the Forester around the back of the house and up through the meadow which had once been a grazing pasture for one of the many dairy farms that had been so prevalent in this area only a generation before. She feared she might be blocked from leaving if she drove out the front gate by the cops who invariably preceded the EMT's. Pam located the overgrown, dirt road she had found while running on the estate and the Subaru managed to negotiate the rocks, brush and garbage that had been dumped along its route. She exited the woods and was in the back of Mendham by its border with Bernardsville. It was woodsy country lanes and with her GPS she worked her way out to Morristown and headed East.

Her paperwork with the help of Matias and then Mikael had been faked. Larry knew her as Alisha Marx, and this is the name she used on all her docs, all her accounts and the debit card she had. She would dump the car, get new docs and it was lucky she had a ton of money which she had withdrawn from her deposit box. She had made a single appearance as Pam Scheider at the Credit Union after getting back after Pennsylvania. She felt that she could get in and out without anyone knowing that she was officially "disappeared," not dead, not necessarily alive, just in bureaucratic stasis until further evidence about her surfaced. She counted on these facts not filtering down to the official institutions she had made use of. She had walked out with a shopping bag full of cash from the money she originally transferred from her trust fund for Rupert's drug deals.

She felt desperate and her anxiety surged and waned. She had absolutely no idea what to do. And then a long shot idea began to take shape in her mind. She had a friend in her pre-Rupert life. They had been inseparable through elementary and high school, but when Pam starting dating boys in her junior year, being a bit of a late bloomer, her friend confessed to her that she was gay and had always loved Pam. Pam was floored and completely speechless and her friend took this to be not only rejection but homophobic bias as well.

They parted and lost contact and then came Rupert and Fairleigh Dickinson and drugs, but she had heard that Laurie stayed in the area and had taken over the running of her family's horse farm after her parent's death in an auto accident. If she still had the council of Mikael and Matias she wouldn't have to take this long shot, but other than turning herself in to the authorities as the "reappeared" Pam Scheider she simply didn't know what else to do. She was not ready to give up her commitment to bring down Rupert and wanted desperately to stay off the grid.

The horse farm was hundreds of acres of gently rolling land south of Morristown. It was almost Trump country down by Bedminster. The farm boarded horses, raised a breed for equestrian that they were internationally famous for, taught riding and even conducted equestrian events for young people and showed horses. When she drove in that evening she was stopped almost immediately by a woman in work clothes carrying a shotgun who skipped in front of her car and waved her down. She couldn't decide if she was security or some other employee. She certainly acted like she owned the place.

"Purpose of your visit? We are not currently teaching classes, or conducting any other public events. I need you to turn off your engine and tell me clearly who you are."

Someone, she was told, had led a prize horse out to the gate in the middle of the night just the night before, loaded him into a trailer and were gone without a trace. The horse had been worth hundred of thousands of dollars. Whoever had done this had assaulted and incapacitated their security people and smashed the cameras scanning the stalls with their most expensive horses.

Pam told her about her relationship to Laurie without mentioning her own name. The woman told Pam her name was Ayann and looked at Pam aggressively and Pam suspected competitively. Pam was struck at how beautiful she was, a tall, slender black woman with the high cheekbones and angular face of a North African. Ayaan scanned her passenger seat and all the stuff Pam had shoved haphazardly into the back.

"Pam Scheider," she said. "Laurie has told me about you. We thought that you were dead."

Time passed by the day, by the week, and then it was a month. Rupert had disappeared completely and D'Altorio didn't know what to do with Ilene. He realized however, that she didn't know where she was because she had worn a hood and hadn't been outside the house or able to see out of the blacked-out basement windows. So maybe she wasn't capable of being the threat he imagined. He had to admit that he'd found her interesting ever since he began dropping in on her at The Exchange, and now having the opportunity to talk to her each day, gradually found his tone had shifted from captor to something more personal, even friendly. Maybe he wished that under different circumstances his relationship with her would become more than friendly.

They kept her in the basement and true to the Raffi's word, fed her well, had good Wi-Fi streaming and there was an elliptical in the corner and a spin bike. They bought her some workout clothes, some bands and dumbbells and a little bench. If nothing else, she worked out everyday. Usually by late afternoon she started feeling anxious and the training seemed to flush the anxiety out of her system. A glass of Pinot Grigio afterward and a couple of episodes of Lucifer and really there wasn't much difference between this and her life in the house in Sussex.

She found herself the next morning groggily waking up in Sussex, on a mattress on the floor in a pretty much stripped to the walls house, which had been so comfortable when it was their house. She was scared and she was shocked. She remembered being handed a glass of wine after her workout last night by a grinning Raffi and how suddenly overcome by fatigue to the point of hardly being able to walk straight, she had laid down. And now she was here and that was all she had to go on.

She got up and her head was suddenly pounding and the room was spinning and she fell back down onto the bare mattress. She had been drugged. They dumped her and she guessed she should be glad they hadn't strangled her and left her in the woods where they had smashed up her car. She was alive and she just wanted to stay that way. She wanted to stay alive and out of other people's business, away from men like D'Altorio and Rupert whose motivations and desires were indecipherable to her. She couldn't decide whether they wanted to fuck her or kill her. Probably both.

She planned to walk out to 94 and see if she could get a ride down to Morris County from a trucker or something. She didn't really know, she just knew she wanted to get as far away from anything that had to do with D'Altorio and Rupert as possible. She walked up the cul-de-sac the house was on and before she could even set foot on the county road a pickup had skidded to a stop alongside of her and a guy with shoulder length hair threw open the passenger door and beckoned for her to get in. When she hesitated and began backing up he jumped out, ran around the truck and grabbed her by the shoulders.

"No, no. Its OK. I work for The Consortium."

He pushed her into the passenger seat and took off for the main buildings. She was crying and he looked over at her and told her that she was safe and that The Consortium would get her back to Rupert. When she screamed, his foot came off the gas and she jumped out of the truck and ran up the hill into the forest that bordered the road. He got out of the truck and stood by the fender and yelled after her.

"No! No! Its cool. You're safe with us. Hey, we'll take care of you!"

She had no idea where she was running to, she was just running. She stopped and put her face in her hands, but instead of crying she screamed again. It wasn't fear. It was frustration. She felt a rage that rose up out of her belly and shocked her with its power. She was furious at the condition of her life which had been corrupted by Rupert and people like Rupert. It was Ilene being crushed by the priorities and issues of other people's lives, which, when it came down to it, really had nothing to do with her. She was not so much an innocent bystander as someone dragged along for the ride. Someone who seemed to incur lots of danger without reaping any of the rewards.

She walked down the hill and climbed back into the truck. They set off more slowly for the main Consortium buildings. The driver phoned ahead and when they pulled up to some modern looking offices in front of ancient hangars, Laurent came striding out, opened the door to the truck and passed an electronic wand up and down her body.

"Sorry," he said. "Have to take precautions. Your Rupert has some scary enemies and I don't want to make Rupert's enemies mine. I mean, I'm willing to help, but me and my business are staying out of the line of fire."

When she looked at him somewhat blankly he frowned and offered his hand to help her down from the truck.

D'Altorio had carried Ilene into the house himself and put her on the mattress. He and Raffi drove up together in the Audi. Raffi was carrying his Uzi with a 32-round magazine, and he had his Beretta and a rifle. It was enough. He felt safe. What could happen? A bunch of potheads from the farm would rush them with their bongs and blow weed smoke in their face? He put her down and she was sprawled on the mattress unconscious, her head twisted and angled down, her knees splayed out like she was at the gynecologist.

He took a minute to straighten her out and put the pack she had when she was abducted under her head. Best he could do. He didn't like this, but maybe after this was all over she'd just go home and manage to evade bastards like Rupert and himself for the rest of her life. Whatever. Throw the little ones back in and see where they go. It was the only option he had now other than surveillance of the usual locations. He knew Rupert was too smart and disciplined in his own insane way to be caught out that way. No. The people around Rupert, Rupert's associates, they were the ones who could be his downfall. They were the ones to start to move on.

He and Raffi hid the Audi and sat up on top of the valley rift and watched as the sun came up and a lone black bear picked its way between the rocks and ambled across the back yard of Rupert's house. He fell asleep and did not wake until Raffi was shaking his shoulder. He sat up and saw Ilene leaving. From their vantage point they could see her make her way up the private road toward Stillwater and the main county road. They saw the truck pick her up and when it took off toward where The Consortium had its base of operations, D'Altorio and Raffi hiked back along the ridge until they were within a quarter mile of The Consortium offices and the main hangar. The ridge they were on rose up at the beginning of what had been the main runway for the old airport and gave D'Altorio a clear line of sight to the offices and parking lot.

D'Altorio took his M40A5 out of its padded bag and slug it over his shoulder. He and Raffi began to slowly descend from the top of the rift and work their way through the tall grass and weeds encircling what was left of the runway. If he could work his way about halfway down the runway on the other side, he'd be across from the parking lot and about 60 yards out. The grass was shorter there by the runway, but was ringed by abandoned trucks and piled up stacks of fencing. After making their way down the runway, they crawled the last 50 yards or so on their bellies and were not seen. He set up his tripod and attached the rifle to it, balanced on a hunk of asphalt from the broken up runway. He peered through the scope and adjusted it for distance.

When the pickup pulled up to the main offices he saw Laurent walk up to meet it. Laurent disappeared behind the truck, but he could see the passenger door open and knew he was talking with Ilene. After a moment he saw Laurent walk out from behind the car and he quickly took a shot which he intended to be a miss. It blew a chunk of asphalt off the driveway right in front of Laurent who dropped Ilene's arm and sprinted for the office door. The guy who drove the truck turned toward the sound of the rifle shot and D'Altorio shot him through the chest. He knew the round would leave a ghastly hole and blow a good chunk of his heart and lungs out of his back. The guy was dead before he hit the ground and he rolled behind the truck. Ilene jumped into the driver's seat and ran him over. She had floored it in reverse, spun the truck around tires squealing, and sent his crumpled body sliding and somersaulting across the driveway. She was headed at full speed out toward the old airport road until D'Altorio blew out her front tire and then put a round through the windshield close to where Ilene sat. It also was meant to be a near miss, and he put another through the engine block bringing the truck to a locked up, fishtailing stop. Three guys ran out of the office entrance and one offered covering fire from behind a low stone wall which ran along the left side of the entrance. Two others ran for the truck. They retrieved a stunned Ilene, pulling her out of the truck and ran back to the building. They pushed Ilene through the door first and then all three frantically tried to jam themselves through the door at the same time. D'Altorio shot two of them in the back of the head and then put a couple of shots into the glass transom above the doors no doubt showering the living with glass and reducing their motivation to confront him again. He could have taken out all three, but his intention was to only do what was necessary to accomplish his aims. He and Raffi stood and Raffi put 32 Uzi rounds into the now abandoned truck, the last few aimed at the gas tank which obligingly blew up with an almost cinematic roar of flame and thick smoke.

"Why did you stop her? Why not let her go?" Raffi asked.

"Rupert's not coming out of his hole unless we force him out. He's going to think that I released Ilene from captivity in order to get to Laurent. And after drawing him out that Ilene had served her purpose and I tried to kill her."

Raffi frowned.

"No, really, it's good. If I wanted to kill her believe me I could have done that quite easily. This is going to make him mad ... furious and that's good. The more emotional he is the more prone he is to making mistakes. He's going to feel more loyalty to Laurent thinking that he saved Ilene."

D'Altorio looked at Raffi who still was scowling.

"I didn't want to hurt her. I like her. You like her. No harm shall come to her if I can help it, but she's a variable that can turn this thing around for us. I've got to use what I have at hand. You get that, right? I mean if fucking ex-Mossad doesn't get that, there's no hope for a guy like me."

D'Altorio laughed and Raffi cuffed him in the shoulder with an open hand. It was a gesture of solidarity and D'Altorio knew what he did was good.

They worked their way back to the end of the runway and

climbed back up to the ridge and walked back to where they had hidden the Audi. They drove the round-about way out of Sussex, up into New York State on 84 coming back into Morris County on the Tappan Zee bridge. D'Altorio felt well satisfied that he had shaken loose a frozen scenario. If the game wasn't in motion again he would come back and take out Laurent. Otherwise, he had nothing particularly against The Consortium or anyone else in the periphery of Rupert's life. He would do what was necessary to accomplish his aims and that was all.

Chapter Twenty-Three

Laurent's runner gave Rupert the cell phone and a new number with which to contact Laurent. When he called, Laurent was near hysteria, but managed to give Rupert a coherent run down of what had happened. At least what he thought had happened.

"I've got three dead Consortium members. What the hell am I supposed to tell the cops? I report a firefight in my fucking parking lot and not only is The Consortium gone but I'm in jail for the next decade or so for conspiracy to sell like a ton of weed."

"Calm down, Laurent. You've got three dead misanthropic hippies, who probably haven't talked to their families or anyone else outside your little weed cult for years. All they've wanted to do is sell weed, smoke weed and grow new and more potent strains. It's not like anyone even knows they're still alive. Bury them under the runway and its business as usual."

There was silence on the other end of the line which Rupert interpreted as his being listened to and his words being considered.

"Everyone there is committed to the continuation of The Consortium as a philosophical life choice and therefore motivated to coverup what happened. You got the best kind of loyalty going there, membership in, lets face it, some kind of weird cannabis cult with a bunch of druggies who think they are spiritual warriors or something. But really, we both know full well, they're just a bunch of feckless hippies looking to remain thoroughly soaked in THC 24/7. I mean I'm all for people making their own decisions about drugs, but you know ... what is it with you guys and weed? Constant use? Do you even remember what it is to be straight?"

Laurent interrupted what looked like it was turning into a rant.

"This guy that attacked us, you gotta take him out. He's gotta pay and I can't have patrols ringing the valley out here looking for snipers all the time." Laurent's voice began to sound frantic again.

"He accomplished what he wanted to accomplish. Believe me, if he wanted you dead he'd have blown your head off with that sniper's rifle. He wants me. He wants to punish and provoke me, and to flush me out. Don't worry ... and listen, you can go on doing what you have always done. You've been a big help to me, and I hope our relationship can continue. I'm telling you he really doesn't care about you one way or the other. He used you to get at me, that's all. The only thing I don't understand is his attempt to kill Ilene. I can't wrap my head around that."

"It may be as you say, but Rupert, this guy's gotta be taken the fuck out. I can't live knowing this bastard is still running around. Please. You've got to do something. Please ..."

"I'm on it," Rupert said simply and hung up. He knew what he had to do now.

When he and E and Scheiner started selling a little weed on the Rockaway market, Scheiner took up with the wife of an older friend of theirs. Rupert hadn't liked it when Scheiner bragged to him about his romantic exploits. He told Scheiner it was bad business. It was the kind of thing that could reach out and bite them in the ass when no one expected it.

Moshe and Rachel lived on the backside of Indian Lakes, deep in the woods behind Second Beach. It was one of those unconverted summer bungalows that they had begun to winterize and expand. Three mornings a week Moshe would leave for a teaching gig at the local County College and Scheiner would appear at the back door, let himself in and quietly shuck off his clothes and crawl into bed with Moshe's wife.

Rachel for reason's incomprehensible to all but her, fell in love with Scheiner. When she admitted this to her husband she asked for a divorce and handed him the preliminary paperwork her lawyer had already prepared. Moshe said he would have to think about it. He went into the bedroom, shut the door and locked it. Ten minutes later she heard a gunshot and he was gone and now

Scheiner was there instead. Later, after marrying Rachel and feeding the drug habit that finally killed her, he inherited the house and rented it for many years until only he and his property manager remembered he even owned it.

When Rupert realized what it was he had to do to respond to D'Altorio, he also flashed on that little bungalow hidden away in the woods behind Indian Lakes. It was like intuition, a gift that made him different than other men.

He rented a car in Stroudsburg figuring that D'Altorio was probably well acquainted with his CRV. Whether D'Altorio had passed on this information to his employers or not he didn't know, so he rented a black Escalade and felt as soon as he climbed up into the driver's seat as though he were back and a force to be reckoned with. Like in days of yore, he would overcome anything arrayed against him. When he drove past Scheiner's bungalow that evening he saw some lights on and a car in the driveway. He repeated this observation over the next few days. Each time the same car was in the driveway and in the evening some lights were always on. Scheiner seemed to have confidence in his ability to hide from Rupert, or maybe he didn't feel he had to hide at all. Perhaps he felt that D'Altorio had Rupert on the run and all of Rupert's energy was being channeled into escape and survival and that vengeance was the farthest thing from his mind. Think again, motherfucker!

Rupert hit the steering wheel with the heel of his hand and laughed. That must be it. His former partners thought he had given up and was on the run concerned only with his own survival. If any of these bastards really knew him they'd know that vengeance was not anything he would ever willingly give up. It wasn't only an emotional reaction, it was a justifiable response to a deceitful and undeserving world.

He waited two days until late on a Sunday afternoon when the people in Northern New Jersey had settled into their homes to football and backyard barbecues, and the streets were relatively quiet. Rupert parked behind an abandoned maintenance building in

Hibernia just off Green Pond Road. He was sure his truck couldn't be seen from the road. He hiked up on top of the hill behind the buildings and walked through the woods until he came to the back of Indian Lakes. There were paths and low fieldstone walls built who knows how long ago and a pond he hadn't realized was back there. It was probably a flooded mineshaft left over from when iron ore had been mined in Hibernia starting from about the time of the Revolutionary War.

When he came out of the woods and into some of the backyards in Indian Lakes, he had to orient himself and yet stay unseen until he shifted up a few lots and came upon Scheiner's place. It took awhile, but his sense of direction was good and he had come out on Scheiner's street.

It would have been a simple matter to sit on a rock up in the woods behind Scheiner's house with a rifle until he saw him at a window or back door, or, lured him into the back yard with bear noises and crashing garbage cans. One shot, one kill, he was a good enough shot to have taken the bastard down no problem at all. That would, however, not have been any fun at all.

He watched the house for twenty minutes or so from the woods and seeing no movement through the windows or sliding glass door in the kitchen he skipped up quickly to the back of the house. He peered through some windows and listened until he could get a fix on Scheiner's location and to make sure that he was alone. He heard a low TV, a toilet flushing, and Scheiner's distinctive heavy footsteps. He heard the groaning sound of furniture accepting human body weight which was probably Scheiner throwing himself onto the sofa in the living room in front of the TV. Except for the TV, there wasn't any other noise.

The bungalow had an old sliding glass door in the kitchen on an aluminum track. It would be a simple matter to lift it out of the track and push it forward until the latch popped out of the bracket attached to the vertical track. He climbed up the wooden steps to the small deck just outside the door. He picked up the handle and put his full weight into the door thinking he'd have enough time to shoot Werner even though he was making some noise. Suddenly he felt the muzzle of a gun between his shoulder blades and without hesitating raised his arms and spun, knocking the barrel off to the left with his right elbow. The shotgun discharged and the recoil knocked it out of Scheiner's hands. Rupert spun completely around and followed this with a left hook to Scheiner's head. Werner Scheiner went down and rolled off the deck. Rupert pulled his Glock, jumped off and held it against his temple as Scheiner attempted to crawl over and retrieve his shotgun. He stopped and looked up and Rupert motioned for him to climb back onto the deck. Rupert kicked in the frame of the sliding door and pushed it into the house where the glass exploded in a million fragments on the tile floor of the kitchen. Scheiner was scowling and very scared and Rupert pointed to the living room. Scheiner walked stiffly from the kitchen looking from side to side, frantically trying to think of a way out of this, but not seeming to find one.

"Don't worry, man, I'll take care of you, man. Listen, we got a big cache of money we hid from everybody. Don't worry. It's yours. It's yours. Yeah. I'll take care of you. No need for this. We all come out of this all right if we do the right thing."

Scheiner was nodding frantically.

"C'mon Rupert, you can't kill me, man. I've known you since we were in like grade school. C'mon, we grew up together. Climbed fucking trees and shit. We gotta work this out. Like when we were friends and shit."

Rupert couldn't take his bullshit any longer. Scheiner sat down on the sofa and put on an expression of great earnestness as though that would convince Rupert that the crap he had just been spouting was sincere. Rupert stepped back and shot Scheiner in the throat. Werner Scheiner choked, grabbed his neck with both hands and coughed up a huge clot of blood. Rupert shot him again in the center of his forehead and Werner Scheiner pitched face forward and was most likely dead before he hit the wooden floor.

Rupert surprised himself. He had planned not so much a speech as an opportunity to rub Scheiner's face in his impending and horrible fate.

"Face the music motherfucker for a life of deceit and evil deeds against your friends and partners," or something like that.

He just knew he wanted Scheiner to realize he was going to die and to have a little time to contemplate how that was going to be. There was nothing he could do about it and he should know who it was that was killing him.

Funny. Werner Scheiner's murder had been one of the main reasons he came back to New Jersey. Scheiner and E were the obstacles Rupert thought he had to remove in order to live the life he wanted and felt he was destined to live. But really, after all that transpired, he had killed him as a response to D'Altorio's chess move and to force a move on D'Altorio's part. It had felt good shooting him. He wasn't confused about that. Killing E would be just as satisfying. But it was no longer the main thing. The game had changed. It was D'Altorio who was now the challenge and the main threat. D'Altorio was the obstacle that when removed would allow him to live and love and work as he wanted to. It was D'Altorio who was now the main opponent.

Laurie was overjoyed to see Pam. Although her current significant other was Ayaan, who she had married and Pam had met at the front gate, she kissed Pam passionately on the mouth and her face was tear streaked. It was reassuringly tear streaked Pam felt after having her life turned upside down by people whose communications at best were dubious.

They knew she had disappeared after a visit to a boyfriend in Pennsylvania and didn't seem to know much more. Laurie had heard about Rupert's reputation as a drug user and possibly a drug dealer when she went to Fairleigh, but that was about it. She had gone to a memorial for Pam organized by their old high school and college friends after two years passed from the time of Pam's disappearance and still no Pam, dead or otherwise, had turned up. Her parents refused to come.

Pam gave Laurie and Ayaan the details of all that had happened, but did not mention the pledge she had made before God and man to shoot the bastard down like a mad dog. Ayaan jumped to her feet and sputtered indignantly.

"This man has no right to continue living. We must do something. Justice demands it; he must forfeit his life for the things he has done."

Pam told them everything.

They pulled the Subaru into an old barn by the main house and covered it with tarps. Pam was given a bedroom in the attic and an old but trustworthy Chevy 4X4 and told she could stay for as long as she needed to. Ayaan told Pam how she had grown up in Rockaway and remembered hearing about a scuffle between some guy named Rupert and another guy at the Exchange from her friends a month or so ago.

"There aren't too many people with a name like Rupert and that's his stomping grounds. The other guy is probably the bastard who killed Mikael. He wants Rupert badly. He tied me up and put a hood on my head. I was so sure he was going to kill me. He's bad. I don't know who's worse, him or Rupert."

Ayaan said that her friend Carl told her how he was walking in the shadows around the side of the bar from the parking lot and had witnessed a big guy shooting at a black Audi.

"Carl said it was over a woman. When he went inside the club his girlfriend, who worked there, told him that the woman in question was their friend Ilene. Her boyfriend Rupert, who she had a breakup with, had evidently changed his mind and come to get her. The other man must have had a different idea about it all. They fought in the bar and I guess it carried over to outside. Carl saw Rupert shoot at the Audi. He took three shots – right in the middle of fucking Rockaway. Very bad! Does Ilene even know what this man did? Does she even know the real nature of this man she thinks

182

is her lover?"

Pam sat up and was staring imploringly at Ayaan and Laurie, "This man ... I don't know, it's like everywhere he goes there's suffering. I don't know what to do, I just know I've got to be the catalyst in stopping him. Whatever that means for me, I've got to do it."

"Let's go a step at a time, honey. The next step is for Ayaan to visit the Exchange and talk to Carl's girl," said Laurie. She looked at Laurie her mouth grim and resolute and gripped her hard around the shoulders. "OK, sweetie? Don't feel alone in all of this. We'll help you."

Chapter Twenty-Four

Rupert called Laurent and asked about Ilene. She was still with Laurent who didn't really know what the hell he was supposed to do with her, or what kind of danger she exposed him to, or his business.

"Calm down, my friend," Rupert said to Laurent, "she's a good girl, she knows not to talk to anyone."

"I want you to know that you were right about the personalities here at The Consortium," Laurent said in a more subdued voice, "and I feel confident that I have some security for my business now and can move on after the unfortunate circumstances of the attack. I feel that you support my business and the mutual interests you and I have insure our loyalty to each other."

"But!" said Rupert second guessing him.

Laurent's voice became shrill. He was obviously scared.

"But that psychotic sniper is still running around alive and free, and as far as I can see, you haven't done anything about it."

"Not true. I'm not going to tell you what went down and probably best for you not to know, but as far as you and your business interests are concerned you can consider it taken care of. Maybe not in the way you would have liked. What I did was in the best interests of us all. Understand? Anyway, listen, can you get Ilene out to me? I want her here. Is this something we can do without risk?"

"I certainly don't want her," Laurent replied. "I want her off my hands as soon as possible and whatever you want with her is certainly none of my business." He said goodbye before Rupert could go over the logistics of the transfer.

His manner showed impatience, and he did not like Laurent's dismissive attitude toward Ilene. But his attitude indicated an unwillingness to stand up to Rupert, which was good. Laurent expressed his anger through passive aggressive language and empty gestures and this Rupert could tolerate because he knew that it was ineffectual and ultimately Laurent would be compliant. "All good," he thought.

He hadn't replaced his security equipment. In the evening he heard some noises at the front of the house that sounded like human activity and not the omnipresent Pennsylvania squirrels and inquisitive bears. He grabbed his shotgun and the Glock and flew out the side door. He circled around the back of the house and the landscaping which consisted of dense rhododendron set atop a thigh-high fieldstone wall. He came out on the driveway on the other side of a sharp turn in the road from his cottage. He walked into the woods just far enough to not be seen from the road and walked back to the cottage parallel to the driveway.

There was a figure sitting on the old hammock by his door, head down and crying softly. Her hands were tied by a plastic strap around her wrists and she had a black hood over her face. He ran up to her, stopped and simply said, "Ilene," before tearing the hood off and shepherding her in through the front door to snip the zip tie. He embraced her there in the kitchen and she went limp with her arms at her sides while he kissed her face and pulled her hard into his chest with his big arms.

He thought her passivity was just exhaustion and perhaps trauma. He wasn't happy with Laurent bringing her back to him this way. What side did he think she was on? What kind of way was this to treat Rupert's girlfriend? It was demeaning and the more he thought about it the more outraged he became. It was another way for Laurent to express upset with Rupert. Had to be. He blamed Rupert for the actions of D'Altorio whom he had no control over at all. Crazy shit. He'd take his time in responding to hostility like this. But he would respond and Laurent would get his, like all the bastards who fucked with Rupert. For now, he needed the guy.

She would not look at him and did not respond to anything he said or asked. He half dragged, half walked her into the bedroom and laid her down and shut the blinds darkening the room. She had been whimpering slightly which despite his usual impatience with such displays he found upsetting. After a couple of hours of checking on her periodically and finding her alternately crying and rolling jerkily from side to side on his king size bed, he thought to use a little of the medicine which had always been such sweet reprieve in his own life. He got out his works and prepared a small amount of dope, drawing it up into his syringe and injecting her quickly before she could see what he was doing. She became calm immediately and was soon sleeping soundly. He left her and did not try to rouse her until the following day.

In the morning she was groggy, but he sat her down at the kitchen table and after some coffee she was talking to him again, depressed and grim, but talking. Rupert was furious at the way Laurent had treated her. All he needed to do was put her in the car and take a trip out to Rupert's hiding place which he was sure would remain a viable hiding place if Laurent had taken even minimum precautions. She wasn't a hostage, or a fucking POW, she was his girlfriend for God's sakes.

Ilene told him that she felt Laurent for all his varied skills as a libertarian, off the grid, weed growing, drug dealer, was in over his head. He was in way over his head. It was an example of someone out of their competency zone making mistakes and someone that Rupert should only deal with within the limits of their business.

"That's the trick," she said, "knowing where people's abilities start and stop. Don't expect them to grow to fit your needs, honey. You should regard this as a learning experience. One that didn't cost you anything but could have easily in other circumstances been disastrous."

Rupert listened, surprised at what he was hearing from her. She had never really talked to him like this before. Although he considered himself a good enough judge of character to usually skirt the disaster other people's incompetence can bring into your life, he felt a new respect for her observations about Laurent. There was something about her he had underestimated. He knew she was intelligent, but her deference to him, which he liked, had always caused him to separate his life with her from the other parts of his life he didn't think she could understand. Maybe that wasn't as necessary as he had thought.

There was a certain objectivity in her assessment of Laurent that impressed him, but of course was not as ruthless as his own. This new side of Ilene, which he had never seen and had not even suspected, appealed to him very much.

When she seemed to run out of gas later that afternoon and began asking him the same questions over and over about how she had arrived there and where she was, it was evident that her symptoms were returning. He brought her back in the bedroom and gave her another injection which she didn't seem to object to. She slept until dinner.

D'Altorio couldn't give a shit less about the death of Werner Scheiner. He was glad he was dead. It was Scheiner he had been most worried about after being threatened by his two employers at their last meeting. He was frankly surprised that Rupert had located Scheiner so easily and seemed to appear and disappear like a ninja in a residential neighborhood on a Sunday afternoon. E was badly shaken and was ready to call off the whole thing and head to Colorado to buy a Pizza place or something. Said he didn't need this shit and would rather just sell a little coke along with his Sicilian and thin crust slices.

Scheiner was nobody's fool and D'Altorio was surprised Rupert had pulled it off so smoothly. There would be no more chess moves, no more fantasies of bringing Rupert to legal and poetic justice for D'Altorio. He was going to have to make a straight run at this guy and create his own advantage. But where the fuck was he? How was he going to find out now? First things first, he was going to have to find out who was with who and where they were. And then, he thought, rethink his no harm shall come to those on the periphery. He had put a shot through the windshield behind which sat Ilene to try to scare Rupert into making a bad move. He couldn't play that cat and mouse game any longer. With a guy like Rupert it could easily get D'Altorio killed. No, he was going to have to go completely ruthless. It was war and if you were with the wrong people, you were putting yourself on the line.

It was an easy matter to post a camera with a high definition zoom almost exactly where he had lain and shot the Consortium members. The Consortium's chronic use of weed seemed to preclude a reasonable approach toward security. A couple of guys were walking around, mostly just keeping the front door in sight. No one noticed Raffi crawl through the weeds and place his camera exactly where D'Altorio had shot from. Raffi was a former Mossad agent and what he saw in the enemy camp put him into absolute and total hysterics.

"Too much weed," he said. "Ate away all their fucking brains." He pointed at his head and laughed hysterically and then screwed up his face in imitation of zoned out weed users.

The feed from the camera at the Consortium was linked to facial recognition software on D'Altorio's laptop which had been fed images of Ilene, Laurent and Rupert. It set off an alarm to alert D'Altorio and showed him live feed of Ilene being hustled out of the front door of the offices in Sussex and placed in the back seat of a Forester. Laurent had walked out with her and sat as his guys strapped her wrists together and put a hood over her head. Curiously, she was treated less like an ally and more like a captive.

Perhaps his attack had shaken up the alliance between Rupert and The Consortium. Good. Less resources for Rupert to call in. What he needed to do now was to find out where the Forester took Ilene. That would be simple.

He sent Raffi up to Newton to await further instructions. On Tuesday morning at nine the Forester was driven out to the front of the building. D'Altorio watched on his laptop as Laurent walked out and climbed into the back seat with a suitcase and a computer bag slung over his shoulder. It was what D'Altorio had been waiting for. Raffi quickly scrambled out of Newton and caught the Forester coming up 94. He forced it off the road in front of the Fredon Municipal building and in a series of quick and economical actions shot the driver and pulled Laurent out the door and dragged him into the back of his van. He was in Morris County with Laurent in front of D'Altorio in forty-five minutes.

Raffi guided him into D'Altorio's office and kicked his legs out from underneath him and Laurent fell awkwardly into a chair on the side of D'Altorio's desk. Raffi grabbed him before he fell sideways off the chair, straightened him up and pulled down his shirt which had ridden up and exposed a soft and protruding belly.

"Sit up straight," he said to Laurent grinning. "Now you looking good."

Laurent looked at him with concern and then turned away to see D'Altorio staring at him.

"You tell me where he is and I let you go. Easy as that." D'Altorio said to Laurent.

"You shot my driver," Laurent cried.

"Flesh wound. Shot him in the shoulder. He can drive himself to Newton Hospital. He'll be fine."

"Really?"

"No. He's dead. We're not leaving anybody behind anymore. You tell me what I want to know because otherwise you'll be joining him in stoner's heaven in about five seconds."

D'Altorio took his Beretta out of the desk drawer and put the muzzle against Laurent's temple. Laurent began shaking and making strangled, crying noises and suddenly there was the ammoniac smell of urine and Laurent's pants were wet and a puddle was forming on the side of his left shoe.

"You'll tell me now or you won't ever be telling anyone anything again."

"If I tell you, then you've gotta get Rupert. I mean you've got to kill him fast. If he finds out I ratted him out, and he will because he's going to hear about my dead driver, he will come after me relentlessly until my business is burning down around my ankles and he blows my head off."

D'Altorio nodded and pushed the muzzle harder into the side of Laurent's head.

"Yeah, he's gonna kill you, he's definitely gonna kill you, so you better give me whatever you can so I can do a good job."

He sat back down at the desk and Laurent told him everything he could about the estate Rupert and Ilene were on and drew a map of the roads and the cottage and how it was situated off the main road and the main house. He gave them everything he possibly could. D'Altorio took notes on his yellow legal pad and afterward looked up and said, "Yes, OK, this is good. Good job," and picked up the Beretta and shot Laurent in the left eye.

His 9 mm Beretta made a neat hole where Laurent's eye had been. A spray of blood and brains spewed out of the back of his head and painted the wall behind him.

Raffi looked at D'Altorio and laughed, "You brutal, boss. You gonna be like one of those Daesh motherfuckers if we don't calm you the fuck down."

Chapter Twenty-Five

When D'Altorio's shot came through the windshield, smashing the rearview mirror and sending glass into her face and mouth, she just shut down. She felt herself being pulled out of the car by The Consortium guys, and when she could not stand, each grabbed an arm and she was dragged all the way up the driveway until she was thrown through the open, front door of the offices. She lay in a heap on the floor as scared as she had ever been in her life. She heard more shots and felt something splattering her legs and feet and was afraid to look down to see what it was. When she did look down her lower body was covered with blood and bits of everything that had come from the skulls of her rescuers. D'Altorio shot them in the back of the head as they struggled through the entrance. Their brains had literally been blown out by the high velocity sniper rounds. She screamed once, then again and couldn't stop until Laurent picked her up and pushed her face deeply into his arm and chest.

Even though she was in Pennsylvania now, safe on a secluded estate, the shooting played over and over in her mind. She could feel the explosive power of the round that smashed through the car and nearly took her head off, and she could see the two Consortium guys lying in the lobby with their heads smashed and blown open and herself covered with their gore. It was like it was happening in the present. She woke often, choking and screaming, caught in a vortex of horror that only pulled her down and down and further down.

When Rupert shot her up with heroin, he promised her it was not enough to become addicted, and everything shifted into warm, sleepy wellbeing and her anxiety was lifted out of her like it had never existed. Rupert told her it was this or benzos, but that heroin was much better. Although both were addictive he was quite familiar with heroin. He knew how to use and not get addicted.

Rupert taught her how to inject the drug properly and she liked the ritual of it and began to shoot up Rupert as well. He showed her his dope box explaining carefully that the sealed vial of powder he kept with his heroin should never be opened. It was an extremely dangerous substance and that even touching it or breathing a bit of the dust could be toxic. When he sold off some of his stash it allowed him to cut the drug in a way that did not compromise its potency.

She made Rupert promise he would give her the smallest amount of heroin possible in order to achieve relief. And she made him promise he would stop giving it to her as soon as she began to feel a little better. But she liked it and Rupert was happy that she did and they enjoyed getting high together.

She had no choice when it came down to it. The dope was good and it was the only thing saving her from being devoured by her trauma. She understood what was happening to her, but had no resources to deal with it other than the heroin. Dope worked and it worked really well.

Then she started having the recurring dream. Each time she had the dream it sent a premonitory chill up her spine and when she woke it had been so realistic that she had to make the conscious effort to remember that it was not part of her history, not part of her memory. It was only a dream, but one which she had to almost forcibly eject from her awareness. It seemed to have an existence all its own.

It disturbed her so much that she didn't tell Rupert until the dream morphed and the blitzkrieg-like attack, which used to stop abruptly at the front door and then suddenly dissipate like a summer thunderstorm, now burst through the door and overwhelmed them in a wave of fire and bullets and men in quasi military gear who overran them and stood over their prone bodies with combat weapons shoved up against their skulls. One of the men stood over her and took off his helmet. He said, while showing her his military shotgun, that he would keep shooting her until she was barely recognizable as a human being. He laughed and laughed and when she screamed he laughed louder until his laughter drowned out her cries. It was D'Altorio, triumphant, gleeful and murderous. He looked at her suddenly curious about her reaction and then backed up while raising his weapon.

"I think they know where we are," she said to Rupert when she finally broke down and told him about the dream. "I think that if we stay here they'll come and they will blow us up, burn us out, shoot us ... it's so horrible. Just a dream and an intuition, but I haven't been able to shake it. It keeps coming and the vision keeps getting worse. D'Altorio, he's like some kind of psycho. He and E and Werner Scheiner. Its such a nightmare. Oh, Rupert! I think the dream is a warning, I think we are in great danger."

Rupert hadn't told her about Scheiner's death, or really any of his previous history and frankly she had not wanted to know too much. Whatever he did now, no matter how aggressive, she was afraid he would rationalize as an act of self defense. But as the Priest in Rockaway used to say to the boys fighting in Sunday School, "live by the sword, die by the sword."

Although she knew Rupert was no innocent, she only had a vague story from him about legal problems over drugs and two former friends, or business associates, or whatever E and Scheiner were to him, who blamed Rupert for everything. She knew D'Altorio was the engine of their vengeance, hence her kidnapping and when that didn't work her attempted murder. It was all a little muddled, but also obviously a war, and she understood that better now after the shooting at The Consortium and now this intuition or nightmare. Who knew what the dream was? A manifestation of her trauma or was it real insight? Who knew? It was all a horrible, horrible jumble that she couldn't get straight in her mind.

She had to talk to someone. She was often alone in the house, deep in the woods, and now had no car, no means to get out of the house and was in fact afraid to leave the property. Rupert had been sympathetic, but his only solution was to dose her more often with heroin. His ability to empathize and talk to her about what she had experienced had been exceeded on the first day of her return. She needed to vent, she needed to tell the story to someone who knew how to listen, and by whose sympathy and attention Ilene could make something coherent out of the madness of all that had happened to her.

She called Ivy. Rupert had warned her emphatically not to call, email or text anyone, but after he rummaged through her purse for her cellphone and could not find it he seemed to forget or loose interest. They had just gotten high and he drifted away to drink coke and watch TV. He was hiding out from some formidable enemies and yet he was constantly out of the house for supplies, for shopping, reconnoitering the county roads around the estate and the main roads into Stroudsburg and the highway into New Jersey. He was a careful man, worried about future business and if the worst happened, escape routes.

Ivy was initially overjoyed to hear from her friend, but then became wary when Ilene made her swear to absolute secrecy. "My life is on the line if you break your promise." She told her everything that had happened, with lots of context regarding personalities and analysis and extrapolation on the motivations of the main players. Ivy was speechless and could not believe what Ilene had gotten herself into the middle of. Ilene made her promise again and again not to break her promise and to keep this an absolute secret. She felt it was good that she had not told Ivy where she was. She hoped that this was enough to protect her and Rupert from any repercussions that might come of Ivy breaking her promise. The only thing Ivy had was her phone number for calling or text. She would always keep the phone with her away from Rupert and perhaps this would be enough to not compromise them.

"Ivy, it is so good to talk to you again, but it reminds me of all I've lost since I met Rupert. I mean I went from living a normal life, dull and ordinary, but I certainly had good friends like you." Ilene whimpered and then was crying and was barely able to blurt out between sobs, "This life I'm living now is a nightmare and I can't wake up no matter what I do. Ivy, I ... I just can't take it. I'm telling you I really can't take it anymore. I don't know what I'm going to do, maybe the only thing I can do, the only thing I have any control over is to just kill myself. I'm afraid. I'm so afraid I have no other choices!"

Ivy was shouting, "Ilene, Ilene," but Ilene had clicked off her phone.

Rupert called Laurent. After no one picked up he called the number he had for the main offices. Usually, a recorded message would pick up right away and would advertise the legal side of the company which was their CBD business and offer company extensions. No one picked up even after several tries and punching Laurent's private extension made no difference.

Bad sign. He didn't know if he completely believed Ilene's premonition, but he had a bad feeling. If Laurent's business was offline then something catastrophic must have happened, and Laurent was the only one who knew where he and Ilene were. He still had the CRV and no one knew he had rented the Cadillac. He left the CRV parked out front in the middle of the driveway, left lights on in the house and a TV on in the bedroom and one in the kitchen. After loading their gear into the Escalade, they were gone within an hour.

What to do? He wanted to finish this. If D'Altorio had taken Laurent then he most likely knew by now where Rupert was. It would be an easy matter to sit with a rifle in the woods each day until D'Altorio made his move and he could pick them off as they approached the house. But D'Altorio was smart and who knows how many he would bring with him. Three guys approaching the house from the front, counting on surprise to accomplish their aims, that would be an easy scenario for Rupert. He knew exactly where he could sit. There was a tree that already had a bow hunter's blind in it and would allow him to make the front of his house a killing field.

This was a scenario that appealed to him. D'Altorio in his greatest moment of triumph seeing it suddenly all evaporate in front of him. Rupert imagined dispatching his cohorts with single head shots and grievously wounding D'Altorio, who in pain and terrible suffering would still be coherent enough to understand what was happening when Rupert walked up to him for the coup de grâce. Pop, pop and D'Altorio's head was a smashed melon on the ground and he could turn his attention to making short work of E.

He and Ilene got a suite for a couple of weeks outside of Stroudsburg at the Hampton Inn. They spent a couple of days taking some walks in the Poconos, having drinks at the pool and eating at the local restaurants and Rupert was quickly bored and frustrated. He didn't like waiting for his enemy to make the first move and then react to him. He liked making events conform to his decisions. He wanted always to be the one who takes action. As he saw it, there was really only one chess move that was open to him. And that was ridding D'Altorio of his now one and only employer, immediately, and before the imminent siege of the Stroudsburg cottage.

E always had a taste for heroin, much like Rupert himself. He remembered when they were teenagers and attempted to shoot dope for the first time in E's bedroom in his parent's house in Indian Lakes. E, not realizing that heroin was injected intravenously, had shot it into the muscle of his arm leaving a small abscess-like bulb of the drug just below his shoulder. It did not readily absorb into his system and when Rupert, laughing hysterically, pointed out his mistake E wanted to know immediately how to do it the right way. Rupert prepared a half of a bag of dope that Werner had sold them and shot up E. E got high but wanted more. Rupert cautioned him that what he had shot intramuscularly was going at some point to be absorbed into his system.

E was belligerent and demanded the rest of what he insisted was his bag of dope and accused Rupert of just trying to get it for himself. E stood, red in the face and shouting, and then it was like a slow motion cartoon transition as the dope in the muscle of his arm was absorbed. He slowly went from anger to total unconsciousness with different levels of slurring and staggering before his eyes rolled up in his head. Rupert watched, scared as hell, as E went to the floor and was unresponsive when Rupert pushed at his shoulder and shouted his name in his face. His breathing was shallow and his lips blue. Rupert pulled him off the floor and put him on his stomach on his bed. He cleaned up any sign of his having been there and left the house without being seen, expecting the news in the morning would be all about E's secret heroin use and how it had killed him.

He heard nothing the next morning and called E's house and hung up when he heard his mother's cheery morning greeting. He was shocked that E pulled through and E seemed oblivious to Rupert's desertion and his own close call during what was actually a clinical overdose that depressed his respiratory and cardiovascular system within a hair's breadth of death.

They both maintained a love of dope although their use would have been described as chipping by hardcore users. Rupert figured that E had probably maintained his old habits perhaps even making a greater commitment to the drug during his time in prison. He would have to be buying somewhere, maybe the only thing he would risk exposure for after Werner's death.

Rupert drove into Dover. He cruised past the spot where he, E and sometimes Werner used to cop dope. It was a low concrete partition between the back of the old movie theatre and the street that the cognoscenti called simply The Wall. There was of course a new generation of dirt bags hanging out there, but they seemed to be upholding the traditions of the place.

He called his buddy James who, although he had moved into legitimate business interests after financing his chain of gyms through the sale of weed and cocaine, still maintained some of his underworld connections in North Jersey. Rupert wanted to know if the head dealer guy at the Dover wall was "resourceful" and a guy who would cooperate with Rupert in a situation he needed to take care of. Was he a guy who could be counted on to do what needed to be done without asking questions and could he keep his mouth shut?

James said yes. Wes was a drug fiend but could be counted on to do anything that would further his abilities to indulge. And, you could put his balls in a vice and wouldn't tell anybody anything. James said he would send word down to expect Rupert.

When Rupert cruised past The Wall in Dover that evening, one of the dirt bags hopped off the wall and walked across the street and down and around the corner. Rupert went around the corner the other way and then pulled up to him on the street and lowered his passenger window. The guy tried to open the door, but Rupert had kept it locked. He passed two, one-hundred-dollar bills through the open window and the guy took it and looked at him.

"You're selling dope to a skinny fuck, my age from Indian Lakes named E?" he asked.

Wes nodded.

"I figured as much. E likes to do things the way he's always done them. I want you to give him this next time he buys."

Rupert handed him a bag of dope he had adulterated with fentanyl.

"You do this for me and I've got one hundred more hundred dollar bills I will give to you. You tell a soul and you die." Rupert showed him his Glock. "Yes? You can do this?"

The guy nodded.

"I hear about his OD and I'll come down here the very next day to take care of you. Ok? Sounds good? Take the money and go to Florida for the rest of the summer. You'll like it there. Lots of dope."

E was dead in a week. He had rented a little bungalow on an estate in Bernardsville and evidently loved to sit on his patio in the evening and drink cognac and smoke weed with the young groundskeeper. When he didn't show for a couple of nights, even though his car was in the driveway, and did not respond to shouts and banging on his door, the groundskeeper opened the door with his key and found E sprawled on the floor. The syringe was still in his arm and the police lab said the drug still in the syringe was some of the most potent they had ever encountered. Luckily, the law enforcement present at the scene had the presence of mind to handle evidence with sufficient protective gear. They told the local Patch reporter that the drugs were so powerful that even touching them could be dangerous.

Rupert drove down to Dover and passed by The Wall the next evening. He met Wes around the corner and produced the roll of bills with his left hand. When Wes leaned in the open passenger side window, he shot Wes in the face with his right hand in which he gripped the Glock he had hidden inside his shirt. Rupert pocketed the money and slowly pulled away from the curb. Maybe Wes wouldn't have said anything, even with his nuts in a vice, or maybe not. The guy was, according to James, a dope fiend after all and Rupert was happy to save the money.

Wes was blown backwards by the force of the shot and his torso was pushed back upright against a retaining wall with his legs crumpled beneath him. He did not look that different than any of the occasional homeless in New Jersey cities except that on closer inspection his head lolled to the side at an unnatural angle and there was a bloody hole where most of his nose had been.

Rupert took a left where the old Army/Navy store used to be and remembered the dungaree jacket he had bought there more than twenty years before. He smiled. E. and Scheiner had accompanied him and it was Scheiner who suggested Rupert buy the jacket. When he turned onto Rt. 46, he was thinking about business and what it was he was going to do about D'Altorio.

Chapter Twenty-Six

D'Altorio wasn't going to get what E and Werner Scheiner had agreed to pay him for killing Rupert. Who cared at this point? Nice to be recognized for your efforts, but now E was dead and the source of his funding had dried up. He didn't absolutely need the money, he had plenty from his years in corporate America. Scheiner and E had been paying his bills which were primarily living expenses and a salary for Raffi and any guys he hired on an as needed basis. He told Raffi it was over. E and Scheiner were dead, Laurent was dead, Consortium weed heads were dead. It was enough and he was backing out.

Raffi helped him clean up the safe house where he had held Ilene and killed Laurent. They pulled out down to the last container of hummus and he gave Raffi a big bonus. Raffi said goodbye and gave him one of those macho Israeli hugs that took his breath away and left him slightly off balance. Raffi grinned when D'Altorio winced and put his hand on his ribs.

"You take good care now, Boss, OK? *Lehitraot.*"

"Yeah, yeah, listen ... goodbye, good luck and have a good life," he said to Raffi somewhat tonelessly.

D'Altorio already had a place out in Denville he had rented as soon as he had heard of Scheiner's death. He had figured it wouldn't be long before E was gone as well and then it would only be him and he was sure he was on the short list of Rupert's inventory of desired dead motherfuckers. And Rupert was certainly on his. He guessed he had failed, not being able to protect E and Scheiner from Rupert, but that had not been his priority. As far as he was concerned their safety was their own concern and his was to draw out and eliminate Rupert.

There was something about this guy that really got to him. Rupert careened through his existence and ruined people's lives if they were lucky. He killed them outright if they weren't. He caused massive collateral damage. There were Ruperts that existed on every level of this world: in the prosecutor's and law enforcement offices in Bergen, among the wealthy people he had defended so that they could continue their entitled exploitation of others of lesser means, and in the avaricious corporate world that like sharks killed and ate and killed and ate. The sharks of this world were programed for one thing only, conforming to the dictates of their predatory and carnivorous natures.

He couldn't repair this world. Quite beyond his abilities. But this guy had become emblematic of all the shit he had seen in his life and for Robert D'Altorio, ridding the world of this particular piece of shit would satisfy him immensely. Taking out Rupert would represent his attempt to come to terms with a life he would have liked to have dedicated to manure shoveling. He felt in this mission to cancel Rupert not so much ennobled as called into service. It was an opportunity to make up for the excesses and the mistakes that characterized his own careening path through life and the casualties he had caused in that pursuit.

He could have assaulted Rupert's Stroudsburg cottage with Raffi and a few of his military buddies, but it didn't seem right somehow. This thing had come down to a personal confrontation between he and Rupert and that was the way he wanted to handle it. He drove out to Stroudsburg and drove round and round the estate that Rupert's cottage was on. The estate backed up onto a nature preserve, camping grounds, and some deep, old growth forest. The rest was surrounded by rural farms and woods. He left the Audi in Butler and rented a mini camper that had a bunk bed, cooking appliances, a toilet and little else. He rented a camp site that had electricity he could plug his camper into and settled in for the night. Forgoing grilling his own dinner like the families on nearby camp sites, he instead brought in some takeout from a Stroudsburg Thai place.

In the morning he brought up Google Maps on his iPhone and located Rupert's cottage and his current location. There was a hiking trail that passed within a couple of miles of the back of the estate on which the cottage was located. He could see the estate quite clearly on his phone as he scrolled around and began his planning for where he might shoot from. He could also see plantings and walls which might provide cover and the road which wound through the woods out to the public roads without ever joining up with the main house's driveway.

The cottage was isolated enough for his purposes. He could hike out on the trail until his GPS indicated he was behind the property, and then bushwack through the woods to get to the back of the cottage. He broke down the sniper rifle and carefully stowed it in his knapsack. He had hiking shoes and hiking gear and with his sunglasses and bonnie hat he looked like ten million other "active retirees" who had found a new life purpose in exploring the natural world. He hadn't shaved in two weeks feeling that his scruffy beard would blur out his features and make him look more nondescript. The constant itching drove him crazy however, and he couldn't wait to shave it.

He went out late in the afternoon hoping to arrive at the cottage at dusk. There wasn't anyone on the trails at that hour. It took him about an hour until his GPS showed him to be behind the cottage. The walk through the woods took about forty minutes, the terrain being somewhat rougher than he had imagined. There were steep ravines and hills that were jumbled up piles of boulders on huge, ancient ledges of rock that allowed only one or two paths through. Google maps was so good that ultimately he was able to come out on a small hill directly behind the cottage. He sat on a rock behind a huge old eastern hemlock with heavy dense boughs and realized that this must have been the way that Rupert killed Scheiner. No one had seen him on a Sunday afternoon when he had suddenly appeared like a fucking ghost, killed Scheiner and then disappeared just as supernaturally. The bastard must have come in through the back door just as he had done. How ironic. How fitting it would be if what he was about to do worked.

He put together the rifle and snapped on the scope. On the left side of the house was a large open kitchen with French doors and floor to ceiling glass windows on either side. D'Altorio figured all he had to do was sit with his rifle until fat boy came down for one of his no doubt many snacks and "one shot, one kill." And if Ilene appeared he would take her out as well. No loose ends left behind. Why take a chance at this point?

He waited until twilight and began moving around the house looking to see where Rupert and Ilene might be. He stayed just far enough out on the property behind brush, behind the trees which ringed the property on the edge of the woods, so that he wouldn't be seen. He saw some lights go on and movement past an upstairs window. It was a male figure, too large for Ilene, but indistinct and impossible to identify with certainty. Must be my target he was thinking. All signs pointed to a green lighted mission as far as he was concerned. He continued his circumnavigation of the house getting ample cover from the landscaping where the property opened to fields and meadow on the right side. He worked his way back to the left side of the house and set up behind a thick tree trunk that had fallen just inside the woods. He had a clear shot into the kitchen. He would just have to wait it out.

The kitchen was dimly lit and when he saw a smaller figure moving around the counter and then stand in front of the large window looking out onto the property, he knew it was Ilene. He needed to take down Rupert first. He was sure that Ilene would be so panicked that she would offer him plenty of opportunities to take her as well. He could always just burst through the French doors and use his Berretta on her after he had taken care of Rupert.

And then he saw a larger figure come up behind her as though to embrace her while she looked out the window. The figures aligned, one directly in front of the other, and he took the shot. He hit Ilene in the head probably just about between her eyes and the bullet passed through and slammed into Rupert's chest. It must have blown an apple sized hole in his sternum and probably passed completely through his body. The round was that powerful.

He couldn't tell for sure though. The round knocked them both back into the dim kitchen, but all he could see were their feet, their upper bodies having disappeared into shadows from the kitchen island. He waited and watched and there wasn't any movement or sound. One shot, two kills. He was proud of himself. Leaving his rifle on top of the tree trunk, he walked up holding his Berretta out in front of him with both hands. The window had a small clean hole through it with a radiating spider web of cracks. He kicked in the rest of the window and stepped into the kitchen. The bodies had been kicked back by the force of the round and were on their backs one partially on top of the other. He hit the lights and gasped when he saw it was two men, one small and thin, the other larger and muscular. They were two men he had never seen before in his life.

He heard the crunch of glass behind him and felt the muzzle of a gun pushed hard into his kidneys.

"Oh no!" he said, as he felt the explosion of the shot in his side and fell as another round hit him in the head.

When he regained consciousness he put his hands to his bleeding skull and was shocked to be alive. Other than the two bodies there wasn't anyone else in the kitchen or in the house. He had a vest on underneath his thick khaki hiking shirt and while he felt like he had been kicked in the side by a fucking horse he was intact. The round to his head looked exceedingly nasty but he had twisted as he went down and the round hit at a glancing angle that his skull actually deflected. It gouged out a long nasty gash in his temple and had lifted his scalp making it look as though it had bashed through his skull and smashed in his head. He guessed that's why Rupert hadn't checked him more closely.

Although groggy, he knew he had to get out of there as soon as possible. He rolled out of the kicked in window and crawled toward the tree where he had left the rifle. Halfway across he managed to regain his feet, grabbed the gun and headed for the deep woods. It took him all night to find his way back to the trail and then ultimately his camper. He drank two bottles of water, threw it up all over the toilet, not being fast enough to lift the lid before the eruption occurred, and fell into the bunk bed angry, his head and side literally throbbing with each heartbeat and utterly exhausted.

When Pam was with Rupert in the McMansion in Greenpond, they had never frequented The Exchange or hung out with his Rockaway friends except of course for E and Werner Scheiner. She felt safe now in accompanying Ayaan to visit Carl's girlfriend at The Exchange. It was early evening and the club was still slow, a few of the bartenders and waitresses were talking in the back and when Carl's girlfriend Stacey saw them. She grabbed the hand of the girl next to her and pulled her out the back door into the parking lot while beckoning to Ayaan and Pam.

"This is Ivy, she's like Ilene's best friend in the whole world. I don't want to know anymore about this shit than I already do, you know seeing the fight and what my boyfriend told me, but Ivy, she's like talked to her and all."

"Who? Said Pam and Ayaan in unison."

"Like Ilene?" Stacey said, rolling her eyes.

Stacy turned and walked briskly back into the club without looking back.

Ivy looked like she was going to cry, "I'm so worried about her," she said. "I'm afraid she's going to hurt herself. And if she doesn't do it to herself then this bastard she's with surely will. I want to do anything I can to help her. But hey, who are you people anyway? Are you like the cops or what?"

Pam explained without identifying herself and without specifics that they had been associates of Rupert's that they were friends of a sort, as much as a person like Rupert could have friends. He had made false accusations against them, ruined their business and reputations, and they knew about his violence and danger to anyone encountering him.

Ayaan said emphatically to Ivy, "Ilene's life is in danger. She is in extreme danger. Do you understand this?"

Ivy told them about her conversation with Ilene in a trembling, rambling and vague recounting that finally Pam interrupted and asked if she knew where Ilene was.

"No idea," Ivy said, "but I have her phone number. Would that help?"

Chapter Twenty-Seven

Alain and Alex had come down from New Hampshire: first to reclaim Ilene's car, and then a second time to help Rupert with his revitalized weed business. After the new business went into what looked like a permanent stall due to his troubles with D'Altorio, E, and Scheiner, they stayed on hoping to pick up some of the dregs of business they had helped Rupert with.

They were staying in New Jersey and had experience in the business having been former employees of Rupert's during his first go round as Manhattan weed sommelier. Rupert's former clowns, now "friends," agreed to come out to Pennsylvania to house sit for Rupert and get a little down time for themselves. Rupert told them that he and Ilene were heading south to Atlanta on a road trip that would take in the Blue Ridge Mountains and some extended time hiking on the trails off Skyline Drive. He had some business contacts in Atlanta that needed personal attention he said, and Ilene needed some personal attention. Might as well kill two birds with one stone so to speak. It was all bullshit of course.

Alain was a small man, his height and weight both about the same as Ilene's. Alex Novik was a robust looking Belarusian, much more muscular and leaner than Rupert, but occupying roughly the same volume of body mass. They were perfect for what he needed, Rupert thought, and easy to persuade.

He set them up in the cottage, showed them his streaming service, stocked the fridge with steaks, corn and craft beer and they were happy as clams. He convinced them to put their car in the detached garage out back and limit their outside activities telling them that he didn't want the estate owner to know that they were there. He had set up a cam in the Bow Hunter's blind across the driveway in the woods, and one behind the house sweeping the tree line from a birdhouse mounted on a fifteen foot post.

He had a sleeping bag, his rifle, handgun, and food he had packed in one of those insulated fabric bags. He set up in the nursery man's shed between the cottage and the main house. It had been abandoned years ago, but was still in good shape. His phone was set to ring an alarm if the cam monitored any motion. He didn't have long to wait. D'Altorio came that evening and although Rupert understood why he had come alone, he was also relieved. It was an easy matter to watch him set up his firing position and then to circle in behind and wait until he took his shot.

It thrilled Rupert to step through the window behind D'Altorio and push his Glock into his side and pause for a second, letting it sink in that he had been taken. When he pulled the trigger and felt the explosion, D'Altorio jackknifed from the upper body and twisted as he fell. Rupert got off another shot before D'Altorio hit the ground. It smashed into his skull at the temple, and when he fell face down, made a satisfyingly thick pool of blood that spread beyond his head and shoulder in neat circles.

"Fuck you," he said. "Ha ha, I won!"

He had three bodies and a car to disappear. He needed Matias, but of course Matias was unable to help him now. He left to get some canvas bags to stuff the bodies into, cleaning supplies, and some accelerant. Stuff the bodies in the back of Alex's SUV and place open cans of accelerant between the three. He'd then park the car on a declining slope that led to a cliff over an abandoned, flooded quarry he knew of near Ridgeway, Pennsylvania. He figured he could ignite the car, let it burn to a fucking crisp and then pull the rocks he would use as chocks and let it drop off the cliff and sink to the bottom of a quarry hundreds of feet deep, where it would likely never be found. It was a recipe for success! He'd have to pry D'Altorio's shot out of whatever wall it had lodged in. He should put that round in a frame and hang it on his wall. It epitomized the sad irony of D'Altorio's life and the luck that characterized Rupert's.

She wanted to go back to her life in Rockaway, bartending at The Exchange and waitressing at the Cafe. It was busy, but easy and she didn't have to think about anything. Here in Stroudsburg with Rupert she was always thinking. Rupert had loaded up the Escalade with his guns and ammo and she knew there was going to be a war at the cottage. This was all a nightmare that she never imagined her life would be caught up in. She felt literally seized and pulled by impossibly strong centrifugal forces, down, down, down into the vortex. This was what Rupert had to bestow upon a vulnerable and naive world, everybody circling the drain. She knew next to nothing about any of these people. What possible motivation could they have for creating such suffering and death? At this point it was the absence of a coherent picture that made her believe that Rupert's unknown history was a lot worse than she thought. In her experience, a lack of information was usually the result of withholding and the reasons for that concealment were never very good.

He left Friday night, and Saturday morning she had to get out of the hotel. She walked down the highway to a diner and ordered coffee and eggs and sat by the window and called her friend Ivy again despite Rupert's renewed warnings about not communicating with anyone.

"Oh My God, Ilene, I can't believe I'm talking to you. I've wanted to call so many times and was so afraid ... for you, for me. Oh My God! You have got to get your ass as far away from that monster as you possibly can. Like right now. Like right this second. You are in such danger!"

Ilene's heart was banging like a drum in her chest. Doom, a constant companion for her, increased even more and it felt like adrenaline and cortisol were rushing through her body in a wash of chemical toxins. Her dissociation was peeling and scaling off, leaving her feeling completely vulnerable.

"Rupert, Rupert, he's a monster, Ilene. Listen, first there was like Ayaan and some other woman telling me how Rupert ruined their lives and then there was this guy, two days later, a detective, saying, you know, he worked for a couple from Morristown whose daughter Rupert murdered. Murdered, Ilene! He murdered people! He's like a monster with a long history. A serial killer psychopath or something. He killed their daughter Pam and a bunch of guys in Ridgeway, Pennsylvania. He killed the first detective they hired to find out what happened to their daughter and he killed another girlfriend and one of his like criminal underlings in New Hampshire. And that doesn't even include what he's been doing since he's been back in New Jersey. He poisons them with drugs, Ilene. Or shoots them if they won't take his poison heroin."

Ivy paused, and when she didn't hear a response from Ilene, who was shocked into silence even though she she had expected the worst, began shouting into the phone.

"Ilene! Ilene! Are you there? Did you hear me? Run! You must run! You can't believe what that bastard has done. Get the fuck out of there right this second even if you have to run down the road in your fucking underwear!"

Ilene took some deep breaths. It occurred to her then that perhaps what needed to be done was bigger than just her individual life and her desires. She was still very upset and yet beginning to be resigned to the reality of what she had been denying for so long. Obliviousness had a cost. Maybe repression had been necessary in order to endure some of the difficult things in her life, but now it was leading her to absolute catastrophe. She was at a turning point and she was going to have to either deal with the reality of the events that were swamping her, or drown. She was not sure which she was truly capable of. She put the phone down and not only clicked off the call but powered the phone off.

When D'Altorio woke up he was dehydrated and had lost much blood. He drove to the emergency room in Stroudsburg and told them that he had been hiking and fallen off a ledge, dropping six feet or so onto rocks where he had gouged his head and smashed his side. He had taken off his vest and changed the shirt in the camper which had been burned by the flash of Rupert's muzzle. They pumped him back up full of blood and rehydrating IV fluid and sewed up his head. They cut off the section of his scalp that had been lifted by the bullet fearing it would become necrotic and cause an infection. It left an open wound that he would have to have surgery to fully close at some later date. Until then they gave him a complicated schedule of changing bandages, cleaning, and applying topical antibiotics and taking oral antibiotics. They shaved his head around the wound. One of the emergency room physicians looked at him suspiciously.

"Are you sure that's what really happened?" he asked. "You fell? I don't know, that wound in your head looks suspiciously furrowed. It's the kind of wound made by a bullet, isn't it?"

When D'Altorio didn't answer, the doctor rolled his eyes and walked away. He had seen a lot in ER. This wasn't something he hadn't seen before.

D'Altorio drove back to New Jersey and returned the camper after a perfunctory cleaning of the toilet he had covered in vomit and the sheets of the bunk full of his blood. He took an Uber to where he had left his Audi and drove to his new place in Denville. He needed some time to recover and get his strength back.

"I was you three years ago until Rupert killed me. At least he thought he did. You and I have an obligation to stop this human horror, this sick man who poisons whoever and whatever he encounters. Do you know who I am?"

"What? What? Who gave you this phone number? Who is this?"

Ilene was beyond shock, she was feeling something more akin to paralysis. With all that had happened to her recently, which already was well beyond her ability to deal with, this phone call dumped a whole new dimension of chaos and insanity she hadn't expected and was barely even able to believe. It was all too much.

"I'm Pam Scheider although you should have been able to figure that out. You must have heard plenty about me by now. You and I have a lot in common, don't we? The question is, what are we going to do about it? Listen, I'm no Sarah Connor but I'm committed to finishing this and ..., well, bring Rupert to some kind of justice. It's like there's a rattle snake loose in the garden. We've gotta stomp the life out of it before the children go play in there. We fed this rattlesnake, we were part of this horror no matter how naive and gullible we were. We've gotta finish this now."

"But you're supposed to be dead."

"No. He doesn't win all the time. I'm proof of that."

Pam told her in detail about Rupert's attempt to cause her to relapse into full blown heroin addiction just because he felt he needed some company when he got high. She told Ilene how he drugged her food and then tied her up and injected her with so much heroin that she tottered on the brink of life and death for days.

"It all comes down to Rupert risking my life because he wanted fucking company. He put my body into massive toxic shutdown, but I didn't die and I ended up having an ally he didn't expect. And now you. I need you as an ally in this battle."

They agreed to meet. Pam would come up to Pennsylvania and they could meet and begin to plan how they would bring this horror show to a close.

Ilene didn't have use of a car and Pam agreed to meet her at a diner on the highway that was close to her hotel. It was risky although she took comfort in how different she looked now. Ilene assured her that Rupert had left the day before and probably was gone for at least a couple of days.

"We'll meet and talk and we'll see what we shall see. Listen, we don't have to act immediately. This guy is smart, we need to do the right thing at the right time."

Pam drove out to Stroudsburg and parked close to the diner. She could see a woman sitting by herself in a booth by a front window.

She was looking pensively toward the highway and then looked down and covered her face with her hands with her elbows propped up on the table in front of her.

Pam entered the dinner and walked over to the table and said simply, "Ilene?"

Ilene removed her hands which were still covering her face and said nothing, but stared at Pam hard. She whimpered a little then and finally stood, began crying and wrapped herself around Pam like Pam was a tree preventing Ilene from being washed away in a flood. Pam tried to disentangle but could not extricate herself from the tangle of arms and the convulsing body of Ilene.

"Please, get a hold of yourself. We have important things to do. Please."

Ilene only began crying harder. Pam finally managed to get her to sit back down in the booth and sat across from her.

"Ilene, I ... We've got something important to do together. Do you understand what I'm saying?"

Ilene buried her face in her hands again and slumped back in the booth. Pam watched as her upper body slipped sideways and she went facedown on the seat of the vinyl bench and draped her arms over her head. She was sobbing, she was whimpering, she was incoherent. Pam was speechless and afraid she had made a terrible mistake in not finding out more about this person.

"I can see that you are not going to be able to help me with what I must do. For your own sake, do not tell Rupert about our meeting. Do you fucking understand what I'm telling you, Ilene?"

Pam got up and stood over her for a minute and slammed the side of her fist down on the table. Ilene did not even look up. Resigned to going it alone she began walking toward the front doors.

"Not staying?" the cashier asked as she passed.

She turned to look back at him and just shook her head. When she turned back to face the doors he was there. Rupert stood on the other side of the glass, fat, arrogant and dangerous looking.

He opened the door and held it for her not seeming to recognize who she was. Pam walked through the door quickly and he smiled as she walked by and then turned his back to her ready to go into the restaurant. She quickly drew the Sig Sauer from her purse and clicked off the safety. She held it out with both hands like she had been trained and pointed the pistol at the back of his head. She had just a second to fire, but time seemed to slow and then her arms began to tremble. Pam's whole body trembled and suddenly she could not fire. All she had to do was pull the trigger. It was a matter of moving her index finger less than an inch and yet she absolutely could not squeeze off the round which would put an end to this absolute abomination of a human being.

Her arms dropped and she transferred the weapon to her right hand. She pushed the safety with her finger and slipped the gun into her pocket. She hurried to her car fearing she would fall apart like Ilene if she remained standing there. Rupert let the door close behind him and walked with the confidence and the ease of the oblivious into the diner.

Chapter Twenty-Eight

When Rupert returned with the supplies he needed he could not believe that D'Altorio's body was not where it had fallen and that the man was obviously still alive. He groaned and punched the wall. He screamed and cursed at the god who presided over all this disorder. Rupert searched the perimeter of the property and found where D'Altorio had entered the woods and escaped. There was a splattering of blood in the grass, but that was all. He had a lot of work to do and he had to do it fast. Who knew what this guy's next move might be.

He stuffed Alain and Alex into separate canvas bags and dragged them out to their car and hoisted them into the back of their SUV. He threw all their belongings on top of them.

He found where the bullet had embedded itself in a wood pillar in the living room. He dug it out and then smashed the pillar with a hammer, tearing it open to the point where the hole the bullet made was gone. With Clorox and a mop he got up all of D'Altorio's blood and the blood from the two New Hampshire guys. He put the accelerants into the back of the SUV, saving a few cans which he put on the counter of the kitchen. He got into his Escalade and headed into downtown Stroudsburg cruising the streets until he found Stroudsburg's equivalent of the wall. After he cruised past the third time, one of the dirtbags who had been sitting on the fender of a parked car peeled off from the rest of the dirtbags and headed down the street. When he was out of sight of his comrades, Rupert pulled up and motioned for him to get in.

"I saw you cruising us," the guy said. "Whaddya want, man? Blowjob, meth, whaddya fucking want?"

"All you gotta do," Rupert said is drive a car out to western Pennsy for me and then I drive you back and you get five hundred

215

bucks. Take a little more than four hours. Think you can do that? You can drive?"

"Yes, of course I can fuckin' drive, man."

"OK then," said Rupert. "No more talking, no more questions. Don't look at anything but the road and you get five hundred bucks for a day's work. Good?"

"Yah," said the dirtbag. "Good."

They drove back to the cottage. Rupert stopped in the driveway in front.

"You drive this and just follow me out. Take us about three hours heading west. Don't worry, go the speed limit, Drive like a little old man and tuck in behind me."

The dirt bag shifted over to the driver's seat. Rupert was going to have to fumigate it when this shit was over. He walked back to the house, got in Alex and Alain's SUV and pulled out of the driveway with the Escalade following. He spent the three hour trip wishing he had taken one more shot and blown D'Altorio's head clean off. Then he would have three canvas bags in the back rather than two.

After the main highway the dirt road out to the quarry was rough in many sections. Dirtbag seemed a little nervous about driving on it. Whether he distrusted Rupert or his own driving abilities was hard to tell and several times he pulled over and Rupert had to get out and tell him the Escalade could handle it and it was just a little further.

When they got to the edge of the quarry, Rupert hopped out and motioned for the guy to join him. As he was walking over to Rupert he paused, unzipped and begin peeing just ten feet away from Rupert. A rivulet of stinking, yellow urine flooded the track the tires had made and flowed toward Rupert's foot. He had to step off to the grass to avoid it. Dirtbag groaned with the pleasurable release. He complained loudly about holding it for the last three hours. There was an unintentional last squirt and he stuffed everything back into his dirty pants before finishing. A stain spread on the front of his pants and he looked down to see what he had wrought.

"Oh, shit," he said.

"You don't have to worry about that anymore," Rupert said as drew the Glock and shot him in the head. The guy fell alongside the SUV on top of the tire track still wet with his own urine. Rupert threw him in the back on top of Alain and Alex. He doused the bodies with accelerant and soaked a rag which he stuck in the gas tank.

The ground sloped down gently to the edge of a cliff which hung high over the quarry. He put a couple of rocks in front of the rear wheels and put the truck in neutral and released the parking brake. It wasn't much of an angle, but enough to get the truck rolling once he pushed out the rocks. He lit the rag in the gas tank and ran back to his Escalade.

The gas tank ignited with a whoomph and then a secondary explosion blew out all the windows when the accelerant erupted. The truck was entirely engulfed in fire. The heat must have cracked the rocks he had placed in front of the wheels, or, the melting tires gave the truck traction over the rocks because the fireball, with the truck barely discernable inside, slowly began rolling toward the cliff. Rupert watched as the fireball plunged over the edge, trailing fire and smoke, and fell until smashing into the water below. Slowly, the fire was extinguished as the truck sank. Soon it had vanished and the water was still. There was silence and Rupert felt the peace and the freedom he always felt when a major problem such as this disappeared from his life. He got a towel out of the back of the RV and draped it over the seat where the dirt bag had sat. He stopped in Ridgeway and had dinner at one of the restaurants he liked when he was a resident so many years ago.

When he got back to the cottage he was exhausted and decided to remove a few more personal items and parked the CRV as close to the front door as possible. Who said you shouldn't burn your bridges behind you. Let the authorities think he was attacked and driven into hiding. He felt, whether they thought much of his story or not, that it gave him some leeway if he had to explain himself to the authorities. He spread the accelerant in the kitchen and threw a match through the smashed in window and got the hell out of there. He could just start to see the smoke and flames through the trees as he came to the end of the driveway and turned left on the public road.

His head hurt like hell where the bullet had grazed his skull. The wound burned and felt like it was tearing open. He imagined it fissuring where they had cut out bits of his scalp and he took another of the Oxycontin they had prescribed for him and resisted the impulse to look anymore. He slept fitfully that night and then drove out to Stroudsburg in the morning. He had his sniper's rifle and his Beretta plus a shitload of ammunition. He hid them in the false compartment Raffi had built into the Audi's trunk. He wasn't coming back until this fucker was dead.

D'Altorio drove out to the estate and stopped at the driveway for Rupert's cottage. From the street he could see that big truck tires had dug up the ground alongside the narrow driveway and that bushes had been driven over and uprooted. It was as though big trucks had pushed through and caked up the driveway with so much mud that the asphalt was almost completely covered. He got out of the car and could smell the wet burned smell of a house fire even from the road.

"Ok, all right." he said, and took the chance and drove up the driveway until he saw the burnt out hulk of Rupert's CRV next to the almost totally destroyed house.

He got out and walked around the driveway looking for something, but he had no idea what that might be. A car pulled up and a couple of guys got out who he assumed were detectives. They had their right hands resting on the weapons holstered inside their jackets and one circled around his right side.

"Tell me who you are right now. Tell me why you are here and perhaps then we can just have a friendly little conversation and you will be on your way in no time at all."

"Ohh, you got me," he said, smiling and putting his hands over his head and waving them exaggeratedly. "You got me. Guilty as charged for the crime of nosiness."

He laughed and brought his hands down to his sides. The cops looked at him.

"I was camping last night and could see the fire from three miles off that a way," he said swinging his arms and pointing to the back of the property. "Yeah, we heard the beeping of the trucks and the shouting of men. Sound carries so clearly out here that you can't believe it. Well, I just came down to snoop around, you know, satisfy the old curiosity." He laughed and was smiling at the detectives. His goofball act seemed to have a relaxing effect on the cops. "Anybody get hurt in this shitshow?"

"Glad to say no although we're not sure what happened here so, don't touch a thing and best if you get underway right now. OK? Guy's car burnt up, but he's got a black Escalade too. Maintenance guy on the estate here told us. He and his girlfriend are probably still around. Who knows what they're runnin' from, right? We'll find 'em."

"Okey Dokey," D'Altorio said and got back in the Audi. "Life's full of fascinatin' stories, right? Always like to hear the details, but you boys look busy, and I don't want to be a pain in the neck."

The cops nodded at him and he drove out to the road thinking about whether it would be possible to drive through all of the hundreds of hotel parking lots in the Stroudsburg/Poconos area looking for a black Escalade. He figured they'd need rooms for at least a week or two stay before Rupert could make a move to a new permanent location. He probably wasn't in too big a hurry to leave. He thought it likely that Rupert believed D'Altorio might not be as committed to the job any longer with his bosses now dead and it was time to just let it all go, especially after Rupert nearly put his lights out forever. His D'Altorio-radar may have relaxed to some degree though he probably didn't want to answer any questions about the cottage so would stay in hiding. He must not have realized the cops knew he had an Escalade.

This guy liked to play chess, but he wasn't purely analytical in how he approached the game. Ultimately, he flew by the seat of his pants and let his feelings guide his actions. Narcissists relied on their guts because they felt divinely directed. But in D'Altorio's experience this guy mostly reacted to the actions of others. A counter puncher. Why would he ever come back to Northern, New Jersey if he was so smart? He's very clever when cornered, but don't expect brilliant strategy.

He cruised a few parking lots of likely hotels downtown and saw nothing. He demanded to see the managers of a few of the hotels and flashed his fake DEA badge. Nothing. He was frustrated and feeling that maybe this guy was going to elude him when pulled up to a red light on the main highway out of town. He was thinking that there had to be another way to do this. He could spend weeks searching the lots and browbeating hotel managers and by that time Rupert would be long gone. He covered his eyes and looked left to where the sun was beginning to set in the west. He looked at the red light above him and his vision drifted over to a black Escalade stopped in the opposing lane with a large, familiar figure in the driver's seat. It was Rupert. If he had his Beretta he would have starting shooting on the spot. He could have emptied all 15 rounds into that windshield and didn't even care if the innocent motherfuckers behind or alongside him were injured or killed.

He stared in disbelief. Rupert was singing happily with his eyes ecstatically closed and didn't even look his way. D'Altorio couldn't hear what he was singing until the light changed and they slowly passed each other in the intersection. He heard the song's jangly guitar and Rupert singing/screaming off key.

Beatles, he thought. The guy loves The Beatles. Incredible. One of the world's most organically melodic, harmonious bands ever, a gift to the suffering psyche of the human race and that's what this one-man apocalypse listens to.

D'Altorio drove until he was out of sight of Rupert's truck and suddenly pulled up onto the grassy median when the lanes were clear, swung the wheel hard to the left and spun the tires for all he was worth. His Audi's back end slid around and skidded off the median and onto the other side of the highway, facing in the opposite direction. The wheels were still spinning with smoke pouring out of the back end until he let off the accelerator and gained traction. He stamped down hard on the gas and accelerated after Rupert. He kept his distance and followed him out to The Hampton Inn further downtown. Rupert pulled the Escalade into the lot and D'Altorio passed the entrance and then took a sharp illegal turn into the hotel's exit. He drove quickly around the building, all the way to the back of the lot and stood behind the car with binoculars and watched Rupert park and walk around the side of the building and enter.

OK. This was good. He knew where the motherfucker was, but what now? The last thing he wanted to do was kick the door of their room in with guns blazing. No. This guy needed to be crushed like a bug, but discreetly. A sharp, clean whack with a flyswatter and scrape the remains off against the side of the garbage. Nothing more to see, just one less cockroach in the world.

He drove out to the convenience store he saw on the way over and bought supplies: lots of water and protein bars and a jug to piss in, came back and set up his observation post in the back of the lot. He got his Beretta out of the hidden trunk compartment. Although he couldn't see everything, he could plainly see the Escalade.

There was a rap on the passenger side window and he saw a guy in a security man's uniform hunched over and looking into this car. He lowered the window, said simply, "DEA," and flashed the faux credentials. The guy who was a twenty something millennial seemed very excited to have happened upon a real-life law enforcement operation in progress.

"Hey, cool! What can I do to help? C'mon I'm gonna make law enforcement my career, man. This is just a gig to get me through school," he said touching the patch on his shoulder. "Let me help bro, let me help."

He walked around the side of the car and D'Altorio powered down his driver's side window and waved him away.

"The only thing you can do to help is to stay the fuck away from me."

The kid looked genuinely hurt and took a step back from D'Altorio as though offended. He put his hand on the roof of D'Altorio's Audi and bent down as if to continue arguing his case. Suddenly a large shape appeared behind him and the kid was smashed in the side of the head with a palmed handgun and pushed back until he fell on his back on the ground.

It was Rupert, who smiled as he shot D'Altorio while he was bending over to grab his Beretta. D'Altorio had placed it on the floor by his foot for quick retrieval. The bullet caught him in his side, but he managed to fire off three rounds while still bent over. Two of the bullets hit the inside of the door and one ricocheted off the door's window frame before burrowing into Rupert's belly.

"Oof," Rupert groaned and fired three quick shots of his own, two into D'Altorio's body and one more to his head. D'Altorio slumped in his seat and his chin fell onto his chest. The seat back where his head had been was thick with blood. There was a slow, even expulsion of breath and his body slackened and seemed to contract. He did not breath in again.

The security guard was crouching on the ground with a hand outstretched as if that could deflect any shots coming his way.

"Please, man I'm just a kid for God's sakes. I don't know who the fuck you are. I don't want to know who you are."

Rupert turned toward him angrily having been engrossed in the spectacle of his dying opponent. He bent at the waist and clutched his belly in pain. The kid squirmed on the asphalt trying frantically to evade Rupert's pistol. Rupert straightened up, spread his legs and slowly raised the Glock. He emptied the rest of his clip into the security guard's chest. After the first few shots he was motionless, but Rupert shot him three more times. He limped back to his room clutching his belly and groaning.

Chapter Twenty-Nine

When Ilene saw Rupert staggering through the front door of their suite she screamed. He seemed momentarily confused until he located the bedroom and collapsed on the bed clutching his belly in pain. His face was splattered with blood and there was a slow seeping wound at his waist.

"I think it missed my gut and liver and passed right through.".

He turned on his side and she could see where D'Altorio's 9 mm had made a neat exit wound in his side.

"If it even nicks your intestinal wall you die of peritonitis. But he's done. I got the fucking guy. Finally. It was worth it. Ilene! We won! We're free!"

He opened his eyes wide and raised one hand, the other still clutched his belly.

"D'Altorio is fucking dead," Rupert announced triumphantly, like it was a negative result from a cancer test, like it was the end of World War II.

"We have to go to the hospital, Rupert," Ilene said calmly although she felt exactly the opposite of calm.

The nightmare was swirling and swirling and she felt like she had vertigo. It was all getting even worse. He had killed D'Altorio out in the parking lot and although in terrible pain he was almost euphoric about the cold-blooded murder he had just committed.

"We have to go to the hospital," she said more urgently. A fantasy formed in her mind. While Rupert was in surgery the detectives dispatched to investigate his shooting would take her back to the station and she could tell them every last thing she had ever known about the monster.

"No, no, we can't do that, Ilene. We gotta get out of here first and then I'll get some medical attention."

He asked for his dope box and she retrieved it and watched as he snorted a substantial line from the small mirror he kept with the heroin.

When she looked at him quizzically he simply said, "Anesthetic."

She threw all their stuff into the Escalade which wasn't all that much. Ilene swabbed his wound with alcohol and wrapped his torso tightly with clean sheets from the closet. The wound was seeping, but he had not lost much blood. He limped out to the Escalade and despite being high and having just been shot, demanded to drive. Pulling out of the hotel exit they saw EMS and cop cars with flashing lights and wailing sirens flying through the parking lot the other way. Hotel guests were streaming out of the entrance to follow them around the side of the building and into the back of the hotel.

He took 80 east and enroute called an old customer, a cardiologist he had a special relationship with, who he had kept well supplied with the heroin the doctor had been addicted to since med school. After the bust, Rupert introduced him to a new supplier, someone discreet, someone who would not exploit a man in his position who was vulnerable to exploitation because of his social and professional prominence. The doctor was effusively thankful and wondered what he could do to repay Rupert.

Collection time. The cardiologist agreed to meet him outside his practice in what had been a private home on Rt 24, which he had converted to office space more that twenty years ago.

Rupert described the wound and the doctor felt he could treat him in his office effectively. It wasn't professional, it wasn't ethical, but if Rupert was to get medical attention and maintain anonymity, it was the best he could hope for. It was a Thursday and the office had closed in the afternoon so the doctor could do his hospital rounds. He had hustled his administrative and medical staff out of the building and met Ilene and Rupert with a gurney and an IV in the back lot. He took them into his examination room and cut Rupert's shirt off with surgical scissors. He x-rayed, he ultra-sounded, he poked and prodded after anesthetizing Rupert, and as best as he could tell the bullet had not done any damage to his internal organs.

He cleaned and sewed him up and sat with Ilene while waiting for Rupert to come around.

"I cannot, however, be absolutely sure if any damage was done to his internal organs. I'll give him some prophylactic antibiotics, but if he spikes a fever you must go to the ER immediately. Yes? You understand? It's the end of my professional life if you or Rupert tell anyone I worked on him, so please - for my family for my patients ..." He looked at Ilene imploringly, then got up to check on his patient, but turned before going into the examination room.

"Really. There isn't anyone else I would do this for. I've had a twenty-year addiction and yet I've been able to live like a normal person. Family. Professional life. My addiction has not destroyed any of these things, and it was because of Rupert. I've had the security of knowing my supply is steady, my identity is secure, and the product is not adulterated."

Ilene nodded. The doctor's experience with Rupert did not change a damn thing for her. She had been hoping against hope that the anesthesia plus the heroin he snorted in Stroudsburg might push him over the line and kill him. It was not to be. Years of drug use had made Rupert resistant to drug combinations and amounts that would kill normal men. He was still groggy but insisted she drive out to Indian Lakes. He knew a guy, who knew a guy who could help them work out a safe and anonymous future.

"I did everything I could to conceal our identities. I always paid in cash. I had fake docs and a fake drivers license, but ... somewhere along the line this all is going to point at me. Connections between The Consortium and me, D'Altorio's knowledge about my identity and my past relationship with E and Scheiner that were probably passed on to underlings. I removed most of those connections, but somewhere, someplace there's gonna be somebody who heard something they shouldn't have heard. And even if that person doesn't come forward, well ... I'm the only one left alive. That alone points to me."

He shook his head. It made him laugh how it had all turned out, and how he was the only one left standing. He grimaced when it hurt to laugh, and his hand went to his gut where the doctor sewed him up. Ilene stared straight ahead, abject hopelessness threatening to overwhelm her.

"Go in the back way to the lake by the mall. I gotta stop at the credit union."

She pulled up to the front entrance and Rupert kicked open the door as the SUV stopped, whacking a guy carrying a laptop in the leg. His arms flew up and the laptop went flying and skidded up the sidewalk.

"What the fuck," he yelled.

He grabbed the door of the Escalade and ripped it all the way open and was about to grab Rupert when Rupert drove his palm into the guy's nose smashing it into his face. His nose split open and began pouring blood down his chin. He fell and rolled onto his back on the asphalt driveway. Rupert stepped over him and stood above his chest. He showed him the Glock.

"One more word, motherfucker and you won't be getting back up." He bent over and said quietly, "Count on it."

The guy stood up slowly and was looking at Rupert, scared, suddenly passive and pointed to his car. Rupert nodded his consent and the guy skipped over and slid into the driver's seat. He started the car and had it backing up before even closing the door.

Rupert took a brief case out of the back and limped into the credit union. Ten minutes later he was back in the car and giving her directions to his buddy's house in Indian Lakes.

"We've got enough for quite awhile. These guys'll set us up and then we can earn again."

She nodded and leaned forward over the steering wheel. She couldn't bear to even see his face. Although wounded he was still a force of nature. She wondered how someone like herself who was so petite and slight could ever go up against a powerhouse like Rupert.

"C'mon," he said noticing her reticence, and the slow withdrawing into herself and away from him that had been happening for a while. "We'll settle in over at Terry's place and get high. He'll let us hide out. We need to recover from this shit and rest up. Let's stream some movies, get some take-out and rest, sweetie. We need some peace and quiet. Yes?" He looked over at her. "OK, hon? That sound good?"

Ilene gave him the briefest nod possible that could still be identified as affirmation. She thought fleetingly that it probably didn't satisfy him. On the left was a huge, old oak with a trunk almost as wide as the Escalade was long. By itself and without any seeming action on her part the SUV started drifting into the other lane and the car was accelerating and heading straight into the massive tree. She felt numb and heard from far away Rupert yell her name and then felt him pull hard at the steering wheel and shake her with his other hand.

"Ilene. What the hell! You're exhausted. Asleep with your eyes open. Damn girl you almost finished off the Rupert saga right here."

She felt as low as she had ever felt in her life. She had no idea any longer of what to do, and everything seemed lost. Maybe he was just too much for her. The only thing she knew for sure was that the heroin made everything all right. She just wanted to get high. She wanted to swim in that warm ocean of sleepy wellbeing forever.

Terry lived on Lake Shore Drive in a house that was a sort of 1960s version of what was envisioned as the architecture of the future. It was a series of five interconnected rectangles, placed at different vertical heights with each consisting of at least several rooms whose exteriors were hung with flat framed boxes of yellow and forest green over grey wood slats. Ugly, somewhat garish, but there was lots of room, beach front property and they were able to park the Escalade at the back of the house out of sight of the road.

"Two weeks and we'll get new docs and set ourselves up maybe out west. This will be like the criminal-world version of a relocation program." Rupert giggled and Ilene looked grim.

She spent two weeks stoned and numb and encouraging him to use more than he ordinarily would have. He was frankly happy to see her wanting to shoot dope since he enjoyed getting high with someone, but he was having his doubts about whether she was going to be able to hack this new life he was about to embark on. Her use was not the same as his. Hers was the only thing keeping her head above water. His was restorative and a reward he indulged in for dealing with all the shit life seemed to throw his way.

He needed a partner not dead weight. He wasn't sure yet about what he wanted to do, but what had worked so well for him before with people who had become a problem would surely work for him again.

Chapter Thirty

She stayed stoned for so long that she was having trouble telling the difference between reality and the stoned out dreams that floated through her consciousness. There was an intermediate state somewhere between wakefulness and sleep, and that is where she would have like to have stayed. It was floaty and warm and self contained. Dope allowed her to feel that she didn't need anyone, emotionally, physically or otherwise. She hadn't ever felt like that before. Everybody in her life had always expended a lot of energy trying to convince her that she not just needed them, but was existentially dependent on them even though she was the one who took care of everyone. Da, her brothers, old and new boyfriends, all the men in her life wanted her running after them, frantically stuck in a never-ending cycle of almost masochistically attempting to validate her very existence through a self negating, self destructive service to others.

It was a product of her family history and the misogynous, authoritarian Catholicism she had grown up with. And as soon as that aspect of her personality was sensed and exploited by the men she dated, there would inevitably be the slow familiar drift toward another unbalanced, unhappy relationship where pleasing her boyfriend seemed to always be somehow just out of reach. The result was a relationship that ended because her partner said with breathtaking unconsciousness that they didn't really sense her as a separate person, but as someone who saw themselves as only a vehicle for someone else's needs.

And as was often explained to her during these break-ups, "I already have a mother. I don't need another one, I need a girlfriend."

Well fuck me if I can't take a joke, she thought and began

giggling. After Rupert told her to "shut the fuck up" because he was watching the Mets in the bottom of the ninth, she walked down the path to the small private beach where she sat alone in a lounge chair. She watched the sun set over the green hills behind the lake in majestic shades of gold, orange and red. The colors bled gloriously into the patchy, cumulus clouds spread out across the horizon, illuminating and giving color to them and making them seem to glow from within.

She heard some children playing on the great lawn of the Clubhouse across the lake from her and the meowing of her host's family cat who jumped up onto the chaise lounge and then quietly sat and witnessed with Ilene the quiet display of a glorious and playful creation. There was the cat, there was Ilene, there were the children across the lake and there was a world manifesting intense and eloquent beauty for their appreciation, and for a time she had the most peculiar sensation of not knowing which one she was.

Afterwards, when it was dark, she walked back up to the house and told Rupert that she would like to get high with him one last time and that in the morning she would leave. She wasn't implicated in any of this, no one had really known she was with Rupert except for D'Altorio and Laurent and they were both dead. She would just go back to her little life in Rockaway and that he would be unencumbered with her forever more. She promised him that she would never speak a word to anyone about what had happened to her during this time and that he could believe this without worry. She pledged her life on it.

Rupert nodded.

"Maybe for the best. I felt you were pulling away from me anyhow. Maybe it's all too much this way that I live. I guess I can understand that, and you're right, for whatever is coming I need to be unencumbered. I need to be mobile and adaptable and I'll need to reinvent myself wherever I end up. So ... perhaps all for the best. We both know that our relationship has about come to an end. We could see it coming. I guess whatever it was that drew us together had begun to fade. Better now than later, when stressed we just begin to hate each other. And who knows what we'd be capable of doing then."

He didn't hate her. In fact, he thought he might miss her. So better to do this the easy way. The easy way was to shoot her up with a little more dope than she was used to. He didn't want to give her enough to make her lose consciousness, just enough to cause her to nod and slur and when she had finally nodded out he'd give her more. Ilene would slip off painlessly and unconsciously into nonexistence. After that it didn't really matter anymore. He was thinking duct tape, garbage bags and enough chains to keep her at the bottom of Indian Lakes until climate change had scorched New Jersey dry. It would be as though she had been subtracted from existence, as though she had never existed at all.

They were sitting in the living room. Their hosts had gone to the Jersey Shore for the weekend. She got up quickly to get the dope box while he turned on the TV, got some water and the bottle of Coke he sipped from when he got high. When he got back there was the syringe and dope in the small metal bowls with handles that he liked to cook in. One bowl contained more than the other, reflecting his body size and years of indulging. Her bowl was substantial though, and certainly capable of producing the effects he was hoping for.

"It's good?" he asked pointing to her dope.

"Yes," she said, "but let me do you first. It's the last time and I'd really like to do it for you."

"OK. We'll get each other off for the very last time together. Like a parting gift." He raised his eyebrows and grinned.

She cooked the mixture in the tiny bowl and drew it up into the syringe. She tied him off and stuck the needle in the prominent vein just below his biceps. Rupert looked down and saw the lid of a vial peeking out from under the coffee table. He looked over at his dope box and saw that the fentanyl had been removed from the place he kept it in the box. It was the last observation he was ever to make.

"Oh no!" he cried.

She pressed the plunger and he gasped, his eyes rolled up into his head and his chin slowly dropped to his chest. He fell back and she could see his breathing was labored and his lips were turning blue. Suddenly, it was as if his presence had gone out of the room. There was a body, which still had some function and struggled through the minimal processes that kept it alive even though consciousness was no longer present.

Finally, she couldn't hear any breathing and his pupils had constricted to tiny, fixed points. She stared at him for a long time. He didn't look like a person any longer. She wondered how it was that she could have ever been so enthralled with this being and to go through what she had. She wondered how the world would be without this force which pulled everything down, this vampire who fed on what was fundamental in other peoples' lives and left only dissolution. She had expected to feel fear and a deep grief for what might have been, but felt only something akin to being unfettered and a lightness which replaced the oppressive weight under which she had endured for such a long, terrible time.

She found the call Pam made to her in the "Recents" list on her iPhone. She pressed the listing to call back and someone answered but didn't say anything.

"New day," she said simply, "all my problems and yours disappeared with the setting sun. He's gone, he's gone, he's gone. We will have a future from this moment on without that affliction, and perhaps there will be some peace for us now."

"Oh, God," said Pam.

Ilene went down to the beach, jumped up and down on her cell phone and threw the pieces as far out into the lake as she could. She was thinking as she walked back up to the house that if she was questioned she'd tell the police that she and Rupert had a violent argument and broke up. After Rupert punched her that was enough and she was out of there. She had been depressed about their relationship for a long time and she found him more and more difficult to get along with. She feared him and wanted to get as far away as she could. He must have taken the drug after she left and she had no idea where he had gotten the heroin, but that he had been going out quite a bit and she suspected he'd been hanging out with some of his old druggie friends. He was an intractable druggie and had a long history as a druggie and everybody knew it. His overdose should not require any further investigation on the part of law enforcement. It should be seen by them as the universe cooperating with law enforcement as it sometimes did, decreasing their paperwork and ending an inevitable future of Rupert mayhem.

She picked up the second bowl of powder, flushed it down the toilet along with the remaining heroin in the dope box. She emptied the fentanyl into a bucket of water. Stirring with a stick, she dumped the bucket in the woods on the side of the house and turned on a garden hose. Ilene washed out the bucket and sprayed down the leaves and brush where she had dumped the drug.

Gathering up her clothes she made sure to pack up all her possessions. She had two suitcases and she packed Rupert's briefcase containing his cash in one of them just below her sweaters and her socks. She was surprised at how much money he still had. The suitcases rolled quite easily down the street and she walked down toward the pizza place and past the blinking light.

There was pleasure in just walking on the street. There was the hardness of the asphalt under her feet, the soft, early evening shadows between and behind the houses and the sounds of cars starting, people talking and TV sets blaring. She didn't feel outside of all this activity anymore. She realized that she had always thought her role in life was to be an observer who watched other people live their lives. Now she understood that she was as integral and as enmeshed in this complex web of human activity as they were.

The owner of the pizza place let her use his cell and she called an Uber. When the driver asked her destination, she said in a firm voice, "Newark Airport, then Atlanta. I should go and see Mum. It's about time. I should have gone a long time ago."

233

CPSIA information can be obtained
at www.ICGtesting.com
Printed in the USA
BVHW041257240922
647922BV00005B/127

9 781952 439414